I0679441

Fealty

Spirian Saga Book 6

Rowena Portch

Fealty

AEON ENTERPRISES, NOVEMBER 2012

www.Aeon-Enterprises.us

Cover illustration and book design by
Aeon Enterprises

ISBN-978-0-9886275-0-5
V1.0_r1

Printed in U.S.A.

ACKNOWLEDGMENTS

Gregg, you are a wonderful mate. Thank you for sticking with me through all my adventures in life. I know it's hard to be married to a female with a gypsy soul. God bless you, my angel. You are and always will be my best friend.

Tyler, my editor, thank you from the depths of my soul for your incredible editing talent. Like a true artist, you've made this story shine. What a Godsend you are.

Daughter, Erika. Your skill of storytelling inspires me to continue writing. I know your own novels will be a huge success. Thanks for your undying support and cheerful spirit. Most of all, thank you for my wonderful grandchildren who make me smile.

Nick, Andrew, and Zach, you are the most gifted sons a mother could ask for. Not only do you encourage me to continue pursuing my dreams, you call when I need to hear the words, "I love you, Mim." Thank you.

To the females in my life, Mum, Evelyn, and Georgian, bless you for the girl time, the laughs, your support, and most of all, your unconditional love. I couldn't make it without you.

Prelude

When you are bound by a fealty, an oath is pledged that cannot be severed lest you bear a fatal consequence.

~ R a e ~

THIRTY YEARS AGO SEEMS LIKE a lifetime. In reality, it is merely a blink in time.

I was barely a woman of thirteen years when my mother, Jenna, sat with me on my bed, the room surrounding us adorned with innocence, joy, and love.

This was not the first time she told me the story of her youth. Each time the words flowed from her lips, I was enchanted. The scent of her still clung to my mind— sweet lemon peel on a bed of fragrant orange blossoms. Her dark mahogany hair spilled sweetly around my arm as she held me close and spoke of her beloved Tishar, a high knight of the Carador realm, a place inhabited by Faeries and other magical beings.

"He was magnificent," she said, her green eyes sparkling like emerald gems in the sunlight. "Fae males are so different than those you find here," she sadly added.

"You loved him?" I asked, my voice soft and innocent—a child not yet stained by the cruelty of men.

"Yes," she answered. "I loved him very much. But," she sighed, "he had a mission to fulfill. Our kind, the Fae, were dwindling. Fewer and fewer children were being conceived. Something had to be done."

"So he called upon the Spirians, children of the Angels," I said, having heard this story before. No matter how many times she told it, I never grew tired of hearing the tale.

"Yes," she said, tugging me closer. "He did. Five of the strongest Spirian leaders were gifted with Tishar's most precious treasures. Four of my slave sisters and I were sent to be with the Spirian males in hopes of strengthening our race."

"Then the bad Spirians came," I said.

My mother's beautiful eyes grew dull with the memory. "The Shadows," she said with spite. "They killed the good Spirian males and their children. They took me and my slave sisters, but they didn't know about the fealty Tishar had formed between himself and the five Spirian males."

"Is the fealty magic?" I asked her, not really knowing what a fealty was at the time.

"Yes," she said. "Tishar wanted to ensure our safety. Anyone who caused us physical harm would die a short but painful death." The distance in her voice alarmed me.

I shrank back a little.

Sensing my discomfort, she pulled me against her, squeezing my shoulders for reassurance. "Unfortunately," she continued, a hardness in her tone, "the Shadows have their ways of causing us pain without causing physical harm."

She turned me to face her; determination and alarming seriousness hardened her expression. "Hide your gifts, Raeiza. Never use them or let others see them. Keep your thoughts and feelings deep in your soul." She shook me to emphasize her plea.

"I promise, Mim," I whimpered, tears stinging my eyes.

She held me close, embedding that promise like a stain that would never wash out.

Chapter 1

- Rae -

FEW THINGS COMPARE TO THE beauty of Edinburgh, Scotland in late May. I typically enjoyed my bike ride home, but tonight, I was late. It was 9:00 p.m., a scant hour before my shift at Malones Pub.

I rode my bike down Lygon Road, past the elaborately landscaped mansions. The Linden trees were blooming early this year; their sweet fragrance welcomed me home as I turned right onto our cobblestone drive.

In the absence of moonlight, our home resembled Dracula's castle with its dark stone walls and dimly lit windows covered in heavy drapes. Short wrought-iron fences guarded the landscape like dark, immovable soldiers. Everything was perfectly in order, just like the man who owned it—my father, Drake Tomei, Shadow leader of Europe and the bane of my existence.

I parked my bike against the stone wall and ran toward the front door. It opened before I could reach the handle. My father's looming figure filled the wide frame. He was a handsome man with peppered hair that he wore short and combed back. As usual, not a strand of it was out of place.

"Good, God, Raeiza; I was worried sick," he said in a thick London accent. His eyes widened as they scanned me from head to toe. I was littered with blood and straw. "What happened to you?"

My father was the only person who called me by that name. I preferred Rae, but he refused to acknowledge that simple request. I gently brushed past him, in a hurry to take my shower and prepare for work. "A mare gave birth. The foal was breech," I called over my shoulder.

I winced as his strong hand gripped my arm and spun me around. "You will look at me as we speak," he emphasized. He stood a good foot above me. His gray eyes peering into mine. "Look at yourself," he said. "You look like a commoner." He turned his head, obviously not appreciating the aroma I emitted. "I gave you a perfectly fine auto and yet you insist on riding that monstrosity on two wheels."

"Father, please, I'm late for work."

"I don't like you working," he reminded me. "There is no need for it." He closed his eyes and shook his head as if summoning patience. "Honestly, Raeiza; you will be mated by the end of this year. Bennet will not permit this foolishness."

My stomach sank at the thought of leaving Scotland to live with my appointed mate in New York City. Bennet Graves was an investment broker. His idea of paradise was the penthouse suite on the top of a high rise. Not much need for a horse vet out there, I imagined.

"I'm finishing my degree, Father."

He shook me. "Why?"

I despised the way he made my spirit cower. It took

everything I had to keep respect in my voice when I answered. "Because, dear Father, you taught me to finish what I started."

Unable to deny that fact, he released me. "Get cleaned up. You smell like a fish pond."

I started up the staircase that curved like a swan's wing up to the second floor. The highly-polished rosewood and brass trim always seemed impossibly bright in this house of anger and resentment.

"Raeiza," he called.

I turned to face him. "Yes, Father."

"Bennet is coming to see you next Thursday. He will be staying for dinner. I expect you to be here."

My stomach felt as if I had swallowed molten lead. I nodded to him.

He raised his chin up a notch, studying me with those cold gray eyes. He expected an answer—a verbal answer.

"I will be here, Father."

It took a moment for him to release me from his stare—a look that could pin and restrain me as fast and hard as iron shackles.

I turned and continued ascending the stairs.

When I reached my room, decorated in white and pale blue, the tears began to flow. I had stood up to my father once long ago; it ended badly for me and resulted in having my mother banned.

He was a cruel and powerful man—a business investor with a heart of cold steel. He handled his acquisitions with the same bitter affection he bestowed upon his family. His charm, money, and absolute power were his only assets, aside from his attractive physique that never failed to lure available females who never stayed long.

Born and raised in London's high society, I was

taught that a proper Shadow female obeyed or suffered consequences. I was passed between my father's acquaintances like a rare, expensive toy. When my mother couldn't stand his abuse of me any longer, she was banned from our immediate clan and sent to a more common clan where she would spend the rest of her days. Two years later, she had died—or so we were told.

Deep down, I knew she was alive—I could feel her, or at least I thought I could. I was her only child, something that seemed to irritate my father, seeing it was the male in a union who determined when his female became pregnant. Picking up her picture from my dresser, I noticed that she looked like me, only older and with shorter hair. Her pale eyes seemed sad as they stared back at me. The picture blurred behind my tears. Things were so different now that she was gone.

I set the picture down, pulled my clothes off over my head and tossed them into the bin. My jeans came next. Everything would have to be soaked. Our servant, Olivia, was a gem at getting stains out and keeping everything impressively clean. She had been our caretaker for as long as I could remember.

Padding my way into the bathroom, I pulled the tie from my hair and shook it out. Long, thick waves of chestnut hair spilled over my shoulders and down my back. Bits of straw floated to the floor.

Like my mother, I had gray-green eyes that looked too pale to be paired with dark hair. I had been pretty once. Now, I purposely avoided makeup and attractive hair styles. I wanted to be anonymous. No matter how hard I tried, though, my efforts never seemed to detract the clan males' attention. They hovered around me like hungry sharks, waiting to be fed.

The shower faucet squeaked with objection as I turned the polished brass handles for a mix of hot and cold. Steam lifted and began filling the large space with inviting humidity. A hot shower was exactly what I needed now. Anything to take my mind off Bennet's upcoming visit.

I stepped into the open space and allowed the five shower heads to saturate my body with heat. Closing my eyes, I buried my head beneath the heavy spray and imagined it was a waterfall in the midst of a lush forest—far away from high society and arranged unions with men who only wanted another precious possession.

The last time I had met Bennet Graves, I was just barely a woman of twenty years. I'd changed since then and wondered whether Bennet would even want me any longer. He needed a gifted, high status female to bear his children. As far as anyone knew, I had no gifts like most Spirian females my age, and I did my best to hide my status behind a simple physique built more for athletic activities than filling out expensive gowns.

Scrubbing my hair with jasmine-scented shampoo, I tried to imagine the ugliest thing to wear during our dinner together. Surely once he saw how homely I could be, he would change his mind about our union.

My father's inevitable riposte to my blatant act of defiance shattered that plan into shards certain to leave me bleeding. I had best play nice and entertain the man who would soon be my mate.

I shuddered as the suds ran down my body and into the drain, mirroring my hopes and wishes.

In thirty minutes, I was dressed in a pale blue sweater and faded jeans. My hair was tied into a braid, still quite damp. When I opened my door, I heard the dulcet sounds of a piano solo coming from the study where my father was no doubt enjoying a snifter of cognac.

Quietly, I made my way down the stairs, praying my steps would go unnoticed. The last thing I wanted was another bout with my father. He would certainly comment on my damp hair.

I opened the front door and slipped outside before closing it softly behind me. So far so good, I thought.

My bike protested with a groan as I kicked the stand up and pushed it onto the drive. In two minutes, I would be free.

Chapter 2

~ Rae ~

THE THREE KILOMETER RIDE TO Malones Irish Pub helped clear my head. I was horribly late, though, and Danny, my boss, would have my head on a platter by the end of my shift, I was certain.

I locked my bike to the pipes that ran up the backside of the brick building. Entering the employee's door, I made a beeline to the private lounge to dump my things and don my apron.

"Nice of ye t'make it in." Danny's gruff voice sounded across the room. His thick Irish accent offered a comforting charm.

I turned to face him, tying the apron around my waist. "Sorry, Danny. We had an emergency at the farm."

He growled, his battered face looking far more fierce than the man who bore it. "Jane's in a fit, out there. I suggest ye take up a shield before facin' 'er."

The scar that ran from the tip of his left brow curved down his face to the crease of his lip. He proudly boasted of it as a trophy from his last boxing match with the infamous Samson O'Malley. Other than that, Danny was a handsome old man with dark eyes as warm as the summer air.

"Thanks for the warning," I said, grabbing a bag of chocolate-covered coffee beans from my locker. Jane would need to be consoled, I was sure. Nothing worked better than her favorite treat.

I walked into the bar to find an unruly crowd giving Jane a run in or two. She held her own like the stoic Irish lass that she was. Her red hair was twisted into a knot at the back of her head. She looked haggard and beat.

Hearing one man's order for gin and tonic, I flipped a highball glass in my hand and filled it with ice.

Jane turned to face me, her pale blue eyes loaded with daggers. "Here already?" she said, sounding more Scottish than Irish.

"Sorry," I said, pushing the bag of chocolate coffee beans into her hand. "I had an emergency at the farm."

She smiled at the gift I had given her. "Apology accepted."

"Hey," the burly man yelled. "Hows 'bout me drink?"

I topped the glass with tonic water and slid the concoction before him.

The man at the end of the bar caught my attention. His name was Seth Dunning, my intriguing distraction who made biochemistry far more tolerable. He was a regular here and quite popular with the ladies. The stories that floated around about him only served to pique my interest to higher levels. Definitely a player, but not a man looking for a solid relationship. Knowing that made him safe, unobtainable, and comfortable at a distance. But he hardly noticed me.

Part of me felt relieved while another part of me craved

to have just one of his smiles aimed in my direction. Fat chance of that, however.

Jane nudged me. "Get his order. Go on." She nudged me harder.

I walked to the end of the bar. Seth's attention was on a redhead with long curls that brushed the tip of her accentuated backside as she took a seat beside him.

I cleared my throat, hoping to draw his golden eyes to me, instead. "Can I get you something to drink?"

He turned to face me, then focused again on the female to his right. "What are you drinking?" he asked her.

"Manny's," she said, her voice seductive and smooth. I wanted to reach out and strangle that delicate neck of hers.

Seth returned his attention to me. "One Manny's and a glass of your house Malbec, please." His American accent seemed so out of place here, yet it was soothing.

I left to fill his order, wondering whether he even knew who I was. He had to have known I was Spirian, one of his own kind yet he seemed more attracted to humans—a real rarity in this pub. Most of the clientele were Spirians. It was a popular hangout for our kind. Humans found the overbearing hum that radiated from us uncomfortable and typically avoided the place. Some humans, however, were drawn to our kind, especially the females.

Seth looked up at me as I lowered the drinks to the counter. He could melt butter in the dead of winter with those eyes, I thought, feeling a flush of heat redden my cheeks.

"Thank you, Rae," he said.

I nodded and scurried away.

Jane rolled her eyes at me. "Do ye know any other

lines than, 'Can I get ye somethin' t'drink?'"

I brushed past her to fill another order of Guinness.

"Thanks, darlin'," my customer said, flashing a stained smile.

I nodded and walked away to update his tab. When I turned around again, I noticed Seth leading the redhead toward the dance floor. A slow ballad began to play. He commanded the female with such confidence that it made me yearn to take her place.

Jane leaned down to speak in my ear. "He's really somethin' to look at, yes?"

I nodded. "Yes."

At 6'4", his muscular frame, dark hair, and alluring shadow of a beard made him downright delicious. Add a good dose of manners and intelligence, and you had a man who made most women weep.

"Take that man and make 'm yours," Jane said.

"No," I simply said, turning to fill another order. That was impossible. I was promised to a male who would have me by the end of this year. The best I could hope for with Seth was one evening. Going by the rumors, that was all he gave to any female lucky enough to snag his interest.

"Rae," a familiar voice called. I turned to see Edmond and two of his friends. He was the son of my father's security man, Jacob.

"Edmond," I said. "What can I get you?"

"M' boys and I are looking for a bit of company tonight," he said, looking me up and down like a vulture sizing up its next meal.

"I'm not available," I said, feeling a familiar pit in my gut.

He reached out and grabbed my wrist, wringing it painfully. I fought back my reaction, not wanting to offer him any satisfaction.

He growled. "Then make yourself available."

"Is there a problem here?" Seth asked, reclaiming his seat.

Edmond eyed the man, obviously taking in Seth's size. In comparison, Edmond looked like a toothpick.

"Just havin' a conversation with the lady."

Seth looked down at Edmond's hand gripping my wrist. I did not want a fight; nor did I want Seth getting involved. Using the skills my brother had taught me, I twisted my arm up and broke away from Edmond's grip.

"I am working, Edmond," I said. "Please leave."

I motioned for Steve, our bouncer, who promptly came to assist. He was an ex-Navy SEAL from the States and a good man. He was one of the few men here who didn't emphasize the rumored fact that I was an ice queen.

"You heard the lady," said Steve. "It's time you and your boys leave."

Edmond jerked his arm away from Steve, keeping his reddish-brown eyes fixed on me. "Later, Rae," he promised.

I shook against the chills that trembled up my spine. This would not end well for me. When my father heard of it, there would be hell to pay and my credit was dry. With shaking hands, I wiped the bar and lifted Seth's empty glass from the counter.

"Hey," he said. "Are you okay?"

I nodded.

He smiled. "That was quite the move. Who taught it to you?"

"My brother—half-brother," I corrected. "He's an Aikido master."

"I like him already."

I turned the empty glass in my hand. "Um, would you like another?"

He studied me thoughtfully, the way he studied the writing board when Professor Ewig explained the mysteries of man. My face heated.

His smile deepened, nearly undoing me. "I'd love one."

Another man, a regular, sat beside him. "Don't waste yer time," he mumbled. "Ye can't tame that ice queen."

I winced, nearly spilling the glass that was horribly over-filled.

"How 'bout a beer for me?" the man asked.

I cast him a stare that was nearly as frigid as the stigma that dubbed me. "Yeah, how 'bout one," I mocked him, matching his common slum accent.

"See what I mean?"

Seth stood and walked away from the man without a reply, taking his glass of wine with him. The redhead he had been dancing with joined him at a table. My chest felt as if it were being squeezed by an unseeable force.

Chapter 3

~ Rae ~

FINALLY, IT WAS 2 A.M. My shift was over and I was beat. I pulled the lock from my bike and stowed it under my saddle. The short ride home always offered time to sort my thoughts. I needed to clear my head. I took a deep breath. The cold, foggy air felt good against my skin.

Across the parking lot, Seth's voice caught my attention. He was talking with the redhead he'd been dancing with, probably arranging where to meet for the night.

Forget about it, I told myself. He's out of my league and far beyond my reach. I turned my bike around and rode in the opposite direction. As I reached the end of the alley, a man stepped in my path.

"Hello, Rae."

It was Edmond, and five of his buddies. My heart pounded, its pulse thumping in my neck. When I tried riding past, Edmond grabbed my handlebars and flung me to the ground.

My left arm fell first as pain tore through my skin.

Edmond reached down and hauled me up from the ground.

"Let's talk about your attitude tonight, Rae," he growled, shaking me till my teeth rattled.

I stomped down on his instep, hammer-fisted him in the groin, and then swung my arm up to back-fist his face before twisting myself free.

Two of his buddies grabbed me from behind. Edmond recovered far too quickly and pounded my face with his fist. My head buzzed and my vision blurred. Another hit sent me to the ground.

"Hey!" I heard a voice shout.

One of the blokes kicked me in the leg as I tried to stand. Pain shot through my hip as I collapsed back to the ground.

"Stay out o'this," said Edmond.

Seth stepped into the light. He was surrounded by Edmond's friends.

I looked around for anything I could use as a weapon, anticipating a bloody battle. Edmond was an aggressive man, so I wouldn't put it past him to cause serious injury when invoked. Seth was dangerously outnumbered. Did he even know how to fight?

In the next moment, I would have my answer.

Edmond moved in first, followed by two others. Seth quickly evaded their blows before flipping them to the ground. In a blink, he was surrounded but holding his own. Moving like the dancer he was, he managed just barely to keep away from the men's grasps.

One of the men picked up a bent metal post. I stood and tackled him against the wall. He swung the post at my head. I fell back into the trash cans, cutting my hand.

Another man ran up the alley toward the commotion.

He was short but stout. Yelling like a banshee in the midst of death, he pulled two men off Seth as if they weighed next to nothing.

I watched the two men fight, downing Edmond and his blokes with quick, easy moves. One man pulled out a knife and sliced the short man's leg. He wailed, yanked the knife from the man's hand, and then landed a blow to his head that rendered him unconscious.

Seth downed three men before going after Edmond. A sharp blow to his temple sent him crumbling to the ground. Seth ended the fight with a rib-crushing kick to Edmond's stomach.

The six men rolled on the pavement, groaning and bleeding.

"Come on," Seth said, pulling my bike up. "Follow me."

The shorter man, who stood barely an inch above my 5'2" height, and I hurried to catch up. He was limping badly from the wound on his leg. My own body felt as if it had endured an encounter with a fast moving truck. My head was still a bit fuzzy.

Shorty had black hair clipped close to his head, and eyes to match. In the street light, he had an aboriginal appeal. His strong, short fingers gripped my arm.

"You all right?"

I nodded. "Just a bit dizzy is all."

Seth led us down the street, past Malones toward the Quartermile development. He turned onto a long cobblestone drive leading into a complex that resembled an Old World castle of dark stone and massive turrets on all four corners.

He punched in a series of numbers on the keypad and the black iron gate clicked open. Shorty and I followed him in.

Seth leaned my bike against the wall next to a wide oak door that led into an impressively large flat.

He flipped a switch and the entire space lit up.

"Wow," Shorty said. "You live here?"

Seth merely looked at him with indifference before gathering towels, a bowl filled with water, and a black leather bag.

"Sit," he said, pointing to the glass kitchen table surrounded by four black leather chairs. The place smelled of sandalwood and clove, like the man who lived here.

The flat was simple, yet elegant in every way. Hard oak floors and cherrywood cabinets. The countertops were pale green and made of a material that looked like granite but felt warm to the touch.

Rosewood furniture added a bit of color. An oak staircase wound up to the second floor, its rosewood banister polished to a shine.

Seth grabbed my arm and hauled me back to the dining area.

"Sit," he repeated.

The hard line in his jaw told me he was not a man to fence with at the moment. He looked at my face with no emotion, and then at my arm and bleeding hand.

"Take off your sweater," he ordered, his voice clipped and stern.

"You don't have to do this," I said. "I'm fine, re—" I winced as he dabbed at my face with a warm washcloth.

"That was the man who came onto you at the pub?" he asked, his golden eyes meeting mine. "Who is he to you?"

I winced again. "His name is Edmond. His father works for my father."

"And the others?"

I shrugged. "I don't know them."

"I could use somethin' t'drink, mate," Shorty voiced, his leg propped up on a chair. His New Zealand accent was thick and unrefined. I assumed he had grown up outside the cities.

Seth looked at him, and then back at me. "Looks like we all could."

He stood, graceful and showing no pain. His lithe body seemed flawless, not even a bruise on his face. I watched as he pulled a bottle of single vintage brandy from an over-hanging cabinet along with three glasses. His black turtleneck sweater was misshapen in some places where he had been grabbed. Only a smidgen of blood marred his jeans where he had brushed up against Shorty.

Amber liquid filled three snifters. He carried them over with ease and placed them down before us.

Shorty downed his in one gulp before slamming the glass down on the table.

Seth shook his head in disgust; then he rose and fetched the bottle from the counter. He poured Shorty another drink.

This time, it was savored.

Seth sipped his brandy, studying the two of us. I could only imagine what was going through his mind as he wondered what the hell he had gotten himself into.

Shorty extended his hand across the table. "I'm Nathanial Dronel," he said. "Call me Nate."

Seth refused the hand and simply nodded. "I am Seth, and this is Raeiza Tomei."

"Rae," I corrected. "Call me, Rae."

A slight smile curled the corners of Seth's mouth. It was a beautiful mouth, full lips and corners that had a natural upward curl to them.

Seth continued with the painful task of cleaning my wounds. When he got to my hand, he frowned.

"This will need stitches."

"Just bandage it up; I'll be fine."

He opened his bag and pulled out a small suture kit. He then retrieved a needle and a bottle of clear liquid. I watched as he sucked the liquid into the syringe.

"This will sting a bit."

"Aren't you only a third-year med student?" I asked, questioning his skills of minor surgery.

"Yes," he replied.

My hand grew numb as he opened the suture kit with confidence and grace.

"They don't teach minor surgery to third-year med students," I said.

"My uncle taught me."

My brow peaked.

"And, I graduate this year," he added.

"You're on a six-year program."

Nate cleared his throat. "He's in the accelerated program."

Seth glanced over at him. "I don't remember seeing you around. Are you a student?"

Nate laughed. "You have a photographic memory and yet you don't remember the bloke who has sat two seats back from you for the past two years?"

Seth frowned.

"You have a photographic memory?" I asked.

"Among other gifts," Nate replied.

Seth sutured the final stitch, ending it in a neat double knot. His work was fine, as if he had practiced cosmetic surgery for many years. He covered the wound with a white bandage, holding it in place with tape.

"There," he said. "Keep it dry and clean."

"Thank you, Doctor," I said, teasingly.

"Your turn," he said to Nate. "Off with the pants."

"I don't typically down m'pants on the first date," said Nate, struggling to a stance.

"I find that hard to believe," I countered, averting my eyes.

"Thank you for the privacy, miss," he said. "I am a bit shy y'know."

"Sit," Seth growled, "before you fall."

The gash in Nate's leg oozed with blood. The muscle had been cut across his quads but not completely through.

"Doesn't look too bad," I said, peering over Seth's shoulder.

"Hand me the dissolvable suture kit in that bag," he said, pointing to the black bag on the floor.

I readied the kit as Seth prepared the injection to numb the area. He offered no warning before piercing the skin.

Nate pressed back against the chair. "Jeeezus," he groaned. "Are you stickin' me with fire?" He downed the last of his brandy.

Seth poured him another. "I need to clean this out."

I jumped up and filled another bowl with clean water. Seth was digging through his bag.

"What do you need?" I asked.

"A syringe to push water through."

I found one and handed it to him. I then retrieved a small bottle of hydrogen peroxide and placed it before him.

His smile was genuine. "You make a pretty good assistant."

"Only pretty good?"

"Do you mind concentratin'," Nate groaned. "Are you cleanin' the bloody thing with sandpaper?"

"Don't be such a baby," Seth said. "We're almost done."

When he syringed the hydrogen peroxide into the wound, Nate ground his teeth and pressed further back into the chair until it groaned in protest. "Criminy. I don't think that shot is workin'."

"I don't have enough to numb it completely. It will have to do," said Seth.

After gloving up, I readied the needle and thread before handing it to him. With great precision, he sutured the muscle together. As he was finishing up, I prepared the external suture kit.

Nate was shaking by the time Seth tied the last knot, fashioned a white bandage similar to mine and said, "That should do it."

With trembling hands, Nate brought the brandy to his lips. "Thanks, mate."

Seth ran upstairs, taking two steps at a time. He returned with a pair of sweats in his hand and tossed them to Nate. "Put those on."

Chapter 4

- R a e -

WE RETIRED TO THE LIVING ROOM where Seth had lit a warming fire. The three of us were exhausted but too amped up to sleep. As I gently rocked the recliner, I worried about my father and his reaction to all this. Surely Edmond would report the incident.

Father and I rarely ran into one another during the week. I often came home too late and was typically sleeping when he left for work in the morning. I wondered whether he would notice my bike missing from the garage. Occasionally, one of my co-workers drove me home, so it wasn't completely out of the ordinary.

I looked over at Seth as he stared into the flames, sipping his brandy in deep resolve. He sat on the white leather couch, leaning forward with his elbows resting upon his thighs.

Nate sat on the opposite end of the couch, leaning back, eyes closed, drink in hand, and his injured leg propped up on the coffee table. His color was pale and he lacked the typical glow in his eyes that were a Spirian's signature.

"You're staring," Seth said without even turning to me.

I quickly averted my eyes to the fire.

He started to stand. "I should drive you both home."

"Where did you learn to fight?" I asked, desperate to change the subject. I didn't want to go home, not yet anyway.

Nate opened his eyes and looked toward Seth, obviously wondering the same thing.

Seth's jaw tightened. "Drew, one of our clan members, taught me."

"He must be very good," I said. "I've never seen anyone move like that before."

Seth leaned against the stone hearth. "He teaches all the men of our clan to fight. And yes, he's very good."

"And your uncle is a surgeon?" I asked.

Seth turned to face me. "He was, before he became the regional leader."

"And what about your father and mother? What do they do?"

Seth reached over and took my empty glass up from the table. "Are you done?"

I nodded.

Nate pulled his glass into his chest as if protecting something precious. "You're from the Gradhun clan," he stated.

Seth froze for a moment before continuing to the kitchen. "I am."

"But it's not your birth clan."

Seth said nothing as he washed our glasses and put the remaining brandy away.

"It's all right, mate; I'm not your enemy."

"What are you then?" asked Seth.

Nate smiled. "A fellow Spirian, mate; nothin' more, nothin' less."

Seth came back and sat on the couch, studying the stout man. "You're a listener," he said, and then cocked his head as if confused. "And somewhat of a seer."

Nate laughed. "Ah, you're good."

Seth's confusion deepened. "Your father is a shaman of the Taluka clan."

It was Nate's turn to frown now. "Your gifts are stronger than I thought."

"So tell me," said Seth. "Why would a Shadow help me in a fight?"

Nate's face lost all expression. "A Shadow?"

"You heard me."

The vibration in the room increased. If I didn't do something, this conversation was going to escalate into the bad side of ugly. I cleared my throat. "Probably for the same reason that you helped a Shadow female out of a bad situation."

"That's what we do," said Seth.

"We?" Nate inquired, sitting on the edge of his seat.

"The Protected," Seth nearly growled.

Nate tossed his head back and laughed. "Ah, yes, the mighty and good Protected. The segregation between good and evil," he said, emphasizing with finger quote marks.

Seth stood, his energy amping higher.

"Easy, boys," I said, standing and moving between them.

"Might I remind you," said Nate, looking around me, "that you, yourself, come from a Shadow clan."

"Not anymore," Seth roared.

"Please," I said a bit more loudly than I had wanted.

"Sit down, both of you, and talk like civilized Spirians."

"Not all Shadows are evil," said Nate, "just like not all Protected are good."

"We are all Spirians," I chimed in. "What we choose to call ourselves has no bearing on anything."

When Seth sat, I lowered myself back into the chair.

"I have never met a Shadow who stood for anything good," said Seth.

That earned him a look from both Nate and me.

"I beg your pardon?" I said.

"I should have let the blokes take you down," said Nate.

"They wouldn't have," Seth boasted.

"Arrogant bugger," Nate sneered.

"And what evil have I bestowed upon you, oh righteous Seth?" I asked.

His eyes narrowed.

"If I'm so evil, then why did you even bother saving me from my own clansmen?"

"You were a female in trouble," he said.

"I'm surprised you allowed us unworthy sorts into your fancy dwelling. It must be hard for you to stew in our presence." I stood and strode toward the front door.

"Where are you going?" he asked.

"Home, where I belong."

He walked toward me. "I'll drive you. It's not safe to be out at this hour."

"Oh, don't worry yourself, Seth. All the evil Shadows are right here in this room."

His eyes narrowed. "Suit yourself."

I opened the door, stepped through, and then slammed it shut, rattling the panes of glass overhead.

My bike was toast. The front wheel was bent and both

tires were flat. I didn't remember it being that badly off when Seth rolled it over here. I couldn't very well push it home in this condition.

The door opened. "I'm sorry," he said. "Please, come back in."

I stepped through the door and walked past him.

Nate was lying back on the couch, his leg propped up on the table again.

Seth walked toward us, rubbing the crease between his eyes. "I was wrong," he said. "I have met Shadows who were good." He sat at the far end of the couch. "My uncle Khalen was born of my clan, and my mother came from another Shadow clan. Both of them are good."

"You are good as well," I said, "when you're not boastful and opinionated." I smiled, trying to lighten the mood.

"He's still arrogant," Nate hissed. He started coughing, soft at first, and then it quickly became heaves that sounded painful.

"Are you all right?" I asked, reaching over to pat his back.

He signed for the restroom, two crossed fingers moving in an arch. Most Spirians know basic sign language, a common form of communication among the young before they learn to telecommunicate.

"Past the dining room to your left," said Seth.

Nate hobbled past me, still coughing as if he had inhaled a hornet.

Our eyes followed him.

"He looks pale," I said.

"He doesn't have a clan," Seth replied.

"How do you know?"

"I tapped his thoughts when I mentioned his father.

His connection to them has been severed."

I didn't reply. There was no need. Every Spirian knew how threatening it was to live without a clan. Those who were forced to live on the outside rarely lived beyond twenty years. Outside of mating with someone from an established clan, joining one was tricky if not improbable. Clans were tight, and allowing strangers to band with them frequently upset the dynamics.

Nate returned to the couch, a spatter of fresh blood marring his already stained shirt.

"Doing all right, my man?" asked Seth.

"Fine, mate."

"How long have you been without a clan?" Seth asked.

"You're startin' to piss me off, Protected."

"How long?" Seth repeated.

"Bit of a dag, eh?"

Seth didn't ask again, but the determination in his eyes caused Nate to squirm a bit.

"Bloody yonks. That's how long."

"How many years?" Seth asked.

"Eighteen."

Both Seth and I knew that Nate was on a downward slope in health. He didn't have much time if he lived much longer without other Spirians.

"You'll stay here tonight," said Seth. "Both of you."

Nate swung his legs around and laid on the couch. "Come 'ere darlin'," he said, patting the leather. "I'll keep ya warm."

I narrowed my eyes at him. "Not on your life."

"Rae gets the room," said Seth, tossing a pillow at Nate's head before turning to me. "Come on; I'll show you where it is."

I followed him upstairs, trying to keep my eyes from

his backside and muscular legs. They filled those jeans with perfection.

Seth turned on the light. "There are extra blankets and pillows in the closet. The privy's in there." He gestured to the room on the left. "There are new toothbrushes in the top drawer, so help yourself."

The king-size bed was topped with a fluffy white comforter and bordered by two maple end tables with two drawers and cubbies stuffed with books. The closet was modest with plenty of room for clothes. In the far corner was an armoire made of similar pale wood.

"Where do you sleep?"

"Across the hall."

I yawned, finally feeling drowsy. "Do you have class tomorrow?"

"Not until noon," he said, turning to leave. "Get some sleep," he added, closing the door.

Chapter 5

- Rae -

I AWOKE TO THE SOUND OF QUIET clanking in the kitchen. The smell of bacon wafted into my room. My stomach growled rather obnoxiously.

Moving proved to be painful. My body was stiff and sore from Edmond's abuse. Each beat of my heart caused my hand to throb. Instinctively, my other hand reached over to cover it. I stopped before any healing could take place. Seth would want to check it this morning, and I didn't want him to know anything about my gifts. Mother promised it would be my undoing should any male ever discover that I was a healer.

Swinging my legs out of bed, I groaned, feeling every bruise and scrape. The fog was thick outside, diffusing the light through the windows. Warmth from the heated oak floors comforted my bare feet as I padded my way to the bathroom.

After relieving my bladder, I found a new toothbrush in the top drawer as Seth had promised and began my routine that started each day. Seth had placed a plastic bag on the counter along with a rubber band, no doubt to keep my bandages dry as I showered. I could just heal my wounds and rebandage them, but feared my energy would be sensed by the other two Spirians in the flat. Instead, I carefully removed my bandages so that they could be reapplied. When I returned home, I would heal the wounds completely.

The spacious shower was stocked with Crew shampoo and soap that smelled of spice—like Seth. Savoring the scent, I lathered up, rinsed, then reached for the small bottle of shampoo, fearing that I would take most of it just to cover my thick hair. The minty tingle of the shampoo felt good to my scalp as I massaged it in. My mind started to awaken a bit. Without conditioner, my hair would be a struggle to brush. I didn't care. This entire experience was worth the hassle. Another long rinse, and I was ready to face the world again.

I stepped out and dried myself with a thick towel that smelled like sage. I used another towel to dry my hair as I returned to the bedroom, I looked toward the valet where I had draped my clothes last night. They were neatly folded. Odd, I distinctly remember draping them over the hanger last night.

They were clean and smelled like fresh lavender, even my undergarments. My face grew warm. Oh God, did Seth wash them for me? When? Why?

After making quick work of reapplying the bandages and donning my jeans and shirt, I looked around for a brush. There wasn't any. I remembered seeing a new comb in the drawer along with the toothbrush.

I heard footsteps ascending the stairs and then a soft knock upon the open bathroom door. I turned around to see Seth standing there with a hot cup of coffee in his hand. How did he know I prefer coffee over tea in the morning? I wondered.

"Good morning," he said, his voice silky and smooth as fresh cream. "I figured you could use this." He set the cup down on the counter. It was black, the way I liked it.

I took a sip and frowned. It had been diluted with water and carried the familiar taste of salt and cayenne pepper.

"Is it to your liking?" he asked, a knowing smile on his arrogant face.

I was tempted to say, "No" just to see him falter, but refrained. "Actually, it's perfect." I took another sip and noticed he was staring at me through the mirror as I struggled to pull the comb through my damp hair.

"You're staring," I said.

"Would you like a brush, instead?"

"If you have one I could borrow, that would be lovely; thank you."

In his absence, I pondered how he knew the exact way I drank my coffee; half water with a pinch of salt and a dash of cayenne pepper.

He returned, brush in hand. "I see you at Peter's Yard every morning at six o'clock. You always order the same thing, coffee with crispbread and jam, fruit and hard cheese."

I frowned, feeling slightly at a disadvantage. This man had a talent for tapping into my thoughts, even when they were closed to him.

Yes, I stopped at Peter's Yard each morning, but I never remembered seeing him. At the very least, I would have felt his presence. Spirians stand out in a crowd like white on black.

"Breakfast is ready," he said, quirking that mouth of

his in a confident, knowing grin. It was disturbing how alluring that was.

"Thank you."

Knowing my hair would take far too long to brush out as damp as it was, I decided to leave it until after I ate. I followed him down the stairs, my perfect coffee in hand.

Nate was already at the table, sipping a cup of coffee and reading the paper. "Bloody hell," he murmured. "Jenico Tomei lost the National Aikido tournament against Rally Evans yesterday. The mangy bloke beat him by one point."

I took a seat beside him, feeling a bit guilty for not attending the tournament. I rarely missed my brother's fights. How could he have lost? I wondered.

"There will be a rematch in September," Nate read.

"Your brother?" Seth asked, taking his seat at the head of the table.

"Half-brother," I replied, looking down at the decorative display of thick-sliced bacon, spinach frittata, cottage cheese with fresh sliced strawberries. "This is quite the spread."

Seth smiled. "Glad you approve."

"I can't believe he lost," Nate said, disappointment lacing in his tone.

Seth said a quick prayer before starting in on the meal.

Praying was not something I grew up with. I wasn't even sure how to pray. Not wanting to seem rude, I closed my eyes, hovered my hands over the meal, and conjured a quick thought of thanks in my mind, though I had no idea whom I was thanking.

Reading Seth's thoughts was like trying to find a pearl in the mud. Nate's thoughts weren't much clearer, though both had mastered the art of shielding their minds.

Seemingly unobservant of the praying ritual, Nate tossed the paper on the floor and dug right in, taking in large amounts of food with a single fork-load. I was tempted to offer him a shovel.

"You're quite handy in the kitchen," I said to Seth, who ate with the dignity of a seasoned aristocrat. His clan had money, that was evident in the way he lived. I never saw him drive, but I was sure he had a vehicle that was just as impressive as his dwelling.

"I did a bit of cooking back home."

"And where is home?" I asked.

"Washington."

I nodded, familiar with the quaint state that boasted of evergreens and abundant rain. "Close to Seattle?"

He shook his head. "Not really. We live on the Olympic Peninsula on Harstine Island."

I wasn't familiar with that area, nor with the fact that Olympic even had a peninsula, wherever Olympic was. When I had accompanied my father on his many business trips, we stayed close to the city. "Is it nice?"

"Beautiful," he replied. "Very green, very secluded. It's about twenty miles from town."

"I bet you miss it."

"Very much," he said, sipping the last of his coffee.

"Do you have a female there?"

He chuckled. "There are many females there."

My face grew warm. "I mean a special female you favor."

The crease between his brows deepened. "Yes, there is."

"Oh," I said, cursing the disappointment in my tone. Damn him for noticing. He smiled. "I'm her templar."

My eyes rose. To be chosen as a templar was an honor

typically reserved for older men of high status. The role of one was to protect the assigned female from harm. If anything happened to her mate, the templar could choose to unite with her himself, or choose another suitable mate for her. "Templar?"

He nodded. "Yes, for nearly four years now."

Even Nate seemed skeptical, having paused his shoveling for a few seconds.

"Aren't you a bit young to be a templar?" I asked.

"Very," he replied, standing. "More coffee?"

I shook my head.

Nate held up his cup and bounced it up and down as if to say, "Keep it coming." The man honestly had no scruples.

Seth filled Nate's cup before refreshing his own. "How about you? Anyone special?"

"Not in my clan," I responded, avoiding the subject of Bennet, my intended.

Seth returned to the table. "Ah, a female with secrets," he hissed.

I ate the last of my meal before standing and carrying my plate to the sink. When I turned on the water to wash the pile of soaking dishes, Seth stood.

"I'll take care of this," he said, brushing against my back as he turned the water off. Tingles prickled my spine as if he had touched my bare skin with feathers.

I skirted around him before turning around. "I should probably go."

"I'll give you a lift," he said.

Nate shoveled the last of his meal into his mouth and dumped his dishes unceremoniously into the sink. "I should bounce, too."

Seth retrieved a set of keys from a peg by the door.

"I'll give you both a ride. Wait outside my door. I'll pull the car around."

Nate and I left through the front door. We heard the lock slip into place.

He fingered my still damp, unbrushed hair. "I like the way your hair smells," he said, holding it up to his nose.

I backed away from him before turning to retrieve my bike. The wheels were straight now, and both tires were inflated. They weren't like that earlier when I was trying to leave, I thought.

Nate started to laugh. "He duped you."

I frowned, suddenly feeling as if I couldn't trust either one of them. Checking my pocket for the tie I used to pull my hair back for work, my fingers found the flimsy elastic band. It had surprisingly survived the violent journey of the washer and dryer, and I was grateful. With practiced ease, I wove my hair into a braid and secured it with the tie.

Nate watched me with awe and a hint of disgust. "I like it better down," he said.

"Then I'll have to remember to wear it up more often," I countered.

Seth pulled around the corner driving a silver Range Rover.

Nate let out a whistle. "Damn, this boy is loaded."

Seth put it in park as the rear door opened. I rolled my bike to the back of the car. He took it from me and easily lifted it into the back.

"Shotgun," Nate called, opening the passenger door.

Seth willed the door shut before Nate could step through. "You get the back."

I smiled at the cheeky Kiwi as Seth held the front door open for me. In the world of Shadows, the females always sat in back.

Nate's eyes narrowed. "What ever happened to respect for males?" he sneered.

"My car, my rules," said Seth.

"The bloody Protected," Nate grumbled. "Always doin' everything backward."

"You're welcome to walk," Seth said, sliding into the driver's seat." With a push of a button, the back door closed and the doors clicked shut.

"And miss this choice ride? Not on your life, mate." He started pushing buttons and turning knobs.

I turned to face him. "Do they not have vehicles where you're from?"

He had a smile on his face that rivaled that of child turned loose at an arcade. "Not as dandy as this one."

A fan turned on, blowing his short hair about and making him squint.

Seth groaned and flipped a switch. The fan turned off. "I'm taking you home first, Nate. Where to?"

"Colinton Road, mate, just outside o'town."

The next few minutes were filled with blissful silence, until the Kiwi opened his mouth again.

"So, the flat, this car, are they yours?"

"No," Seth said, almost as if he were embarrassed by the admission. "They belong to my uncle Khalen."

"Too bad," Nate admitted. "I was 'bout t'make you my new best mate."

"God's miracles never cease," I said.

Nate leaned forward until his lips were inches from my ear. "Careful, Rae. I'm startin' t'think you like me."

Seth growled, eyeing Nate through the mirror.

Nate sat back in his seat, keeping his eyes trained on Seth. "Easy, mate. I was just playin'." He stared out the window and grumbled, "It's not like you have designs on her."

In another minute, Nate pointed to a farmhouse on the left. "Turn left up here."

Seth slowed and took the turn onto a worn dirt road.

"Good enough," said Nate. "I c'n hoof it from here."

Seth stopped before a large barn that looked as if it were struggling to support its last few trusses.

Nate opened the door, made a graceful exit, and then slammed the door shut, before leaning in through my window. "Ta, mate, Rae. Try not to miss me too much." His breath smelled of coffee and egg.

I wrinkled my nose. "Goodbye, Nate."

"See you around," said Seth.

He turned the car around and headed back down the dirt road.

"You don't suppose he lives there, do you?"

Seth shrugged. "Not my concern."

His words would have had more tenor if he hadn't looked back in the mirror so often.

"He saved us both last night. Surely that means something to you?"

"Yeah," he said, "Where to?"

I gathered that was his way of saying the subject of Nate was now closed.

"I live on Lygon Road, just past Lauriston Place."

Chapter 6

~ R a e ~

GESTURING TO THE CIRCULAR PARKING space in front of the gardens, I said, "You can drop me off here." My father would be at work, so I felt relatively safe allowing Seth to park so close. Normally, I would have asked him to drop me off along the street.

He leaned forward and looked up at the looming house that towered above the others in the neighborhood. "Nice place."

I snorted, immediately wishing I hadn't. "If you like overly florid dungeons."

He looked at me skeptically before exiting the SUV. After removing my bike, he refused to allow me to roll it up to the garage.

"I can take it from here," I assured him.

"Your hand is healing. You shouldn't be using it."

I had forgotten about the wound, having done some healing on it to stop the throbbing pain. Not enough to hide the scar. I wasn't sure whether he would be checking it this morning. A small part of me wished he had cared enough to do so.

I led him into the parking area that wound its way underground. After parking my bike out of the way, he followed me to the lift door. I pushed the button but the door refused to open. I pushed it again. "That's odd."

After a moment, the door rattled, then slid open, revealing my father and brother. My heart slammed in my chest when they walked out of the lift.

I stepped back into Seth, nearly knocking him off balance. He caught my arm and steadied me.

"Um," I stammered. "Seth, this is my father, Drake, and my brother, Jenico." The hum in the air intensified. Bringing a member of the Protected clans was strictly prohibited. According to my father, it was akin to inviting priests to a séance.

Seth extended his hand. "Rae speaks highly of you," he said.

I most certainly did not.

My father noticed my shocked expression and smiled. "Yes, I'm certain she does."

Jenico reached out and shook Seth's hand. "Pleasure to meet you, Seth."

"Don't you have somewhere to go?" Drake growled, staring straight at his son.

"Excuse me," he said, skirting around me. He gave my shoulder a reassuring squeeze before continuing through the garage.

He had moved out of the main house several years ago. I often envied him that and wished that my father would allow me to do the same. Unfortunately, unmated females were under their sire's charge and not permitted to live in a separate dwelling.

The lump in my throat tightened. "Thank you for

your help, Seth," I said, hoping he would take the hint and leave.

"Anytime," he replied, keeping his eyes trained on my father. The hum between the two males was intense and made my innards rumble like pregnant storm clouds.

"Were you with my daughter last night?" Drake asked.

"Father—"

His energy blast brought me to my knees and held me there.

"You will not speak, Raeiza. Not now."

Seth's jaw tightened, his lips grew firm. Angels above, don't let him overreact, I thought.

"Your daughter was attacked by five males last night on her way home," Seth explained, somehow keeping respect in his voice. "She was injured. I tended her wounds and allowed her to stay in a spare room until I could drive her home."

Drake looked down at my bandaged hand. My bandaged arm was covered by my sweater. He held Seth's stare for a grueling moment before offering a slight bow.

"Thank you for tending to her. You're a doctor, then?"

"A student," Seth responded.

I squeezed my eyes shut. This was not going well at all.

"A student?" my father drawled. "Of?"

"Medicine."

Another long pause. "I see."

"I graduate next year," Seth added.

"Have you any designs on my daughter?" my father asked.

I tried to struggle against his bind, but as usual, it was impossible. My mouth opened but nothing came out.

"No, sir, I don't."

"Good. She is to be mated this year so I wouldn't want her—compromised."

What he really meant was that he didn't want me lying with a Protected one. Shadows, on the other hand, seemed to have free rein of me. I struggled to keep the contents in my stomach. Father's bind made it difficult to swallow.

"Rae is a friend, sir, nothing more."

Hearing those words hurt more deeply than any punishment my father would certainly issue. Of course Seth had no designs on me. Did I honestly think he did? He had never made a pass at me; nor did he show me any sign of interest. I was stupid to hope for anything more.

A shrewd smile lit my father's calculating expression. His gray eyes glimmered under the soft glow of the garage. "We have an understanding then."

My father released his bind on me. I stood with shaky legs and mouthed the words, "I'm sorry," to Seth.

His smile warmed me.

"Inside, Raeiza," Father said, pointing to the lift doors.

"I'll find my way out," said Seth.

My father stepped into the lift with me, watching as Seth made his way to the exit. As the doors closed, I felt the cruel grip of my father's hand. This was going to be a bad day.

-Seth-

I HEARD THE LIFT'S DOORS CLOSE and its rapid ascent. Then, the hair on my neck tingled; my nerves stood alert and poised. Cool air drifted all around me. I turned to find Jenico standing behind me.

"Don't be alarmed," he said.

My Land Rover was parked in the garage. Odd that I hadn't heard the sound of its engine. It made the impressive array of luxury cars dwarf in its presence. I was surprised it even fit through the door, let alone down the narrow path descending underground.

This garage was huge and could easily store fifty or more vehicles. Why would anyone need so much space? I wondered.

"I took the liberty of moving it down here, which is better than doing what my father had suggested." He tossed me the keys.

"And what was that?" I asked.

Jenico's green eyes were soft but held a certain distance to them. He stood at a mere 5'10" tall, much shorter than he had seemed during his fights. I towered above him but could feel his strength. This man could take me down if he chose to do so. I gratefully sensed that was not his intent.

"He wanted the car destroyed."

Tapping his mind, I quickly learned that he was a very skilled elementist. He could melt that car as if it were a stick of butter and then remove any traces of its existence. That explained how he was able to move it here without our knowledge.

Given his gifts, I wondered how he ever lost a fight with a human when he could make the man feel pain without raising a hint of suspicion. A Shadow would have no qualms about cheating. This man was not a typical Shadow.

"I appreciate the alternative," I said.

"I wish to speak with you. Do you have a moment?"

Studying him for a minute, I felt no reason to avoid the

male. If he wanted to harm me, I would not be standing here now. "Sure."

He led me to a flight of stairs that ascended to a pair of French doors with ornate windows and brass trim. It seemed a waste to have it open to a dismal garage.

Inside, the flat was spacious with minimal furniture, a simple coffee table, and a kitchen built for one. Oak floors were softened with colorful rugs. Two rooms led off from a single corridor that was wide and decorated with pictures of Jenico fighting various opponents.

"Can I get you something to drink?" he offered.

"Coffee, if you have it," I said, staring through the large picture window looking out at the massive gardens in the back. The scent of white sage permeated the place, reminding me of Drew's meditation temple.

"Go ahead and take a gander, if you like," he said, gesturing to the corridor.

I walked down the spacious hall, looking at the pictures of Jenico fighting. He stood like a mountain and studied his opponents as if they were puzzles begging to be solved. He looked small compared to most of them. Jenico was not a muscular man, per se, but a very powerful one. His movements resembled those of a cat, graceful, low, and precise.

I continued down the hall. A very large room to the left was empty in the middle. The floors were covered in rubber mats. Free weights filled the back wall. On the opposite wall were kick bags, punch bags, and a wooden dummy with several odd looking arms sticking out of it.

The far room was his bedroom, something I had no interest in seeing.

Jenico came down the hall holding a cup of coffee and a cup of tea. He handed me the coffee. "I'm not sure how you like it."

"Black is fine," I said, following him into the living room where we sat on comfortable winged-back chairs upholstered in navy blue cotton.

"How do you know Rae?" he asked, sliding the short coffee table between us.

"She's in two of my classes and I see her at Malones Pub occasionally."

"She likes you," he said, sipping his tea.

I looked up at him, saying nothing. Whether or not the statement was true, I was not in the position to act upon it. She was to be mated and I was not in the market for any sort of relationship, especially one with a Shadow female.

Jenico smiled. "No response?"

"The fact is moot, is it not?"

"I love my sister and I want to see her happy."

"She said she was your half-sister."

He nodded. "Yes, we have different mothers. Father has many mates but is rather choosy in who bears his children."

"Most Spirians are," I said. The coffee was bitter and strong, just how I liked it.

"Rae's mother was—special." Jenico met my eyes as if willing me to tap his thoughts.

I did, of course, but none of them made much sense. "Tell me about her." I'm not sure why I wanted to know. None of this was my concern; nor did I want it to be. But, the words flowed out of my mouth like a willful breeze.

"She is one of the original Fae slaves bestowed upon us from the good knight Tishar."

I chuckled. "You speak of fairytales, my man. That story is a myth that has been passed down for many generations."

He shook his head. "Not exactly. Jenna, Rae's mum, is the last of the original five slaves. She is bound by a fealty that both protects her and vows her loyalty to Spirian males. She was a gift to my father from his father in hopes of strengthening our race.

"So Rae is only half-Spirian?"

"Yes," said Jenico. "But she is special and too damn good for the likes of Bennet Graves, her bloody intended."

"You sound as if you disapprove?"

Jenico sipped his tea, obviously trying to get a handle on his emotions. "Rae doesn't want this," he growled.

"She is strong. I've seen that side of her. Why doesn't she stand up to her father?"

"She's tried and has paid dearly for her efforts. No doubt, she is paying now for her actions last night," he seethed.

"That was not her fault."

Jenico's eyes turned dark as rich emeralds. "She refused Edmond. Until a Spirian female is mated, she is available to any male of her clan, should her father make it so."

"Only in the Shadow clans," I said, trying to keep the anger from my tone.

"The division between our clans is so vast," Jenico said almost distantly.

After a long moment of silence, I said, "How can I help her?"

His eyes pierced mine. "Take her. Make her your own."

I set my coffee cup down and stood. "I am not a Shadow. We don't just take what we want without any consideration of others."

"There is no doubt she wants you," he said. "Give her what she wants."

"I'm not looking for a mate; nor do I sport any notions of challenging a far more experienced male to claim rights to her."

Jenico stood and walked to the door. He flung it open. "Then watch her die," he hissed.

I eyed him as I left his flat, feeling the wave of energy he emitted. "You are her brother," I reminded him. "Do something for her, if you can."

"I just did," he sighed.

Chapter 7

~Seth~

FOR THE NEXT TWO DAYS, I avoided the pub, and I hadn't seen Rae in class. At home, her scent still lingered in the room—lilac and clove. Her hair clung to my brush—deep chestnut with black and copper highlights. The toothbrush she used remained where she had left it.

Forget it, I reminded myself. This is a bolt of lightning I don't want to offer any ground to. She is just another female—a Shadow female, I reminded myself.

Nate nudged my arm. "Hey, you here, mate?"

The muddled sounds of the surgery was nothing more than white noise in my mind. The other students in the theatre were quiet, observing as Dr. Thorton demonstrated a proper appendectomy.

"Yeah," I said, running my hands over my scalp. The acrid scent of alcohol, iodine, and blood did little to clear my mind. It seemed Rae was all I could think about. Her delicate London accent lulled my thoughts, and those incredible gray-green eyes were heavy and deep with a history I didn't want to know. For such a young spirit, she carried the weight of many hard years.

We watched as Dr. Thorton closed the wound, recounting the technique in vivid detail.

As we stood to file out of the theatre, I noticed Nate was limping.

"How's the leg?"

"Good," he lied. "Healin' nicely."

"As nicely as the wounds on your face?" I mocked.

Nate waved his hand as if to dismiss the issue. "I'm hungry. Do you want t'grab somethin' t'eat at the pub?"

"How about we go to Peter's Yard, instead?"

Nate frowned; then his face grew solemn. "Avoidin' her, eh?"

"Who?"

"You know who, you bloody piker."

"Piker?"

"Yeah. You're givin' up on her."

"There's nothing to give up on," I admitted rather coldly.

"Whatever, mate. Peter's Yard it is, then. I'm starved."

The place was packed. Nate and I were tucked into a corner table, surrounded by chatty females and teens looking to kick off a bit of dust.

A young female, who had waited on me several times before, sauntered up to the table, a beaming smile across her delicate face. She shrieked as one of the teens reached over and pinched her backside.

Nate stood and had the teen's arm twisted painfully behind his back in a blink. "Touch her again, mate, and this arm will resemble rubber. Feel me?" He tightened his hold to emphasize his point.

"Yeah, yeah," the young man sputtered. "I feel ye."

"Let him go, Nate," I said. When he didn't respond, I

touched his shoulder, sending a bit of energy for emphasis. His eyes snapped to mine. "Right."

The waitress' face grew bright pink, contrasting her pale blue eyes and blonde hair, tied loosely in a short braid. She nervously wiped her hands on her apron before setting two menus before us.

"Thank you, Lisel," Nate said rather formally. He was oddly out of character today.

"Would ye like t'hear our specials for t'day?" she asked, her lovely Irish accent blooming under Nate's hungry stare.

"That'll be beaut, love."

I suddenly felt more hungry for air than food at the moment.

Lisel rambled on about the day's specials, finally ending with the fresh dessert of the day—apple crisp.

Nate spilled out his order in a serenade of euphemisms and a blatant display of his healthy appetite as if it were foreplay.

When she finally turned to me, I simply ordered the lamb stew special and iced tea.

She scribbled my order, looking a tad disappointed before she left.

"Mind telling me what that was all about?" I asked him.

He still wore that smitten look on his face like a polished trophy.

"She's a beauty, yeah?"

"She's a human," I reminded him. "As in, off limits."

Nate frowned. "I'm not lookin' to mate her, and besides, you bed the humans often."

"I bed them because I don't want them," I said through clenched teeth. "Judging by the look on your face and your protective tendencies toward her, I can guess where this is going."

"How's this any business of yours, mate?"

"A friend of mine died when a Spirian male tried to make her his own." The thought of Jade spilled through me like acid in my veins. When Khalen found the male, he ended his life with a mere thought.

Nate obviously read my thoughts. "He can do that?"

"Efficiently," I said. "Jade thought she was in love with the male. The male was definitely in love with her. He never pleaded with Khalen; he just sank to his knees as if his very life had deserted him."

Nate's face paled. "There are times I curse being a bloody Spirian."

"Are you sure you want to give your heart to someone you can't possibly have?"

"Like Rae?"

My jaw tightened. "We're not talking about Rae."

"Why not?" asked Nate.

Lisel returned with our iced teas and a bowl of soup for Nate. When he didn't return her smile, she seemed disappointed.

"Tell me about your family," I said, deliberately changing the subject.

"Don't have one."

His thoughts were shielded, but easy to extract. Still, the picture of his past fell together like a jigsaw puzzle with missing pieces—too many missing pieces.

"What happened to your mother?"

Nate's jaw popped with tight cords, his dark eyes dimmed. He continued to sip his soup.

Lisel delivered a massive serving of cornbread to him.

"Thank you, love," he said, keeping his flirtations in

check.

I watched as he tore the thing apart and smothered it in butter and honey. His first bite resembled a wolf tearing into a juicy leg. Just when I thought there couldn't possibly be any room left in that mouth of his, he took a second bite.

The teens paid for their meal, offering Nate a wide berth as they left. The chatty females also took their leave. The place grew blissfully quiet.

"You have gifts," said Nate, "but you're afraid to use them. Why?"

Lisel dropped off my stew and Nate's beef sandwich with a huge side of chips. She motioned for another gal to refill our iced teas.

This time, I was the one to thank her. She beamed me a smile, then glanced over at Nate. He kept his eyes trained on me.

"Because nothing good can come of them," I said.

"You don't know what you don't know, mate."

"That's profound, coming from you."

He stuffed his mouth with beef and bread, and then added a few chips to top it off.

The stew was a bit gamey for my taste, but flavorful and filling.

"Why were you banned from your clan?" I asked him.

"We're not doin' this," he said, stuffing another bite into his mouth.

"I can't help you if I don't know who you are," I said.

"Who said I wanted your help?"

"Your failing health," I growled. "Have you looked in the mirror lately? Death is all around you."

Nate scoffed. "Everyone dies, mate, even us Spirians."

"Damn, but you're stubborn."

We ate in silence for some time. Finally, Lisel brought us both an apple crisp and hot coffee.

"It's on the house," she said, smiling sweetly.

"My mum was Teaka," Nate said once Lisel had left us. "She was beautiful, sweet, and loving beyond measure. Because of her gifts, she was forced to mate Danube, but she was already pregnant with me."

"And Danube didn't know it?"

Nate smiled and shook his head. "No. Teaka could shield with great efficiency. He thought I was of his blood."

"Who is your real father?"

"Huli."

"The Shaman?" I clarified.

"Yes."

Another moment of silence passed between us. It wasn't until our coffees were refiled that he continued.

"Teaka and Huli were in love. Some things cannot be shielded. When Danube discovered the truth of me, he killed my mother and tried to do the same to me. Huli prevented it, but it was only a matter of time before Danube would overpower him."

"How long did Huli protect you?"

"Nearly twenty-five years. When it was evident that Danube would destroy the clan to get to me, Huli pronounced me dead, and sent me away."

He coughed to clear his throat, his eyes glistening with unshed tears.

"Do you ever hear from him?"

Nate nodded. "Sometimes. He sends me what money he can, and short missives laden with encrypted words that only I can understand."

"Surely he knew you would soon die without a clan?"

"He is a visionist," said Nate, turning his coffee cup in his hands as if to warm them. Then, his dark eyes met mine, connecting with my soul. "He saw you and told me to find you."

My chest tightened. That a Shadow had seen me in a vision, gripped me to the core.

"No worries, mate," Nate smiled. "My father is a good man. He taught me to treat all people with respect, despite their spiritual beliefs. He had five wonderful females, all who were happy to be with him."

"And what of Danube?"

Young Lisel came to refill our cups. "C'n I get you anythin' else?" she asked, her sweet eyes on Nate.

A sad smile crept over his face. "No, love. Thank you."

When he turned back to me, his lips grew firm. "For now, he believes me dead."

He glanced up at the clock. "I need to be at the garage in half an hour."

"Garage?"

He tossed a few bills on the table. "Yeah, Mac's garage. It's where I work."

I added my money to the pile while standing to leave. "I'll see you at the pub tonight, yeah?"

I hesitated for a moment. "Don't know yet. I have finals to study for."

He scoffed, "Piker."

I RETURNED TO MY FLAT AND picked up the phone. The conversation I was about to have could go one of two ways. It could be helpful, or disastrous. Khalen was a good man—a bit high strung at times, but good nonetheless.

It was 9 p.m. in Washington. He was no doubt enjoying a drink with his family. The month of May, being mostly rainy in Washington, he was likely to be inside by a warm fire.

I missed the clan and reciting stories to the children. Often, I would wake up with my three younger siblings sprawled out on my bed. The memory made me smile.

"Hello, stranger," a familiar voice said.

"Khalen. How are things?"

"Good," he said. "Haven't heard from you for a while."

"Finals," I said. "The next two weeks will be grueling."

"But that's not why you're calling."

Intuitive as always, I thought. Few things slipped past my uncle, even when masked by idle conversation.

"Are you familiar with a Shaman in New Zealand named Huli?"

A long pause and then the sound of movement as if he were walking to another room.

"What about him?"

"He told his son to find me."

"And why would a Shadow leader send his son to find you?"

I filled him in on the details of Nate's surmise. I could feel the tension build over the phone as I spoke. Khalen had the same dislike for the Shadows as I did, having a nasty history with them.

After a moment of silence, Khalen said, "I've spoken with Huli at council meetings. He never mentioned a son named Nate. That isn't even a Spirian name, let alone an aborigine one. What are you getting yourself into, Seth?"

I cleared my throat. "I'm not sure Nate is his real name. Like I said, Danube thinks he's dead. Taking a human name makes sense to me."

"Huli is a peaceful man and has never been any trouble to our clans. Did Nate mention what his father's vision revealed?"

"No. I sensed that Huli knew Nate would need a clan to join."

More silence. "And choosing a Protected clan would ensure his son would be safe."

"Exactly," I confirmed.

"Do you trust this young man?"

"He hasn't given me reason not to."

"I trust your instincts, Seth; you know that. If you believe this Shadow is trustworthy, then act on it. By what you have told me, he doesn't have much time."

"He will not be willing to change his...lifestyle," I said, not really wanting to go into the details of wanting multiple females.

"Understood," said Khalen. "Keep your instincts sharp, Seth. Did you want to move into the penthouse? It will offer you more room."

"That won't be necessary, Uncle Khalen. The flat is already too large for my needs."

"We'll see you soon at Darius', yes?"

"Yes. I'm looking forward to it."

"Bring Nate. I want to meet him."

"Of course."

"Bye, Seth."

"Bye." I hung up, feeling as if the conversation had gone much better than expected. Khalen had calmed considerably over the years. For that, I was truly grateful.

Chapter 8

~Seth~

IT WAS LATE. I SAT back and rubbed my tired eyes. The books that surrounded me lay open, beckoning my attention. I had none left to give.

My phone vibrated against the glass coffee table. I reached over and glanced down at the ID: Unknown.

"Yeah," I answered.

"Get down here," said Nate. "There's somethin' you ought t'see."

"Here?"

"The pub, y'drongo."

"Nate, I'm tired."

"I'm tellin' you, y'need t'see something."

I growled. "Fine. Be there in a few."

I threw on a pair of blue jeans, a white pullover sweater, and a pair of black Mezlans. It wasn't the most stylish ensemble, but then I wasn't out to impress anyone tonight. I simply wanted to see whatever it was that Nate wanted me to see and get out of there. With any luck at all, Rae wouldn't be working.

Not in the mood for walking tonight, I pulled out my blue gray Audi A4 and headed down the road.

Malones parking lot was cram-packed. I picked a spot on the far end and made my way inside. I could hear the band play a lively Celtic tune sung in old Gaelic. The song told the tale of an ancient Druid who was hunted for witchery, though I doubted anyone in this establishment would even know it. This was more of a rock-and-roll crowd who went wild whenever a U2 song was played.

I walked in through the front doors to find a rowdy bunch, all gearing up for finals and summer vacation. Jane was working the bar, along with Danny. Rae was nowhere in sight.

Come to think of it, Nate was nowhere in sight, either. I scanned the dance floor for a short, stout man with really bad moves. Next, I studied the bar for annoyed females. No traces of Nate, anywhere.

I walked toward the bar and took a stool near the end where I always sit. Jane poured me a glass of Irish whiskey—Bushmills Black Bush.

"It's paid for, love," she said, giving me a wink.

"Have you seen Nate?" I shouted over the din.

She nodded, then gestured upstairs. "Topside. He wants you to join him."

I took my drink and headed for the private rooms upstairs.

When I turned the corner at the top of the curved staircase, Amber, the young female I had danced with several nights past, caressed my shoulder.

"Hey, handsome. Did you need some company tonight?"

I peeled her hand from my arm. "Not tonight, Amber."

Her pout was quickly replaced by a new spark of

interest toward the far side of the room.

"Your loss," she said, making a beeline toward a tall man with a buzz cut and military duds.

I wove my way through the elite clientele who frequented the place toward a private room in the back. The room cost 500 euro to rent for the evening, making me wonder how Nate could afford it.

I entered the curtained off area to find Nate and Rae sitting in the far corner table. The deafening din of the music was muted here to the point where conversations could actually be heard without shouting.

When Rae saw me coming, she quickly looked down.

"You called him?" she hissed to Nate, trying to slide away from the table.

Nate gripped her arm to keep her from leaving. He peeled up her long sleeve to reveal bruising all around her wrists. He then lifted her chin to show me her battered face, split lip, and two darkened eyes.

My energy amped up. The drink in my gut suddenly felt like acid. "Who did this?" I growled, far louder than was necessary.

"Stay out of this, Seth," she said. "My father has already issued a warning. He won't offer a second."

"Danny told her to go home and she refused," said Nate. "I brought her up here, instead, so we could talk."

"Did you ride your bike here?"

She shook her head. "No. Father destroyed it. I took the bus after he left for work."

I downed the rest of my drink. "We're going to my place."

Rae jerked her arm free from Nate and stood. "No, we are not!"

I tossed my keys to Nate. "Blue-gray Audi A4, far

corner slot. Bring it to the back entrance."

"Right," Nate said, leaving his unfinished drink on the table. He stopped short and handed me a credit card—my credit card.

My eyes narrowed. "You stole my card?"

"Not exactly, mate. You dropped it during the fight the other night. I simply forgot to return it to you."

"Perfect," I mumbled, knowing now how he managed to pay for this bloody booth.

Rae's eyes widened as I walked toward her.

"What are yo—" she screamed as I hauled her over my shoulder. "You are not carrying me out of here, Seth."

I walked toward the back entrance and pushed the door open. She struggled against me as I carried her down the stairs.

"Damn it, Seth, put me down."

The door leading out to the parking area was wired to an alarm. If I depressed the handle, all kinds of attention would be directed at us—something I didn't want right now.

"Don't open it," she warned.

Instead, I willed the door open without depressing the handle.

Nate pulled the Audi around, refusing to relinquish the driver's seat.

I willed the back door open, set Rae down, belted her in, then closed the door. Using the gift Khalen had helped me develop, I bound her with energy to keep her from doing something stupid.

"I can't move my arms," she hissed, wiggling madly to free herself.

I slid into the passenger side and instructed Nate to take us to my home.

"Ugh," she screamed. "You bloody bound me?"

"Will you stay in the car if I remove it?"

"Damn it, Seth. Remove this bind immediately."

"Soon enough."

Nate didn't hide his smirk as he raced the Audi out of the parking lot and onto the street.

"Easy, Nate. I don't want to attract any unwanted attention."

"This ride is a beaut."

"I trusted you," Rae said to Nate, staring at him through the mirror.

His smile darkened to seriousness. "And you should continue to do so."

She looked away in disgust. "I don't trust any male," she quietly said.

My heart felt weighted with that statement. There was so much sadness in her voice. What had she been through? I wondered. Her thoughts were closed to me, a feat not easily done. Shields were nothing more than an inconvenience to me; they always had been.

Again, I probed her thoughts. What came back was nothing short of a nightmare. Pain, humiliation, disgust. I fought to keep my stomach from purging.

I directed Nate to the parking area. He reluctantly killed the engine and handed me back the keys.

I turned to face Rae, still staring out the window. "Are you willing to walk like a lady to my flat or must I carry you?"

Gray-green eyes loaded with daggers stared back at me. "I will walk."

I removed the bind, a nice little trick I had acquired from my uncle while he trained me to develop my other gifts.

"How did you do that?" she asked, shaking off the tingles that typically followed such a bind. "You are not a clan leader. That gift is only reserved for those who lead."

"I acquired the gift from my uncle Khalen. Never really had to use it until now."

She glared at me. "I'm honored—really."

I opened the back door to my flat and flipped on the light switch.

Nate walked straight to the kitchen to get himself a drink. "Do you not have any beer?" he asked, peering into the refrigerator.

"No beer," I said.

He rummaged through my cupboards, pulling out various bottles of liquor.

"By all means, make yourself at home," I mocked.

"Just tryin' t'help out, mate."

Rae walked into the living room and settled on the recliner. I stoked the fire I had started earlier that evening before Nate had called.

She eyed the display of books I had sprawled out on the couch. "How many classes are you carrying?"

"Too many," I said, smiling.

I gathered the books and piled them neatly on the bookshelf.

As she sat back and admired the fire, I noticed the dark coloration just below the hem of her jeans. Her feet were slightly swollen, which explained why she wore sandals.

I knelt down before her and removed the sandals from her feet, now marred with shallow indentations from the straps. Her ankles were bruised and looked as if they had been bound with chains.

"Who did this to you?" I asked, gently rubbing the

marks on both ankles.

"Please, Seth. Stay out of this."

"Who?" I growled, forcing my way into her thoughts.

Images of Edmond and his blokes hovering over Rae sent me back. I landed on my ass, eyes wide and heart pounding as if the devil, himself, were after me.

Nate came into the room with a drink in hand. "You all right, mate?"

I stumbled to my feet and met Rae's eyes. They were glistening, tearful, but steadied with stubborn resolve.

The anger welling inside me rumbled like thunder. I had to calm down before my amped up energy shattered every glass within a twenty-foot radius. I walked to the kitchen and splashed cold water onto my face, wetting the front of my sweater in the process.

I returned to the living room with two glasses of Bordeaux. I handed one to Rae. She took it with a shaky hand.

"Your father allowed this?"

She took a sip, her chin raised a notch. "It is our way, Seth. Until I am mated, he governs over me. I must obey."

"I thought he wanted you pure for your intended," I spat.

She scoffed. "Pure? No, Seth. Not pure, just untainted by Protected blood."

When I didn't respond, she continued.

"I'm a Shadow. You may think our ways are wrong, but they are our ways. Nothing will change that. I am tainted, used, and fed up with everyone's opinion of me."

My eyes narrowed. "Forgive me for thinking more highly of you than you do of yourself, Shadow. My mistake."

She stood and carried her wine back to the kitchen.

"Are we done here? I need to get home."

"Yes," I said. "I can see why you are so eager to return there."

She dumped the wine down the sink and placed her glass on the counter. When she tried to leave through the front door, I stopped her.

"I'm sorry," I said.

She jerked away from me. "I don't need your sympathy; nor do I want to hear your apology."

I placed her sandals down by her feet. "At least let me drive you home."

She was silent as she donned them. I sensed it took all that she had just to keep it together.

"I don't want your help. I want you to leave me alone, Seth. Understand?" Her eyes pierced into mine. "Leave me alone."

I opened the door and allowed her to leave.

Nate stared at me as if I had lost my mind. "Go after her, you dolt."

"No," I said, closing the door. "She's made it clear. I'm to leave her alone."

"Piker."

I returned to the couch and sipped my wine. The fire danced and laughed like cruel memories of my past. Memories of when my father would beat my mother for various reasons. The cruel way he would treat other females when his temper was out of control. I shook my head, trying to clear the unwanted drama from my mind.

"Why must Shadow males be so cruel?" I asked.

"Not all of them," said Nate. "We are not all bad."

After a moment of silence, Nate continued.

"My father, Huli, is a good man. He has many mates, yes, but all of them are treated with respect and adoring love. He would never allow such treatment of any being in his clan, children included. Now, Danube, on the other hand, was a real tosser. He'd beat me simply for bein' in the same room."

More silence, filled only by the soft flames licking wood.

"Y'need to help her," said Nate. "She can't help herself. You know that."

"She doesn't want my help."

Nate hissed. "She doesn't want you to get hurt."

"Like she said, Nate. She's a Shadow. This is her way of life, be it good or bad."

"For a man who is academically brilliant, you sure are daft." He sighed and rubbed the creased area between his eyes. "Look, she likes you and you like her."

"She has a poor way of showing it," I said. "And my attraction to her is purely physical. She is nice to look at, but I'm not willing to risk my neck to save her from a fate she has all too willingly accepted."

Nate stood as if preparing for a fight. "Like your mother accepted her fate?"

My jaw tightened, forgetting that he, too, had the ability to pierce through my shield.

"I'm sure she enjoyed being beaten by your father or she would have changed it, yeah?"

I set my glass down and stood to square with him. "She had no choice! He would have killed her."

"Does Rae not face that same choice?"

"Damn it." I grabbed the keys from the counter and headed for the garage.

It didn't take long to find Rae. She had only made it two blocks when I spotted her walking. I pulled over.

"Get in."

"Sod off," she said.

I blocked her path with the car and put the thing park. "Please, get in the car."

"Leave me alone."

I closed my eyes and took a deep breath. "Look, I can make you get in, or you can do it on your own. It's your choice."

Feeling my energy begin to peak, she stopped walking and sighed. "If it were my choice, you would leave me alone like I asked."

"That's not going to happen."

"So, then, I have no choice."

"Not with this."

"Not with anything," she mumbled.

I opened the door and waited for her to settle in. She said nothing to me as I slid into the driver's seat. Her anger was palpable.

"If my father sees you with me, he'll kill you."

"I have no doubt he'll try."

She pressed her lips together and shook her head. "You're a fool, Seth. Please, stay out of this. My father is powerful and ruthless beyond measure. The mere scent of you on me will send him over the edge."

"You're smart, and gifted," I said. "I have seen your ability to shield. Use it on him. Don't allow him to—"

"Not him," she said, shaking her head as if reliving a horrid nightmare. "He'd know. He'd—"

"Hey," I said, placing my hand over hers. "It's all right. We'll get through this."

"Why do you care?" she said, trying to pull her hand from mine.

"Because you need my help."

Her hand went limp in mine like a balloon that had

been deflated.

"Right," she said. "A helpless female drawing upon the valor of the Protected."

"Something like that."

"Let me out here," she said, pointing to the corner just before her driveway. "Father may be home and I don't want him to see you."

I did what she asked. The sadness of her eyes tore through me like a jagged blade. At that moment, I would give anything to feel the warmth of her hand in mine again.

"Goodbye, Seth."

I watched her walk down the driveway without looking back at me. I had to be crazy to pursue this, I thought. Another hopeless endeavor—something I seemed to be drawn to—like a moth drawn to the flame that eventually kills it.

Chapter 9

~Seth~

NATE WAS GLANCING THROUGH my pathology book when I returned, no doubt looking for lung disorders. His injured leg was propped up on the coffee table, a drink wavering in his hand.

"How's the leg?" I asked, pouring myself another serving of wine.

"A bit achey, but fine."

"Let's see it."

He stood and downed his pants. I wasn't surprised to see he had gone commando. I focused on the swollen wound over his thigh.

"Sit," I said. "It's infected."

After cleaning the wound, I pulled down my supply of tinctures that Elle kept me well stocked in. She had been the only woman I had ever loved, aside from my mother and siblings. When she mated Drew, it nearly undid me. Becoming her templar, as honorable as that is, was like a consolation prize—a craving I could touch but never taste.

I opened the bottle labeled Herbal Antibiotics, and placed two droppers worth into a cup. I added lemon juice and honey, per her instructions, and hot water.

It smelled like stale athletic socks that had been stored in a plastic bag for a week. The taste was even worse. I added two shots of whiskey just to make the concoction tolerable, before taking it to Nate.

"Drink this," I told him.

He smelled it, then shook his head in disgust. "Bloody hell. Are you tryin' t'kill me? What is it?"

"Echinacea and goldenseal. It's for the infection. I added a little Dr. Jack to get you to drink it."

While he endured the medicine, I smothered his wound with antibiotic salve that Elle had made, and dressed it.

"I have a proposition for you," I said, cleaning the mess from the table."

Nate immediately covered himself with his pants, eyes wide. "What kind of proposition?"

I rolled my eyes. "How would you feel about living here with me?"

"I don't swing that way, mate."

"Nor do I, you fool."

I ran upstairs and returned with a pair of sweats that I tossed to him. "You need other Spirians around you, or you will die. I have a spare room you can use if you like."

"Can we stock the refrigerator with beer?"

"Yes," I said, feeling suddenly exhausted. "I'm heading for bed. Use the spare room if you like; it's clean."

AFTER A QUICK BREAKFAST, WE took the Land Rover to Nate's house to pack his things. He lived in a small flat above a garage surrounded by old tractors, trucks, and various tools that had succumbed to years of rust and idle aging.

A sweet old lady using a cane came to meet us with a pitcher of lemonade. Her Australian Shepherd accompanied her, carrying a bag in his mouth.

Nate quickly relieved the old woman of her burden, and helped her sit at the patio table that was clean but well used.

"Ye lads look thirsty," she said, her voice shaky but calm. "Spikey there has a few glasses." She gestured to the dog who had set the bag down by her feet.

Nate placed the cups on the table and began pouring.

When the old woman noticed the items in the car, her frown deepened. "Are ye leavin', Nate?"

"I'm movin' closer t'school, Shelby, but I won't be far. I'll still help you with repairs and such."

"Oh my," she said, shaking. "I'll miss ye, lad." Her fragile hand reached over to Nate's.

"Shelby, I want you to meet a friend of mine. This is Seth. I'll be moving into his flat."

Her face grew pink, causing the delicate network of veins to darken under her pale skin. "Oh," she said, as if understanding something that was clearly uncomfortable.

Having read her thoughts, Nate quickly clarified. "No, Shelby. We are straight—just friends."

"That's nice," she said with an audible sigh. "I'm sure those women you spend time with would be sorely disappointed if you had turned sides."

"Well, they needn't worry and nor should you." He patted her hand.

"The fields will be ready to harvest soon," she said. "Will ye be helpin' me?"

"Don't I always?" Nate said.

"You're a good lad," she laughed. "Always willin' t'help this old woman."

Nate pulled out his wallet and shuffled through the bills. "Here's two months rent, Shelby. That should last until you can find another tenant."

She waved her hand and scoffed at the gesture. "I don't need that, lad. Besides, you've done quite enough around 'ere t'pay for several months rent. Ye dun't owe me a thing."

"I've ordered the part for the tractor. I'll be by to fix it later this week, yeah?"

"Thank you, lad."

Her pale blue eyes focused on me, scanning me from head to feet. "Yer a handsome one."

I hid my embarrassment by taking a long draw of the tart drink. "Thank you, ma'am."

She laughed. "And shy at that, eh?" More laughter.

We sat and talked with her for about an hour before Nate talked me into unloading a flatbed full of hay into the loft before we left.

It didn't take long, but the exertion caused Nate to cough up blood. Not wanting Shelby to witness the gore, he ran behind the barn.

"Oh. Is he all right?"

I took her arm and escorted her back to the patio. "He's fine. Just a few allergies, that's all."

"My beloved Ben, God rest his soul, suffered badly from them as well." She glanced over her shoulder with sympathy. "Poor lad."

"Thank you for the lemonade," I said.

"Ye come back an' visit, now, yes?"

"Yes," I said. "We'll be back."

She patted my hand. "Ye're a good lad."

Nate stumbled back to the car and slammed the door shut, obviously in no condition to say his goodbyes.

Shelby looked at me with knowing eyes. "Ye take good care of 'im, yes?"

"I will."

She turned and sadly retreated back into the house.

When I got into the car, Nate was wheezing. Blood spattered the front of his shirt.

"Christ. We need to get you some help."

He forced a smile. "I know a good doctor."

"This is beyond me, Nate, and you know it."

"Take me home and let me rest. I'll be fine."

I put the car in drive and headed down the road. In two weeks, I would be leaving for my uncle Darius' place in Uig. My aunt Skye would be there. She would be able to heal him, I was sure. Khalen would know what to do after that.

"How did things go with Rae?" Nate asked.

I shook my head. "She is unreachable."

"Interesting choice of words."

It was time to change the subject. "So, how did you meet Shelby?"

After a moment of silence and exhausted resignation, he finally answered. "She brought her car to the garage. I fixed it for her."

"For free, no doubt."

He smiled. "You seem surprised."

"Not really."

"Careful, Protected. This is a Shadow you're talking to. No tellin' when I will turn into the evil spirit that lingers in my blood."

"Touché," I said, remembering my previous opinions of Shadows.

My mind wandered to memories of my sister, Tria, who had tragically died before I left for college. She had always been mean-spirited since the day she was born. Even when she was nice, it was for her own personal gain. My mother had known. Sadly, she thought if she could take Tria away from the Shadow clan, she would change for the good. It didn't turn out that way. Tria was miserable living with the Protected and didn't bother to hide that fact. She had done a lot of damage in her wake.

Her death was hard on my mother, but it brought me relief. For years, I had kept her evilness to myself, shielding it from Khalen. I had vowed loyalty to him and had no right to protect Tria. When the truth finally came out, the clan had been shattered. My mother and stepfather parted for a brief time. The separation nearly destroyed us all, me and my younger siblings included. Thank God, Aidan saw the light of things and gave her another chance. Still, there was a distance between them that I wasn't entirely convinced could be healed.

Trust was such a fragile vise that when crushed could only be restored with time. Even then, it would never be quite as strong as before—ever.

Nate started to snore, his head propped against the window. I pulled into the garage and started emptying the vehicle of his things, which were few.

Sometime during one of my trips, he found his way into the house and collapsed on the couch. I wondered whether he would survive the next two weeks.

Chapter 10

~ R a e ~

THE KIND GUARD AT MUSSELBURGH Race Track smiled as he recognized my pale blue BMW 328i. He was a dark-skinned man in his sixties with peppered hair and large brown eyes. I rolled down my window.

"Hi, George."

He removed his hat. "Well, hi, Ms. Tomei. Not ridin' your bike, today?"

"It's out of commission for now," I said, not bothering to mention how my father had disintegrated it into a pile of ash with a wave of his hand.

"That's too bad," he said, looking genuinely sad. "I know how much you enjoy riding it."

He flipped a lever that opened the gate. "Your brother is in barn eight. He asked me to direct you there."

"I know the way, George. Thank you."

He waved as I drove on past. The track was busy with activity, no doubt getting ready for the day's races, which would begin in two hours.

I drove past the hot walkers loaded with young horses,

some prancing and kicking up clouds of dust. I parked along the side of barn eight and made my way through the dark corridor that separated the fifty stalls.

Jenico smiled as I walked toward him. When he saw my face, that smile crumbled. I had done my best to cover the bruises with makeup, and my sunglasses did a fine job at hiding my eyes, but the barn was dark and I was forced to remove them in order to see.

I was tempted to heal the bruises and cuts but did not want to spark my father's suspicions. He almost seemed happy to see the marks when I came home each evening. It made me sick the way he fingered each one as if it was a testament to the power he held over me.

Jenico took my face in both his hands and tears began to well in his beautiful green eyes.

I backed away. "Don't."

"God, Rae." He closed his eyes and clenched his fists. "This is so wrong."

I turned my attention to the fine colt in the cross ties. After introducing my scent to the young horse, I glided my hand along his elegant neck and down his strong back.

"Who's this?"

"Rambo. He's my new recruit about to run his first race, providing you can fix him."

"Fix him?"

"He's not striding out. I turned him loose in the pen this morning, and he moves as if he's tight in the middle."

Unlike most horses under training, my brother's horses were always taught ground manners and were a pleasure to work with. He simply would not put up with any horse with an attitude for causing harm, especially to me.

I ran my hands over Rambo's back and legs, observing his minor reactions. Satisfied that he was sound, I began applying pressure to his vertebrae. When I reached T6, his entire left side began to quiver.

"I think he pulled a rib out," I said, running my fingers along the bones.

"Can you fix it? His race starts in three hours. I won't run him if he's in pain."

I smiled. That was just like my brother. He was more concerned with his horses' welfare than the money they ran for. His clients didn't feel the same and often tried to force him to run a sore horse anyway, despite his opinion.

"Yeah, I think I can."

I massaged the area first, trying to relax the spasming muscles. Rambo responded by lowering his head and closing his eyes part way. When he started licking his lips, I knew he was ready for the adjustment.

Lifting his left front leg, I slowly stretched it forward, holding the pastern area. When he completed the stretch himself, I carefully crossed his leg over his chest. A subtle pop preceded a groan from Rambo. When I released his leg, he gave his body a good shake.

This time, when I ran my hand over his vertebrae, there was no reaction.

"That should do it," I said. "Give him a moment to settle before working him."

Jenico offered the colt a carrot and an apple slice before giving his neck a good rub.

"Thanks, Rae."

I smiled, trying to ease my brother's inner pain. "He looks like a fast one."

Jenico shrugged. "Don't know. He doesn't try very hard during training unless another horse comes close. Today is more of a trial jaunt to see what he's got."

We both picked up a brush and began grooming the

colt in silence.

"I'm sorry about your bike, Rae."

I shrugged. "It's just a bike."

"Can I buy you another one?"

I shook my head. "No, you cannot. Father would have your head on a stick if he ever found out. Besides, I can afford to buy my own. I just need to decide where to keep it so he doesn't find out." I winked at him over Rambo's back.

"He went to meet Bennet in Glasgow this morning."

My gut twisted at the thought of sitting across from Bennet Graves. His eyes always wandered over my body as if he were assessing his next business acquisition. I tossed the brush back into the bucket, startling Rambo.

"At least he's a handsome man," said Jenico.

"Nico, please. I don't want to talk about him."

He frowned, deepening the crease that seemed a permanent feature on his handsome face. I walked around to stand before him.

"Don't fret for me, Nico. I will make it through this— we both will."

He looked up and blinked back the tears I knew wanted to flow. His big arms wrapped around me like a huge comforting blanket, strong and familiar. He was the only male I trusted. The only male I would ever trust.

"If your mother were here, she would never allow this," he said.

"Yes, and look what that defiance did for her."

"She frightened Father. That's why he sent her away. I wouldn't doubt that he was the one who had her killed as well."

I closed my eyes and shook my head. "Shh, Nico. Don't talk like that."

"I'm tired of this, Rae. I'm tired of all of it. Father runs this clan with fear, not respect."

"I know."

"I want to change it."

"Soon," I said. "You will be leader of this clan soon, Nico. You just need to stay on his good side and do what he says."

He brushed his thumbs over my swollen eyes. "This has to stop, Rae. I cannot sit back anymore and see you suffer such treatment."

I pulled his hands away. "We both know there is nothing you can do. I will not have you endure the same retribution that killed my mother."

"Are you working tonight?" he asked, trying to keep his emotions reined in.

"Yeah."

"I could use a sparring partner later. Are you game?"

I shook my head. "Not today, Nico. I have finals to study for and I still need to stop by VetMed to check on that mare and her new foal."

"All right," he said. "Maybe later, then, yes?"

"Yes." I smiled. "I'm going to need something to beat on before that cursed dinner with Bennet."

His face beamed. "You know where to find me, darlin'."

Chapter 11

-Rae-

JANE GREETED ME IN THE EMPLOYEE lounge. Her pale blue eyes studied me from head to foot. "Well, ye look better." Her soft hands brushed my face. "How ye feeling?"

"Better," I said, breathing in the familiar and somewhat comforting aroma of Danny's personal brew. Its scent of oak, teak, musk and honey seemed more pungent today.

I placed my keys, bag, and sweater into my cubby, pulled back my hair, and donned the black apron that would smell like a spill mat by morning.

Danny came around the corner with a cracked mug in his hand. He studied me with those dark eyes of his, the concentration of it all making his facial scar twitch.

"Gonna tell me who hit ye, yet?"

"No," I said, taking the cracked mug from his hand and tossing it in the bin. "I've seen what those fists of yours can do."

Danny was a boxer in his day and was quite a sight to watch in action. His last fight with Samson O'Malley had earned him that lovely mark on his face, making him look somewhat disfigured. He wore the scar like a shiny badge.

"Was it yer brother, lass?"

I turned sharply to face him. "Heavens no. Nico would never hurt me."

Danny laughed, knowing full well my brother's kindness toward me. "Well, let's hope he's feelin' the fight during the rematch, eh?"

I rolled my eyes and made my way to the bar. As expected, the place was busy and promised to keep me hopping till the end of my shift. I looked forward to the exhaustion that would certainly follow.

Jane nudged me. "Seth is at the end of the bar, lass. Go and serve him, yes?"

Jane typically handled that end of the bar when Seth wasn't there. She had a strange notion that he could like me if given the chance. Apparently, my feelings toward him were more transparent—except to him.

Nate sat beside him, looking less pale than the last time we had talked. He smiled as I approached.

"Well, look at you, love. You look radiant tonight."

I rolled my eyes and shook my head. "To you, Nate, every female looks radiant."

He pursed his lips and cocked his head. "Perhaps."

I laughed. "What can I get you boys?"

"Monteith," said Nate. His usual. Danny had to bring in the lager from New Zealand just for Nate, it seemed, since he was the only one who ever ordered it.

Seth looked distant in thought, as if he wanted to be elsewhere. "How about for you, Seth?"

"Black Bush with a drop of water."

His eyes never touched me. Was he angry?

When I returned with their drinks, the two of them

seemed to be deep in conversation. The crease between Seth's brows deepened as I placed his drink before him. Still, he did not look at me.

"Bring us some chips, love, eh?"

"Extra crispy?"

Nate smiled. "That'll be beaut."

Seth continued to look down, drawing figures through the condensation on the polished bar.

Well, my conscience chimed in. You did tell him to leave you alone. He's merely doing what you asked him to do.

And since when did Seth ever listen to anyone? I rebuked.

Jane was kind enough to bring Nate his chips while I filled several orders for the tables upstairs.

"Hi, Rae," said a familiar voice.

The hairs on my neck vibrated like the tail beads of a rattlesnake. I looked up to find Edmond and his five blokes staring down at me. I dropped the highball glass in my hand. It shattered, mirroring my nerves.

In a blink, Seth was facing off with Edmond, Nate standing close behind.

Steve, our bouncer, came between the men, holding them apart with outstretched hands. He was a large man, but dwarfed by Seth and Edmond as the energy between them amped to deafening proportions.

"Take it outside, boys," Steve said.

"No," I countered. "Seth, please. Stay out of this."

"Outside," he growled to Edmond. "Now."

I had felt that kind of energy before. Nothing good could come of it.

Jane came over to help clear the broken glass. "They're the ones, yes?"

When I didn't answer, she simply placed her hand on my shoulder. For a human, she certainly knew when to leave things alone.

I felt the hum of energy all around, making me shudder. Other Spirians in the room felt it as well and all grew quiet. The humans continued along as if nothing were out of the ordinary. Those who were not numbed with alcohol rubbed at their temples, no doubt fighting an ensuing headache.

Moments later, Seth and Nate returned. The hum died down. One look at their faces and I knew that what happened could not be reversed.

"What have you done?" I whispered.

Seth's eyes met mine for the first time this evening. They were nearly glowing like the sun. "What should have been done the first time they harassed you."

"Nate," I said, pleading. "Please tell me."

He covered my hands, his were shaking. "They won't hurt you again, love—ever."

I covered my mouth with my cold, trembling hand. "Oh God. If Father finds out."

Seth stood and gripped my arms. "No trace, no witnesses. He won't know."

"What if he asks me?"

"Tell him the truth, Rae. Edmond came to see you, and then left. You don't know what happened to him."

"But I do."

He shook me, his hands digging painfully into my arms. "No, you don't." His voice was low and disturbingly dark.

As if sensing my fear, he released me, took up his drink, and wandered toward the center of the room.

"Give him a moment, love," said Nate.

"What happened out there?"

He shook his head. "You don't want to know." He downed the last of his beer. "Bring us another round, yeah?"

I nodded.

They had settled at a table with two women. A dark redhead stood and massaged Seth's shoulders. The other was talking to another gentleman. I was very tempted to spill Nate's brew down the back of the redhead's shirt. Instead, I set the drinks down before the men and then presented Seth with a plate of cheese, meat, and fruit.

"Thank you," I whispered into his ear.

He eyed the platter before turning to face me. "You're welcome."

"Come dance with me, Seth," the redhead purred.

He removed her hands from his shoulders. "Not tonight, Jasmine."

"I'll dance with you, love," said Nate.

The redhead looked at the short man like a woman on a diet would a carrot over a double fudge brownie cake.

Nate didn't seem to care. He led her onto the dance floor like a prize he was eager to flaunt.

"Are you all right?" I asked Seth.

"I will be," he said. "Thanks for the platter."

"I figured you needed something more substantial than extra crispy chips."

He reached over and grabbed my hand. His grip was hard at first, and then softened around my fingers.

"What are you doing for breakfast, tomorrow?"

"I have go to VetMed first thing in the morning, but after that, I'm free."

"Perfect. I'll take you."

"Um, I'll meet you at your place, okay?"

His face tightened. He released my hand. "Yes. Okay."

"Eight a.m.?"

He nodded. "See you then."

What are you doing? My conscience scolded. Getting involved with this man is like signing both of your death sentences.

He's a player, I reasoned. He's not looking for a relationship.

And what are you looking for? my conscience replied, as if talking to a promiscuous hussy.

Kindness, I thought. That's all, just a little kindness.

Jane smiled as I approached with a new bounce in my step.

"What's the craic? Have ye been sippin' Danny's brew?"

I laughed. "No."

"What's it, then?"

"Seth asked me out for breakfast." The words flowed from my mouth as if I had just won a prize I had been aiming for my entire life.

"Well, it's 'bout bloody time."

Chapter 12

~ R a e ~

I **PARKED MY CAR IN THE GATED** lot and walked to Seth's flat entrance. I was a tad early, but I didn't think he would mind. Straightening my pink cashmere sweater, I took a deep breath and knocked on the hard oak door.

Moments later, Jasmine, the voluptuous redhead, answered the door wearing a silk gown—the same silk gown Seth had offered to me the night I had slept over. My heart sank and threatened to cease working altogether.

"Hi," she said.

"Um, is Seth—"

Jasmine laughed. "He's indisposed at the moment. Would you like to come in and wait for him?"

I shook my head. "No. Just tell him I came by."

Jasmine looked at me as if I had marbles for eyes. "Uh, okay."

As I turned to walk away, I heard the door close. My vision blurred. I was a fool—a bloody hopeless fool. How many times had my mother warned me about not trusting males? I should be used to this, I thought. Males of our clan often laid with multiple females.

Somehow, I thought Seth was different. Given his past history, I had no idea why I would think that. He was a player; I had known it from the start. Why was I so shocked?

I drove past the flat toward the slowly opening gates. Through my teary peripheral, I saw a half-naked man running toward me, shouting my name.

I continued past the gates and accelerated down the road. He's a player, my conscience repeated. Then, I remembered what Seth had said last night when I asked if he was all right.

"I will be," he had replied.

Of course he would. All he needed was a bit of female companionship. He seemed to be attracted to the fiery red-headed women. I must seem like quite a bore in comparison.

I turned onto A701 and let my auto fly. The road was empty and flat. If a copper stopped me, it would only serve as a needed distraction. Perhaps if I mouthed off, he would arrest me. Wouldn't Father be proud of that?

Damn them all to hell, I thought, shifting into a higher gear. The engine roared and pitched forward like a grayhound who had been pent up too long.

VetMed was only a kilometer beyond Musselburgh Race Track. It wasn't far enough away as far as I was concerned.

Ben, the groundskeeper, hesitantly waved as I sped on past, leaving him in a wake of dust. When I parked, I sat there, allowing the dust to settle.

Ben stood outside my door. When I exited the car, he waved his hat around, coughing and gagging rather dramatically. He had moved here from Alabama where he was raised as a groom. His dark skin suggested a Nigerian heritage.

"Sorry, Ben."

"Girl, ye came blastin' through here so fast I thought my overalls were going to tear away from my body."

"Just blowing the cobwebs out," I explained.

"Yeah, well, I think ye blew them onto me." He brushed at his dusty overalls and slammed his hat against his leg.

When I didn't reply, he followed me into the barn.

"Can't be a tough day," he said, sounding quite puzzled. "Just barely past eight."

I snagged a pair of coveralls from the peg above my cubbie and donned them over my clothes. "How's the colt?"

"Won't eat. His eyes are swollen shut now."

I hurried my pace down the corridor, ignoring the snorts and nickers of greetings from the many horses I had treated. Normally, I would offer them all carrots during my rounds. Today, I had an agenda.

"Did the vet say anything?"

Ben shrugged. "He thinks the colt is allergic to somethin'."

I rolled my eyes. When I reached the stall where the mare and foal resided, I talked softly to the mare and slid the stall bolt open.

Ben waited outside while I examined the foal.

"You said he hasn't been eating?"

"Not like a normal foal."

I ran my hands over the foal's rib cage. He was severely underweight. "Did Dr. Gannis give him anything?"

"Some kind of milk substitute. Doc says the foal is allergic to his mama's milk."

"Is he taking it?"

"No, miss, he's not."

"Bring me a bucket of warm water and a few clean rags, could you, Ben?"

"Sure thing."

The foal's eyes were so swollen shut, it was difficult to determine the true nature of the cause. I wondered whether the good doctor even took the time to clean the eyes before making his assessment. Dr. Gannis was a good man, but he often jumped to conclusions without cause. He and I rarely saw things on the level.

Ben returned with a bucket and some rags.

"Steady him for me?"

Ben wrapped his large arms around the foal's neck and steadied his muzzle, being careful to stay out of my way.

I had to smile. "You make a great assistant, Ben."

He returned the smile. "Thank ye, miss."

It took nearly a half hour to clean the discharge from the foal's eyes. Upon closer inspection, I noticed the lower eyelid was rolling inward.

"What do ye think, miss?" Ben asked, clearing away the bucket and soiled cloths.

"It looks like Entropion."

Ben's expression resembled a young boy who had just eaten a bug. "Oh, what a damn shame."

Untreated, the condition would lead to blindness. Surgery was an option, but the foal's condition was too weak even to consider it.

"Ben, I have a solution of eyebright in my cubbie. Would you mind fetching it for me along with two eyepatches?"

"Not at all, miss." He left, taking the bucket and cloths with him. That would give me a few minutes to offer a healing to the foal. With any luck, the improvement would be contributed to the solution.

Closing my eyes, I drew my energy inward and covered the foal's eyes with my hands. I stopped when I sensed another Spirian nearby. As far as I knew, the only Spirians who visited this facility were my brother and I. It was one of the reasons I had chosen it to serve my residency. Dr. Gannis could be a bit of a pain at times, but he was manageable and seemed to respect my opinions.

"Don't stop," a familiar voice said. My heart pounded at the sound of it—Seth. Had he witnessed the healing?

"I'm not sure what you're talking about." I turned so he couldn't see my fear.

"You're a healer," he said. "Why would you hide that from me?"

"Your mistaken, Seth. Please leave."

"I know what I saw."

"No, you don't."

Ben came around the corner with the items I had requested. I took them from his hands.

"Thank you, Ben."

The old man looked between me and Seth and grew visibly uncomfortable. "If you won't be needin' me, miss, I have some work to tend to."

"No, Ben. I'm fine. Thanks for your help." I forced a smile.

He returned it hesitantly, spared Seth another speculative glance, and then took his leave.

"You shouldn't be here," I said to Seth.

"We had a date, remember?"

Anger replaced my fear. If I couldn't change his belief about my ability to heal, perhaps I could distract and anger him enough to forget what he saw. Yeah, right, my conscience chimed in. The man has a photographic memory. I'm sure he'll forget everything. I turned to face him. God, he looked great in that white pullover. The jeans weren't too bad either. Then, I remembered that bloody redhead and my anger rekindled full throttle. "That was before you decided to sleep with Jasmine."

"I what?"

"You heard me." I turned my attention back to the foal who was now quite skittish from all the aggressive energy floating about. I tried calming him with little success.

Seth opened the stall door and stepped inside. He approached the foal with the same confidence he approached his women.

"Shh, now," he softly said. He rubbed the colt's withers and slowly worked his way down between his spindly front legs.

With slow, almost liquid movements, he rubbed the inside of the colt's front leg. His mare nickered softly, smelling Seth.

She didn't take well to strangers touching her colt, but she seemed comfortable with Seth. If she were the least bit alarmed, she would have taken a chunk out of him by now.

The foal's eyes relaxed and his head dropped. Seth moved up his neck and under his head. When he placed a finger between the foal's upper lip and nose, the colt pressed into it, relaxed and looking half-asleep.

"How did you do that?" I asked.

"My aunt Skye is great with horses. She showed me a few things."

"Can you steady him while I tend to his eyes?"

"For as long as you need," he said. There was a hidden meaning in that statement, but I wasn't going to go there—not now.

I applied the eyebright solution and covered the eyes with a see-through mesh patch. It enabled the colt to see, but helped keep out dust and debris. I used surgical tape to discourage the lower lid from folding under. Most of the infection came from irritation from the eyelashes that scratched the cornea. With the little bit of healing I administered, he should be better by morning.

"You should give him one last healing before we leave," said Seth.

I could see my conscience now, grinning and gloating about how she told me so.

"It's just Reiki," I lied.

He smiled. "Fine, call it what you want, but I think he needs more."

Since the cat was out of the bag, I might as well let it run free, I thought. Closing my eyes, I gathered my energy and directed it toward the colt's eyes.

When I finished, I opened my eyes to see Seth smiling.

"Please don't say anything," I said. "Nico is the only one who knows."

His jaw tightened. "Nico?"

Was that jealousy? I wondered, stifling a laugh. "My brother, Jenico. He prefers me to call him Nico."

He relaxed some. "Well, it's wise of you to keep that gift hidden in the midst of Sh—your clan and strangers."

"You sound like you speak from experience."

His expression changed as if a dark shadow loomed above him. "My aunt Skye is a healer."

That got my attention. Very few Spirians had the gift, and those who did rarely lived long enough to tell of it. No one really knew why the healers had been killed.

As usual, Seth's thoughts were closed to me. "You have

something to say?" I asked.

He shook his head. "It's nothing. Forget about it."

We exited the stall and secured the door. He took the items from my hand and insisted on following me around as I checked on my other patients.

"Does Bennet know?" he asked.

"Know what?"

"About your gift?"

I shook my head. "No, like I said, Nico is the only one who knows."

He grabbed my arm and spun me around to face him. There was a hardness in his eyes. "Can he shield his thoughts?"

I winced and tried to pull my arm away. "Yes, he can."

"I'm sorry," he said, releasing his grip. "It's just that..."

He remained silent for a moment.

"What?" I prompted.

His lips tightened and the cords in his jaw flexed. "I know how ruthless some males can be to acquire a female with such gifts."

I leaned against the stall, rubbing the gelding's head. "Did something bad happen to your aunt?"

He paced, staring down at the ground as if looking for a hole to crawl into.

"Oh, for Pete's sake, Seth. If you have something to say, spill it." I opened the stall door and began taking the gelding's vitals.

Seth remained silent as I recorded my notes and exited the stall.

He followed me to the next stall, watching as I tended to my tasks.

I glanced up at him. "Are you going to talk to me?"

"My father was not a good man," he finally said.

I scoffed. "Like mine is?"

"He was a Shadow, through and through. Before Skye was mated to Khalen, my father tried to take her from him."

I stood and met his eyes. They were dull and dim with memories that had been buried too long.

"What happened?"

"Khalen killed him." His words were spoken with an odd reverence of sorts.

I exited the stall and closed the door. "I'm sorry," I quietly said.

"I'm not. The world is a better place without him in it."

I finished my rounds, slipped my stethoscope back into my pocket, and shed my coveralls.

"How badly does Bennet want you?" he asked.

I shrugged, hanging my coveralls on the peg and closing my cubbie. "Bad enough to pay my father a billion dollars."

Seth's eyes widened. "A billion dollars?"

I narrowed my eyes. "Are you saying I don't measure up to the cost?"

His reaction was worth the cheap jab and I stifled a laugh.

"Of course you do, and much more."

I rolled my eyes. "You can always counter the bid, if you're interested."

He stiffened. "I will not pay for a mate."

That hurt. He may as well pierce my gut with a pitch fork and twist the throngs to finish the assault. I forced in a breath.

"That's right," I said, "you can have anyone of your choosing. Why would you stoop so low as to pay for a female when you can have your pick for the price of a smile?"

"When I am ready to mate a female, it will be her choice."

"How noble of you."

I stepped around him and opened my car door. He slammed it shut.

"Are we having breakfast?"

I arched my brow at him. "What? Did Jasmine have other plans?"

"I did not sleep with her."

"So, she just happened to stop by your place this morning and slip into your well-used guest robe?"

I could feel his energy ramping up and knew I was close to crossing the line. At the moment, I really didn't care. I was used to hotheaded males.

"She was Nate's guest, not mine. I was loading something into my car when you came to the door."

"Nate's guest?"

"Yes. He moved in with me yesterday morning."

"Oh," I said, lacking a better reply. Nate must have been the half-naked man running after me this morning.

"Would you like to see what I was loading into the car?" His voice was softer, now.

I glanced over at the Range Rover, feeling rather guilty for assuming so much. "Sure."

He took my hand and led me around to the rear of the vehicle. When he willed the door open, my mouth dropped open.

Inside was a brand new Raleigh Venture 4, an upscale model of the bike my father had destroyed. This one was pearl white.

"Are you taking up biking?" I asked.

He squeezed my hand. "It's for you."

Trying to remove my hand from his unyielding grip, I blinked back the tears stinging my eyes. "Why would you do this?"

"Honestly?"

I nodded.

He quirked a smile. "You're a much nicer person when you're not forced to drive everywhere. And, judging by the skid marks in front of my place, the town is safer as well."

That earned him a glare. "Oh, nice."

Thinking about the fine gift, I frowned.

"What's wrong?" he asked.

"I can't bring it home. My father would know where it came from."

"Keep it at my place. You can park your car and use your bike without Drake ever knowing."

I doubted that. He would find out eventually. "He's a dangerous man, Seth. I worry for your safety."

"Don't," he said, his forehead creased. "Come on. I'm hungry."

Chapter 13

~ R a e ~

I FOLLOWED HIM BACK TO PETER'S YARD and parked my car next to his. He walked beside me and possessively wrapped his arm around my waist.

When I tried to move away, he pulled me closer.

"Do you think this is a good idea?" I asked.

"Why? Are you ashamed to be seen with me?"

"Don't be stupid. Of course I'm not ashamed. My clansmen reside in this town. If word gets back to my father about this, he'll have both of us destroyed."

Seth smiled. "Not when you're worth a billion dollars."

He opened the door and followed me in. It felt as if every eye in the place turned toward us. Part of me was thrilled to be seen with this man, while another part of me screamed that it was a bad idea.

"Hi, Seth," a blonde woman chimed. "Sit anywhere you like."

Seth took my hand and guided me to a corner table by the windows.

The blonde sauntered over. "What c'n I getcha?"

Seth looked over at me. My voice got caught in my throat. "C—coffee," I stammered, not used to being able to order for myself in the company of a male. The men in our clan always took that liberty and demanded to place their orders first.

"Coffee," Seth said, far more confidently.

His golden eyes studied me. "Get used to being treated right."

My comfort level plummeted. I started to stand. "This is a bad idea."

"Please sit," he said. "Stop running from me, Rae."

I stifled a laugh. "Running from you?"

He reached over and held my hand. It felt right, but so wrong on many levels. When I tried to pull away from him, his grip tightened.

Again, I laughed, tears starting to blur my vision.

The blonde came back with our coffees. When she glanced over at me, she frowned. "Um, I'll give ye a moment, yes?"

"Thank you, Ginger," said Seth. Of course, he knew her name. It seemed every female in town knew him or of him.

"You're stronger than this," he said. "I've seen that strength. Where is it now?"

I closed my eyes and shook my head. "Can I be blunt with you?"

He released my hand and pulled something out of his pocket—a small container of cayenne pepper. "For your coffee," he said.

I frowned, taking it from him. "Thank you."

"Let me tell you what I think is on your mind," he said.

I arched a brow. "This should be interesting."

"You've wanted me for so long that it has become more of an unobtainable dream."

"How very humble of you," I sneered.

He raised his hand. "Let me finish."

I nodded my acquiescence.

"It is true that I'm a player, like most young Spirian males. I am not looking for a mate."

I felt my face betray my pain. Not surprisingly, it didn't escape his notice. He lifted my chin and his eyes seemed to glow like the sun.

"For some reason, however, I feel very drawn to you, Raeiza Tomei. To the point where I'm willing to die for you."

I pulled away from him. "Don't say that."

"You want me," he continued, "but only to the point of having me for a night, maybe two. You want to feel what other women feel when a man treats them with kindness. You are not looking for a man who will challenge your intended. No, you have already resigned yourself to that horrid fate."

I felt my face pale. He had read me correctly. Somehow, hearing the words spoken made it sound so shallow and pathetic.

You are pathetic, my conscience confirmed.

"Well, I'm here to tell you that I want more," he said. "I want you."

I shook my head. "You don't know what you're saying, Seth."

"Probably not, but that's how I feel."

He handed me a menu. "What are you having?"

Just like that. Guts spilled, the ground was stained, and now he was ready to eat.

Ginger returned to fill our cups. "Ready?"

"Egg sammy," I said.

"Sausage or bacon, love?"

"Sausage."

Ginger looked over at Seth. "And for you?"

"Poached eggs over crumpets, bacon, and a side of fruit."

Ginger tapped her pencil against the pad. "Be right up."

I leaned toward him. "You aren't supposed to want me," I said quietly.

"But, I do."

This had gotten messy far too quickly. My head reeled with horrid scenarios—my father trying to kill Seth. Bennet trying to kill Seth. My brother maiming Seth.

"This can't happen."

"It already has."

"Then, it needs to stop before it's too late."

"Fine," he finally said. "Allow me to enjoy our breakfast together, and I will not bother you again. Agreed?"

"Ever?"

He smiled, obviously enjoying what he thought was a game. "That's up to you."

"Don't play with me, Seth; not about this."

"I'm not playing."

Damn his coolness. I sipped my coffee, unable to meet his luminous gold eyes—a light that would soon fade once my father caught wind of this.

Ginger returned with our meals. Seth said a quick, silent prayer, and then ate with such dignity that it was almost an art.

"You're staring," he said, a quirk of a smile on his lips.

"Are you as methodical with everything as you are with eating?"

He chewed, swallowed, sipped his coffee, and then wiped his mouth while pondering the question. "Yes."

I ate my sandwich, allowing my imagination to go wild. I had heard women talk about him and his fabulous lovemaking skills. What would that be like? I wondered. To have a man who actually took his time with a female, and ensured her satisfaction? Judging by the way he danced, I could only imagine what he'd be like in bed.

Then, there was the way he touched that foal. My mind reeled with the possibilities.

"Your thoughts are intriguing." He smiled, eyes alight with mischief.

"I shielded those thoughts, Seth."

"I could recount them for you, word for word, if you'd like." His smile broadened.

"You are in rare form this morning," I said, looking at him over the rim of my mug. "The last I heard, you were not looking for a mate, and rumor has it that you only sleep with a female once."

He sat back and pondered that for a moment before answering. "That rumor is true."

"I will not be just another notch in your belt, I assure you."

"Yet you claim you can offer me nothing more." His brow arched as if he had just parried my thrust.

"We both know that's true," I said sadly. I pushed my half-eaten sandwich away.

Given the way his brows knit together, he was thinking far too much about this issue. It was time to change the subject.

"Are you ready for finals this week?"

"I believe I am. You?"

I laughed. "I could use some help with diagnostics and

lab prep."

"Nate and I are studying on Thursday. You're welcome to come over. Perhaps I can help you?"

I frowned. "I can't."

"Ah, the anticipated dinner with Bennet," he drawled.

"I have to be there," I said, not enjoying his mockery.

"The only thing you have to do is die, Rae. Everything else is optional."

"Yes, well, there is time enough for dying, young Seth."

I had no idea how old he was, but I was certain he was younger than I. Taking note of his cringe, I continued. "I'd rather enjoy my life and would like to see it extended for as long as I can."

"Point taken," he said coldly, sipping his coffee.

The man was moody as a mare in heat, I thought.

Ginger strode on over. "C'n I get you two anythin' else?"

"I think we're done," said Seth.

Without another word, he paid the bill and escorted me back to my car.

"Thank you for breakfast," I said.

"You're welcome. I'll park your bike in my garage. You know the code to get in."

"You still want me to have it?"

He turned to face me, his eyes more brown than gold now. "Yes, I do."

"Thank you," I said, softly, feeling as if this were goodbye.

He nodded, opened my door, and then waited for me to slip into the seat. After he closed the door, I opened the window.

"I wish things could be different," I said.

His lips grew thin. "Me too." He tapped my door.

"Take care of yourself."

I nodded, closed my window, and drove away.

Funny how one minute, I could feel on top of the world and everything was right, and the next, I could see it all crumble in front of me.

Did Seth honestly think I had a choice in this matter?

Chapter 14

- Rae -

I DUCKED, **BARELY DODGING NICO'S** staff. I countered the attack with an upward thrust followed by a spin. He caught the back of my knees with his staff and sent me flying to the padded floors.

"Never turn your back," he chided.

I stood and readied myself for his next assault. Our sparring sessions were like therapy to my soul. Nico never attacked with malice in his heart, or with any sort of intention for causing me pain. His goal was to teach me self-defense, and he was good at it.

After felling me five more times, I was done, lying there on the pads, panting like a spent puppy after a long run.

His strong hand reached down. I grabbed it and allowed him effortlessly to haul me back to my feet. For such a strong man, he demonstrated nothing but gentleness toward me. I wondered why he hadn't landed a good female by now. Lord knew there were plenty to choose from. They seemed to swarm all around him after every match, even if he lost.

I removed my padded helmet and vest and then tucked a strand of damp hair behind my ear.

"Thirsty?" he asked.

"Very," I replied, following him into the kitchen.

He pulled out a pitcher of lemonade from the fridge and filled two tall glasses. I smiled as he plunked a skinny pink straw into my glass, following it with a ripe raspberry.

"Why do you spoil me so?" I asked.

He lifted his glass to me as if in a toast. "Because, my dear sister, you deserve it."

I frowned.

"Uh, oh. What's that look for?" he asked, sitting beside me at the bar. He placed his hand over mine. "What's on your mind, sister?"

"Nothing."

"Hmm," he moaned. "The standard response from a female when her world is crashing about her shoulders."

I narrowed my eyes and shook my head. "Don't be so dramatic."

He smiled. "I saw you riding a bike yesterday."

Tingles numbed my lips as the blood drained from my face.

"Don't even try to deny it. I know it was you."

"It was a gift," I said. "I only went for a quick ride."

I remembered seeing Seth and Nate through the windows. Both of them had been heads down in books and papers, no doubt studying for the upcoming exams.

"A gift from whom?" he asked.

"I don't want to say."

When I tried to stand, Nico held me down. "Rae, have I ever given you reason not to trust me?"

"Never," I admitted.

He said nothing, staring at me with those vivid green eyes that could easily bore into my soul.

"Seth," I said with sadness in my voice.

Nico smiled. "You like him?"

"Honestly?"

He turned to face me more squarely. "I wouldn't have it any other way."

"He is the only man I have ever wanted, but I can't have him."

"Leave this clan, Rae. Do it now before it's too late."

My eyes grew wide. "I can't, Nico; you know that. Father has bound me. He will think nothing of ending my life should I desert him."

"Seth will not protect you?"

"He is young, Nico. There is no way he can stand up to Father, let alone Bennet."

"Then he is not the right man for you."

My shoulders slumped.

"Does he want you?"

"He said he did."

"And he knows the risks?"

"Again, he is young. He doesn't know what he's getting into, Nico. Please, stop talking about this."

I stood and walked to the living room.

He grabbed his glass and followed me. "Has he bonded with you?"

"No," I said rather tersely.

Nico frowned. "Are you certain?"

"What difference does it make? Nothing can come of this and you know it."

"Maybe, maybe not. All I know is that you cannot continue living this life. It's killing you from the inside out. Once this union with Bennet comes to fruition, I will lose you forever. I don't want that to happen, Rae."

"I see no way out of it."

"Go with Seth."

"No."

"Why?" he asked.

"Because. I don't want him killed because of me." I thought of my mother. She had died for me, for standing up to my father. He had sent her away, and then had her killed.

He looked at me, reading my thoughts. His mouth grew tense and thin. "Your mother was sent away, Rae, but I don't believe she's dead."

I sank down on the couch. "Have you seen her?"

He sat beside me. "I feel her, sometimes. I think she was at my last match."

Part of me felt numb like a limb that had shriveled and died. "I miss her," I mumbled.

"She loves you, my sister. Seeing you mistreated is torturing her, I'm sure."

A moment of silence pressed us into our thoughts.

"Go with Seth," he said.

"I won't sacrifice him," I replied, my voice much harsher than I had intended.

"But you're willing to sacrifice yourself?"

"Yes."

"Ugh," he growled. "Stubborn female."

"Look," I said, "if you want to save me so badly, why don't you stand up to Father?"

He shrank back. I knew I had thrust that dagger deep, but it was too late to pull it back out.

I placed my hand on his shoulder, grateful that he didn't shrug it away. "I'm sorry, Nico."

"Don't be," he said. "I deserve that."

"No, you don't."

"I should have gotten you out of here the first time Father made you available to the clan. You are a female of status and not one who should be used by any miscreant looking to blow his fire. Damn it, Rae, I should have been here for you."

I knelt down to look into his eyes. "God, Nico, you are the only male who has been here for me. Don't you see that. I confide in only you."

When he didn't respond, I moved closer to him, wishing I could heal his tortured heart. "You have to stay on Father's good side; you know that. He is running this clan into the ground, tearing it apart with greed, power, and dominance. When he is gone, you will take over. Please don't risk that—not for me."

"I hate not being able to help you."

"You do help me," I pleaded. "You shield me from Father and keep him out of my mind. Without you, I would be in worse condition, and you know it."

We sat in silence for several minutes. I sipped my lemonade before placing it on the table. Birds chirped outside. The clock on the wall ticked away the time that held us all within its illusion of urgency. My hands twisted together.

"He's good with horses," I said.

"Who?"

"Seth. He helped me with a foal." I smiled and stifled a laugh. "He nearly had the young in a full sleep while I tended his eyes."

"Tended his eyes?" Nico asked cautiously. He knew I was a healer and worried that I may have exposed something I shouldn't have. He had a right to be worried.

"He knows," I finally blurted, not convinced it was the

right thing to do.

"Knows what?"

"About my gift."

"How?"

"I started healing the foal's eyes before I sensed Seth was there in the barn. He said he felt my energy."

"Oh, Rae," Nico said, running his hands through his hair. "Can you trust him?"

"Yes," I said. "I'm sure Nate knows as well."

"Who's Nate?"

"Seth's friend. He shares some of our classes."

"Did Seth tell him?"

I shook my head. "No. Nate is a seer and a listener. He can blast through shields, even those that Seth puts up."

"Hmm," said Nico. "I couldn't read Seth's thoughts and I can typically break through most shields. He has a strength about him that he keeps well hidden."

"He is just so young," I said. "Probably half my age."

"Why does that matter?"

"He isn't mature yet."

Nico stood and carried our empty glasses to the sink. "According to whom?"

"Most Spirians don't mature until they are past forty, Nico; you know that. This is why they are prohibited to take a mate before then."

"And you, my dear sister, are you like most Spirians?"

"I'm half-Fae."

He smiled. "Well, we won't hold that against you."

I narrowed my eyes, following him into the kitchen. "Meaning?"

He cleaned the cups, sneering. "Don't judge others by what is considered the norm. Seth is mature enough. Like I said, he has a strength about him that rivals most males triple his age, if he is, indeed half of yours."

"Strong enough to face Father?"

Nico shrugged. "If Seth has bonded with you, there is no telling what he might do to have you."

"How would I know?"

"He will be protective, possessive, and his eyes will glow their true color."

I smiled, "You sound like you speak from experience."

"I am a male, Rae. I have not found a female who causes me to show such traits, but I know quite a few males who have. There is no question."

"Father is that way with me," I sadly admitted.

"He is your father. It is his nature to protect and possess you until you are mated."

My face reddened a bit. "Other males have also shown those qualities when they have me."

I could sense his tension as he turned to look at me. "What I speak of is different, Rae. Trust me."

I frowned, not comfortable with his sudden coldness. "Well, the point is rather moot. Bennet will not relinquish his rights to me—not when he's paid Father so much money to have me."

"We shall see," he said.

Chapter 15

~Seth~

DIGGING AROUND THE REFRIGERATOR for something to eat, I asked Nate over my shoulder, "Another beer?". We had been heads down in textbooks for nearly three hours to the point where my head felt ready to explode.

"Yeah, mate, that'd be beaut."

I tossed him a bottle of Monteith, which he carelessly opened on my coffee table.

"The bottle opener is on the end table," I reminded him.

"Ah, yeah. There it is."

I shook my head, grabbing a bottle of Borolo and a wine glass from my cupboard. After opening the bottle, I poured a serving into my glass, swirled it around a bit, and then carried it back to the living room.

The place looked like a preschool room with books, colored markers, and colorful anatomy pictures scattered about the floor and tables.

Nate took a long swig of his beer before scratching

his head.

"Take a break," I told him.

He moved a few books off the couch and sank down, cold beer in hand. He rolled the bottle across his forehead. "Let's go to the pub," he suggested.

I glanced up at the clock—ten o'clock. "Don't you have class first thing tomorrow?"

"Not, 'til nine."

I sipped my wine.

"No worries, mate. She's not workin' tonight."

"Who?"

He huffed. "The female you've been thinking about all night, y'dolt."

I didn't respond. There was no point. Nate was one of the few people who could read my thoughts whether I wanted him to or not.

"You said you worked things out with her, yes?"

"Sort of."

"Did you give her the bike?"

"Yeah, it's in our garage."

"Our garage?" He swigged his beer as if anticipating juicy details.

"Long story short, I want her, she wants me, not gonna happen."

"Not gonna happen?" he asked, mocking my American accent.

"She's promised to another man, remember?"

"Petty issue."

I glanced at him. He was serious. "Petty?"

"Take that female and make her your own."

I laughed. "Just like that?"

He swigged another gulp. "Yeah, mate. That's what I'd do."

I sipped my wine, trying to imagine this half-pint of a man facing off Bennet Graves to tell him that the woman he paid a billion dollars for was now off limits.

"And what makes you think she would want me to do that?"

"She's a female. Since when do they know what they want?"

I rolled my eyes. "Would you say that to her face?"

Another long swallow. The last of the bubbles drifted into his mouth. "Hell no. I've seen that little bit fight."

"She doesn't want me involved," I said. "I am going to respect her decision."

Nate stood, taking his empty with him. "It's a wonder you're as lucky as you are with the women," he said, considering fetching another brew.

"I thought you were going to the pub?"

He glanced over his shoulder and closed the refrigerator door. "I have better luck finding female companionship when you come along."

"Really? And why's that?"

"You get'm hot and heavy with your dancing, and I get'm after you reject their advances."

His expression changed as if he were suddenly enlightened. "In fact, mate, I haven't seen you take a female since we rescued Rae that night from those blokes in the alley."

I sipped my wine without reply.

"Have y'lost your mojo?"

My next sip was more of a gulp as I drained my glass. "Just saving my energy for finals," I lied.

"Yeah, I bet. That explains your endless thoughts of gray-green eyes, long mahogany hair, cocoa skin, and legs that make your groin ache."

I carried my empty glass to the kitchen. "Let's go," I said, having heard enough of his ceaseless yapping about my thoughts.

MALONES WAS QUIET TONIGHT, with only a sparse crowd and a mellow band playing ballads sung in classic Gaelic. Avoiding the bar, I chose a table next to the dance floor, hoping to find a partner who wanted only to dance.

Nate returned with two drinks in hand—a beer for him, and a Scotch for me.

"Any good prospects?" he asked, sliding into the chair across from me.

"If you're not too choosy, there are plenty."

He scoffed. "As long as they know how to pleasure a man, that's good enough for me, mate."

I shook my head, then froze as if a wave of nitrogen washed over me. There on the dance floor was Rae, laughing and having a good time with a bloke I had seen in chemistry lab. His name was Mike, a human, nice enough, but he was dancing far too close for my comfort. I stood and made a beeline toward them.

Nate followed my stare. "Uh, oh. Hang on, mate. Think about this for a mo—shit."

I barely heard his chair slide out as he followed on my heels. "Easy, mate," he said, gripping my shoulders. "He's human—hardly a threat."

I tapped the human's arm. "Mind if I cut in?" It was more of a command than a request.

The human looked at Rae, then back at me and Nate. Reluctantly, he released his hold and stepped back.

"That was unnecessary," said Rae.

I curled my fingers around hers and gripped her waist,

pulling her into me.

"This is not a good idea," she hissed, trying to pull away.

"And dancing with him was?"

Her gray-green eyes flashed and narrowed. "He is human, Seth, and we were dancing. That's all."

I swung her around to the center of the dance floor. She followed with elegance and moved as gracefully as a butterfly.

"I thought you had studying to do?" I asked.

"I did. I needed a break. What are you doing here?"

"It was Nate's idea."

The song ended. When she tried to walk away, I pulled her in close. "Not yet," I whispered.

A slow melody poured from the band, accompanied by a deep male voice singing, "You are Mine"—an appropriate tune for the moment.

As I pulled her in tighter, I felt the connection between us. "We fit well together," I said.

I felt her swallow hard. Her hand began to sweat in mine.

The male sung, "Titim isteach i mo lámha, mo ghile, agus lig dom tú a chosaint. I gcás go bhfuil tú mianach."

I pulled her in tighter against me. Through that embrace, she felt the emotions the song had invoked in me.

"What is he saying?" she asked.

I closed my eyes and breathed in the fresh scent of her hair—jasmine and clove. I sang the words in English close to her ear. "Fall into my arms, my darling, and let me protect you. For you are mine."

She stiffened against me. "Seth," she said, her mouth against my chest.

"Shh," I said. "Just let me enjoy this dance."

When she relaxed, her body molded to mine, moving with my every step like an extension of my body.

The song ended too quickly. She pulled away.

"I'm a bit warm," she said. "I need some air."

I led her to the door where several people huddled to enjoy a smoke. We walked past them toward a bench across the street.

"You're quite a dancer," she said, still looking a bit flushed.

"It helps to have a good partner," I said.

"Where did you learn to dance like that?"

I smiled at the memories that surfaced. "Our clan dances a lot when the weather permits. One of my clansmen named Ian, showed me a few moves."

"And how did you learn to speak Gaelic?"

"It's our foundation language," I said. "Khalen ensures that all children are taught to read and write it."

She cocked her head, her beautiful eyes reflecting the moonlight like silver mirrors. "I thought you were American?"

"Our clan is Scottish."

"But you live in the Americas. Why?"

Goose flesh began to form on her arms.

"Come; let's get you inside. You're getting cold."

"I'm fine," she said.

I thought back on the many stories I had heard about my family and why they had migrated. All I could recall were bits and pieces that didn't make sense.

"We will have to ask Khalen when we see him," I said.

"We?"

"I'm spending summer break at my uncle Darius'. Khalen will come to visit. I want you to meet him."

She stood. "I can't come with you."

When she started walking back to the pub, I followed her. "Rae, stop."

She shook her head. "No, Seth. I can't. This is getting too—"

I pulled her around to face me, my grip much tighter than I had intended.

"Come with me," I said.

"No."

I released my hold and watched her walk inside.

Moments later, Nate and another man nearly twice his size were tossed out the door.

"Take it outside," Steve yelled.

Nate pounded the larger man with an effective punch to the stomach. The man curled. Nate followed the blow with a nice hook to his temple and his opponent crumbled to the ground.

I walked over and pulled Nate back. "That's enough, my friend."

"Tosser," he spat.

"Come on," I said, pulling him back. "We're going home."

I TIED THE LAST STITCH in his forehead, before covering the three-inch scar with a bandage.

"What is it with you and fighting?" I asked.

He rolled a cold beer over his face. "The bugger was pressin' me."

"So let him."

"Like you allowed that human to dance with Rae?"

My spine stiffened. I gathered the rubbish and tossed it into the kitchen bin.

"Ooh, I take it things didn't go well for you?"

"I'm tired of chasing females who have no interest in me," I said.

"No interest?"

I poured myself a glass of wine from the bottle I had opened earlier.

"You sound like a man scorned," said Nate.

I sat on the recliner, thinking about feelings I had stuffed away for the past few years.

"What was her name?" asked Nate.

"Elle," I said.

"You're a bit young to bond with a female. How long ago was this?"

"Three, almost four years," I said.

"Um, and counting, I see," he replied smugly. "What happened?"

"I wanted her, she wanted someone else."

"You think the same of Rae?"

I sipped my wine, watching Nate stir the fire before adding another log.

"Rae believes she has no choice. She doesn't want me involved."

"Well, given the way you wanted to rip that human's head off for dancing with her, I'm guessin' you've bonded with her, mate."

"Like you said, I'm a bit young to be bonding with any female."

Nate shrugged. "My father always said that age is merely time's way of proving mortality."

The crease between my brow deepened. "What's that supposed to mean?"

"It means that man places too much weight in the measurement of something that doesn't exist. In short, your age means squat. Don't use it as an excuse."

"She did," I hissed.

"Elle?"

"Rae."

Nate laughed. "She's barely a hair older than you in Spirian years."

I sipped my wine. "I asked her to come with me to Darius'. She said no."

"Ah, best give up, then, mate. It's hopeless. Let her go and move on."

The glass in my hand shattered, spilling wine over my fists, mingling with my fresh blood.

"Bollocks!" Nate yelled, jumping up and grabbing a roll of paper towels.

"Too much glass to remove by hand," he said. "Best get you to the sink to wash it out."

I stood, feeling numb. "Devil take me," I said. "I just don't care."

Nate held my hands under the cold water, doing his best to clear my wounds of the tiny shards of crystal.

"Some of these will need stitchin'."

"Leave 'em," I said.

"Don't be such a dolt."

I pulled my hand out from under the water and wrapped it in a towel. "Look," I said. "Women of my clan get to choose their mates. If Rae wanted me, she would have chosen me."

"What makes you think she hasn't chosen you?" asked Nate, gathering the broken shards on the floor.

"I told her how I feel; she said no. End of story. I'm done. From this point forward, I want nothing to do with females."

"Ever?"

"Ever."

"Good," he said. "Then I'll take a chance on her."

I turned to face him. "Meaning?"

"I'll take that female for my own."

The energy in the room amped up in response to my feelings toward that notion. "Like hell you will," I growled.

Nate stepped back and raised his hands. "Easy, mate. I was just eggin' you. You've bonded with her, no question."

The adrenaline rush had my head spinning and cramping with pain. My feelings for Elle had been just as strong, or at least they seemed as strong at the time. That was years ago. All I truly remembered of that time was the pain in my chest when she had given herself to Drew.

When I had become her templar, that bond to her was the closest I would ever be to finding a mate, I was sure.

I had allowed Rae to burrow under my skin, a Shadow female with an intended mate—perfect.

"Don't give up on her, Seth," said Nate, his voice sounding like that of an elder. His face, too, seemed different. In a blink, that look was gone.

Nate smiled. "Stay put. I'll get some bandages."

Chapter 16

~Seth~

JENICO LEFT A MESSAGE on my phone to meet him at Musselburgh race track at ten this morning. How he had obtained my number was one mystery; what he wanted to talk about was quite another.

The guard stopped me at the gate. He was a tall dark man with a genuine smile fit for a toothpaste ad.

"Good morning, sir. Who are you here to see?"

"Jenico Tomei."

The guard flipped through the pages on his clipboard. "And your name, sir?"

"Seth Dunning."

He slipped a badge into a plastic holder and handed it to me. "Keep this on while you're on the grounds."

I fastened the badge to my shirt.

Next, the guard handed me a map he had highlighted with yellow ink. Leaning into my window, he traced the route with his thick finger.

"Take this road to the first barn." He pointed to a building just past the hot walkers. "Park here," he pointed to an area on the map. "You'll find Mr. Tomei in this barn, near stall number nine."

I took the map. "Thank you."

"Have a good day, sir." He tipped the navy blue hat that matched his uniform and stepped away from my car.

I drove past the hot walkers. Only one was in use with three horses still dripping from a recent bath. I parked between two pickups that looked as if they had just been driven off a showroom, all shiny and new.

I left the car unlocked, figuring the place was not a particular hangout for thieves.

The barn was well lit, but still quite dark compared to the bright morning sun. I gave my eyes some time to adjust before venturing down to stall nine. The hairs on my neck tingled and stood erect. There were Shadows here, many of them.

As I made my way past the bobbing heads of nickering horses, the feeling grew stronger. What was I walking into? I wondered. Jenico didn't strike me as a conniving sort, but then, he was the son of a Shadow leader.

Judging by the way the energy in the barn wavered, the Shadows knew I was here—show time.

Jenico stepped out, stiff brush in one hand, curry brush in another. He plopped them down into a bucket by his feet. "Glad you could make it," he said, smiling.

Shadows moved around me like a hazy buzz.

Jenico's smile broadened. "Don't worry about them. They work for me."

I gave him a speculative look. "Somehow, that doesn't give me the warm and fuzzy."

Jenico laughed, tossing me a soft brush he had chosen from a bucket. "I hear you're very good with horses."

I caught the brush, following him to a stunning black

colt standing quietly between two cross ties.

"This is Rambo. He ran his first race not too long ago."

I began brushing the colt's opposite side, using the techniques my aunt Skye had taught me; flick, smooth, flick, smooth.

"Thanks to Rae," said Jenico, "he strided out beautifully and took third place."

The horse's coat gleamed like polished ebony with indigo highlights. He stood with one back leg relaxed, his massive rump rippling with corded muscle. He was obviously in great shape.

I remained silent, allowing Jenico to talk while I kept my senses sharp.

"My sister likes you, Seth."

The hairs on my neck felt like ridged needles now. "I think you're mistaken."

Jenico chuckled. "Rae is like a precious gem to me. I know her every flaw, her worth." The last word was spoken with emphasis.

I said nothing.

Jenico came around and took the brush from my hand. "What are your feelings for her?" he asked point blank. He tossed our brushes back into the bucket.

The muscles in my jaw worked. I met the man's eyes; they were green and sharp as daggers. "My feelings are irrelevant."

"Come," he said, walking toward a stout man who looked rather exotic; Asian with a Spanish mix.

"Take care of Rambo," Jenico ordered the man. "Then get Siscat ready for a run, yes?"

The stout man nodded.

Jenico continued to lead me down the barn. He stopped before a door with a window and unlocked it.

We stepped inside a small office with a simple desk, three chairs, and four filing cabinets. In the far corner was a coat tree with three hats hung upon it and a dry rain slicker.

"Please, sit." He gestured to a chair across from his desk.

My chair was lower than his; not without purpose, I was certain. This man liked to exude power over others. It was evident in the way his stable crew addressed him.

After waiting for me to sit, he lowered himself in his own highbacked chair and steepled his hands before him—the standard posture for those who wanted to claim control.

I sat back. "Is there a reason you asked me down here?"

"Have you bonded with my sister?"

The bold question imbalanced me. I blinked, met his green eyes, then glanced away.

I could feel his smile. Still, I could not bring myself to look at him; nor could I answer his ridiculous question.

"Your refusal to answer me confirms my suspicion."

That got my attention. "Your suspicion?"

Tapping his fingertips together, he formulated his words. Unfortunately, he was about as good at shielding his thoughts as I was. Tapping his mind or his intentions only provided confusing fragments. It was a common trick I had often employed.

"I'm guessing the answer to my question is yes. You want my sister; however, she has somehow convinced you that she does not feel the same."

"I know she feels the same," I said. "She is just too intimidated to act upon it."

Jenico's smile broadened. "And where does that leave you?"

"Where should it leave me?"

"If you have indeed bonded to her, which I suspect you have, then I would expect you to fight for her."

I scoffed. "Against your father?"

His eyes brightened. "Why not?"

When I didn't reply, he leaned forward. "Unite with her, Seth. Make her your own."

I hissed. "We do not take our women. When we unite, it is a mutual desire—one done with ceremony."

Jenico slammed his hand upon the table. "It is no wonder the Spirian race is declining. If every male waited for the perfect female to agree to anything, let alone a union, we would be extinct by now."

"Which explains why you are still single," I countered.

He closed his eyes and took in a deep breath, clearly trying to stay in control. Shadows were not known for their patience.

"What are your intentions?" he hissed.

"To let her decide."

"She can't decide," he roared. "Bloody hell, are you really this dense? Can't you see what's she's up against?"

"What do you suggest? Should I kidnap her? Toss her in the trunk of my car and whisk her away until her father tracks us down? And then what? I fight for her honor. If I win, I'll be damn lucky. If I lose, Rae will pay the price for my insolence. How, pray tell, will that save your sister?"

Jenico stood and started pacing.

"Look; I know you love her," I said. "But this has to be her choice."

"She will never make that choice. She fears too much for your safety to even think about her own."

The thoughts from his mind formed a picture that made *Sleeping with the Enemy* seem like a family flick.

When he noticed my expression, his eyes softened. "Now you see. What she is being forced into will surely break her spirit beyond repair."

He offered more images. Rae's mother and her demise. Rae crumbling after learning of her mother's death.

I stood and leaned over the desk, fighting the wave of nausea threatening to rise.

Jenico placed his hand on my back, as if trying to absorb my pain. "I'm sorry I had to share that with you. For some reason, our forefathers have made us enemies, but we are really only two sides on a single coin. One is worthless without the other. Together, our value increases. I'm asking for your help; one Spirian to another."

I turned and met his eyes. "You sound like my roommate."

"Nate?"

I nodded. "He is a Shadow, but his intentions are pure."

"Yes, Rae told me about him."

I stiffened.

Jenico laughed. "As in passing, my friend. She has no designs on him whatsoever."

My shoulders dropped a bit and my breath deepened.

"Now," said Jenico, "imagine Bennet's hands all over her, forcing her to do things she has no interest in doing."

My fists tightened. "I won't imagine that."

"Exactly," he said. "If you give up on her, you won't need to imagine it."

My jaw worked itself into tight cords as my mind fell back to when Drew made his intentions for Elle known. I knew I could not compete with him. He was perfect for her. I was too young and not nearly gifted enough. When I had told Khalen about my feelings, he never laughed or doubted the seriousness of those feelings. He had simply stated the fact that Drew was a better choice for her.

A low growl escaped my throat like an old soul desperate to free itself from a young body pining for a female it could never touch.

"A man never knows his true worth," said Jenico, "until his mate is threatened."

Even though Rae was not officially united with me, I still felt protective of her as if she were, and Jenico knew it. Was I really that transparent?

"I will bring her with me," I finally said.

He bowed slightly. "Thank you."

I nodded, then stepped out of the room, wondering how in God's world I would accomplish that feat. Rae would not be willing to go, and her wrath was not something I wanted—ever.

Chapter 17

~ R a e ~

IT HAD BEEN AN UNUSUALLY calm night at the pub so Danny was thinking about closing early. Seth and Nate sat at the end of the bar, drinking brandy and talking about the upcoming final exam.

Seth had kept the wolves at bay all evening. The energy he emitted had every human feeling queasy, including Steve the bouncer. Other Spirians avoided the bar completely and treated me with kid gloves, all the while keeping their eyes trained on Seth.

Despite my many pleas for him to calm his intentions, he did not. Nate was clearly amused by the display, dishing out harmless flirtations my way just to rouse Seth's temper.

"We'll be closing on the hour's half. Can I get you two one last drink?" I asked.

"No, we're good," Seth answered.

Nate stared down at his empty.

I poured him a half shot and continued cleaning the bar, ignoring Seth's growl.

When Nate and he had finished their drink, Seth

leaned over the counter. "I'll be waiting for you outside."

"No need," I told him. "I rode my bike."

"I know," he said. "It's in the back of my car."

I stepped back, hands on my hips. "It was locked."

His smirk indicated that locks were mere inconveniences, nothing more. He had been trying to get me to talk to him all evening. My avoidance had apparently reached its end.

"I might be a while," I warned him.

He looked at Danny as if they had an agreement of sorts. My eyes rested on Jane, who just smiled as she continued wiping down the bar.

The corners of Seth's mouth curled up. "I'll see you soon."

I watched as he and Nate walked past Steve and out the front door.

I growled in frustration, tossing the chairs up onto the tables with more strength than was necessary. Thank God they were made solid from sturdy oak or they would be in shambles from my anger.

"Dang, girl," Steve commented. "What has you so flustered?"

"Domineering men who think they own me!" I screamed back.

"Whoa," he said, backing away, hands held up as if I were holding a gun to his head.

Danny laid a firm hand on my shoulder. "Go home," he said. "I'll finish up."

I looked at the chairs I had haphazardly tossed upon the tables. Tears burned my eyes as I held them back.

"Thank you," I whispered.

Not sparing Jane a glance, I ran past her, grabbed my things from my cubbie, and considered using the front door. If I ran fast enough, Seth wouldn't even know I had left. He would certainly be waiting for me to exit the back door.

I walked back past Jane, Danny, and Steve, who wisely opened the door for me without saying a word.

Slinging my knapsack over my shoulders, I quietly made my way down the street, careful to stay out of plain sight.

As I rounded the corner, Seth stepped in front of me. "Why are you avoiding me, Rae?"

My shoulders slumped as I sagged against the cold brick wall. He lifted me up and led me toward his car.

"We need to talk," he said, opening the back door and urging me inside. There was no use trying to open the opposite door to leave.

When he slid in beside me and closed the door, I shivered against the cold. He reached for the climate controls and turned up the heat.

"Where's Nate?" I asked.

"He walked home. Look at me, Rae."

I did as he said. Gold eyes staring back at me looked as if they belonged to a man nearly three times his age.

"Tell me you don't want me and I will leave you alone."

Fully intending to do just that, I squared my shoulders and met his intense stare. "I don't...." The words tangled in my throat like spiny vines. I cleared my throat. "I—"

"Say it," he commanded.

I looked away. "Don't make me do this."

His hand brought my chin back up. The warmth of his breath feathered across my skin like silk. It smelled of brandy mingled with the spicy odor of Seth.

"This cannot happen," I said. "I won't allow it to happen."

"Too late," he said, drawing nearer. His lips, full and soft, lingered so close to mine as if begging me to meet him halfway.

On its own volition, my betraying body closed the distance, despite my mind screaming for it to stop.

At first, the kiss was gentle and sweet. Every ounce of reason told me to pull away, but I couldn't. When his hand reached around to the back of my head, I knew it was too late. The kiss deepened.

Just as he did with his dancing, he equally knew how to seduce with his lips. The kiss was far better than I had ever imagined.

When he pulled away, we were both breathless and the cab was suddenly too warm. I pressed the button to crack open the steamed-up window.

"Now," he said, forcing me to meet his eyes. "Tell me to leave you alone, forever."

"I can't. But, we both know the reality of this situation. The direction you're pulling me in is akin to signing your death warrant. That, I won't do."

"Death is inevitable for all of us at one point in time. If I die to save someone dear to me, my life will have meant something."

"My mother died trying to save me, Seth. It only made matters worse. Please don't make me suffer that again."

He frowned. "Is your faith in me so shallow?"

I choked a laugh. "Seriously? Are you telling me that you can defeat my father and the male who has laid claim to me?"

He growled low and deep. "Does he have claim to you?"

I nodded. "A billion dollars worth."

"Do you want him?"

I slammed back against the chair, closing my eyes in frustration. "No. I don't want him. But you know as well as I do that what I want doesn't matter."

"It matters to me."

I turned to face him. "What is this sudden interest you have in me, Seth? Only days ago, you wouldn't give me the time of day. So many nights, I watched as you left with one female after another, wishing one of them could be me."

His eyes softened. "I wasn't ready for you."

"Ready?"

"I've always been attracted to you, Rae. There are other pubs in town. Why would I always come to this one?"

I shrugged. "There is a greater selection of Spirian females at Malones?"

"No," he said with a hardness in his tone. "I came because of you."

"Then why did you treat me with such indifference?"

"Because I didn't want you for just the night, and I wasn't ready to commit my heart to one female."

"So what changed?" I asked.

"The thought of another man having you is driving me insane. When those six blokes had their way with you, I nearly came undone. It was then that I realized you were the one female I had to make my own."

"But you can't, Seth. I cannot belong to you—ever."

The gold in his eyes deepened. "Do you trust me?"

I thought about that for a moment. Did I trust him? He had protected me more than once. He knew about my gift of healing; was that his motivation for wanting me? "I don't know," I quietly said.

"Fair enough," he replied. "I would like to earn that

trust."

I looked down. "I'm not sure I can trust any male."

He brought my chin up with his warm hand. His golden eyes bore into mine. "We shall see."

"I should probably get back home. Father is no doubt waiting up for me."

"I'll drive you."

"Just take me back to your place. I left my car there."

We rode in silence as he held my hand, which seemed so small in his warm, protective grip.

"It will be all right, Rae."

Things hadn't been right since my mum left, I thought, thinking back on the events that had caused the uproar. I had defied my father. He had lashed out with a vengeance that rivaled my worst nightmare. The physical punishment was nothing compared to the pain of being used by his friends.

When my mother lashed out, it was the last time I ever saw her. Father wasn't the same afterward. Nothing was the same.

"Can we have breakfast tomorrow?" he asked.

I shook my head. "I need to go to VetMed in the morning."

"Dinner?"

I felt my face grow pale. "Bennet is coming to our home for dinner. I have to be there."

His grip tightened around my hand. Even as he pulled up to the security gate to enter his code, he refused to relinquish his hold on me.

"I can escort you."

I blinked a few times. "Escort me?"

"To your dinner," he explained, his face calm and serious.

"Are you out of your mind?"

He said nothing as he parked his Rover under the carport.

I exited the car and followed him to the back, where he proceeded to remove my bike.

"I'm being quite serious," he said, rolling my bike to the far end of the carport.

"Well, no, you cannot escort me. My father would have you served as the appetizer."

He half-smiled as if doubting that fact. "I'm leaving for Uig early Saturday morning. I want you to join me."

I propped my fists onto my hips. "I gave you my answer already."

"Either meet me here, or I will come find you."

My blood grew cold. "You wouldn't da—"

"Don't say it, Rae. You know I will."

"Please don't."

He closed the back door, pressed the key fob to lock the car, then turned to face me. "You had your chance to be rid of me. All you had to do was convince me that you didn't want me. You couldn't."

With that, he turned and started walking away. If my jaw had opened any wider, I could have captured butterflies.

What was I going to do now? Jenico was right. Seth was bonded to me. There was no way this situation would end well for either of us.

I dug the keys from my pocket and unlocked my car. Father would be waiting for me to get home. I had to clear my mind before entering the house or he would suspect something was wrong, and his suspicions were not easily derailed.

Chapter 18

-Seth-

NATE OPENED ANOTHER BOTTLE OF BEER. "This is supposed to be a celebration, mate."

I continued to sip my glass of Borolo while staring into the fire. It was Friday night, finals were over, and I had been looking forward to spring break—until tonight.

Nate waved a cracker loaded with goat brie and a fresh basil leaf in front of my nose. "I know you like this bit of fluff."

I took the cracker from his hand. "Thank you."

He made a face and then reached for the greasy pizza rolls with a hungry smile. "Ah, now this is good eatin'."

Not wanting to dampen his jovial mood with my bitter feelings, I shook my mind of Rae and her unwanted house guest. "How's the shrimp doing?" I asked, smelling the aroma of bacon.

"Grillin' up nicely, mate. Should be beaut in a few."

I took another sip of wine, wondering whether Rae was doing the same. They would be serving the first course about now, I was sure. Was Bennet treating her well? Was her father? Jenico said he would be there to watch over her, but his hands were just as tied as hers when it came to their father.

"Give it a rest," Nate chided. "It's just dinner. She's goin' t'be fine."

"Yeah," I said, refreshing my glass of wine. "She's caught between two males who clearly don't respect her wishes. How do I know Bennet won't want to unite with her for dessert?"

Nate rolled his eyes. "If you're that concerned, why not go over there and take her away?"

"She asked me not to."

"And, of course, you do exactly what she wants you to, yes?"

"Jenico texted me and said he would let me know if things got out of hand."

"He's a good man then, yeah?"

"Yeah," I said, sipping my wine.

"I'll go pull the shrimp off," he said, placing his sweaty beer on the table. I reached over and moved it onto a coaster.

Moments later, Nate returned with a platter full of bacon-wrapped shrimp and a spicy sauce he had made for dipping.

He lowered the plate onto the table, slapped his hands together, and rubbed them with childlike anticipation.

"How do you think you did on the finals?" I asked.

He sat on the sofa and loaded a small plate full of shrimp and sauce. "Good, thanks to you."

"Glad to hear it. They'll be posting grades tomorrow. Did you want to check them before heading out?"

"Sounds good," he said, crunching into a bite.

I loaded my own plate and dug in. The tender morsels

were generous with flavor and the sauce added a tang that complemented my wine.

I glanced down at my phone—no new messages.

Nate choked a laugh. "You have it bad for her, yeah?"

"I'm worried, that's all."

He guffawed. "Lord spare me the penance of bonding with a female."

I finished my shrimp and stood to carry my plate to the kitchen. Really what I needed was an excuse to move and fix my mind on other things.

Nate watched me with tired eyes. "You're a real buzz kill, you know that?"

I headed for the stairs, phone in hand. "I need to make a call."

Nate shrugged before loading his plate with another helping.

I closed my bedroom door and dialed my uncle Khalen's number. He answered on the second ring.

"Seth, how are you?"

"Good, Khalen. Looking forward to seeing everyone soon.

Khalen laughed. "Not enough drama in med school?"

"More than I can handle, but I do miss my clan."

"Understandable," he said. "We are hard to live without."

I had missed his humor, dry as it was. "Will mother be coming with you and Skye?"

"Yes, of course. Gabrihen will be joining us later this week."

A smile lit my face. These reunions almost made the daunting schedule of med school worthwhile. I really enjoyed summer break.

"I miss everyone."

"Yes," he said. "I know you do."

"I'll be brining another Spirian to Uncle Darius'."

Silence.

"Another?"

"Yes, beside Nate, the man I talked to you earlier about."

"Who?"

Ah, the dreaded question. How was I going to explain that I was intending to kidnap a Shadow female destined to mate with a powerful man by the end of the year? Oh, and by the way, her father will no doubt seek vengeance for taking his daughter.

"A female."

More silence.

"Anyone significant?"

"No," I lied, not wanting to get into the whole speech about how I was too young to bond with a female. Lord knew I had heard it enough to last my lifetime.

"What are you not telling me, Seth?"

Damn his cursed instincts, I thought. I cleared my throat against the tightness that Khalen's demanding tone typically inspired.

"She's a Shadow and will be in trouble soon if I don't take her away from here."

Long silence this time. "Explain."

"Um, I'd rather wait until I see you," I said.

"Will this, so called, rescue place the clan at risk?"

"Possibly."

Big sigh on the other end. I could imagine Skye placing her calming hand on his shoulder, trying to keep his anger in check. She was one of the few people who could pull off such a feat.

"Khalen," I said, "this is important to me."

"You mean *she* is important to you."

"Yes," I confirmed. "She really is."

"Seth," he sighed. "God has surely placed an old soul into a young body."

Long pause.

"Very well. Bring her along. I'm eager to see the female Shadow who has purloined your soul."

"Thank you."

"Is this something I'm going to regret?"

"Possibly."

"Well," he chuckled. "Darius did say things were getting quite dull out there."

I smiled, picturing the burly Scot saying just that.

"I'll see you tomorrow."

"Yes. We're leaving tonight.

"Safe journey."

"You too."

We hung up. Typically I was eager to reunite with my clan. The surge of energy that followed was like wine to the soul.

I thought of Nate, living so long without a clan to call his own. I could not even imagine such a fate. I also wondered whether he could make the changes required to join our clan. After observing his promiscuous love life, I seriously doubted he would ever consider monogamy as a life choice.

I descended the stairs to find Nate sucking on a fresh brew and eating the last of the shrimp.

"Ah, he emerges," he said with a full mouth.

My phone buzzed, indicating a new message was received.

Take her with you tomorrow.

I texted him back. *I intend to.*

Somehow, I knew Rae wouldn't meet me here in the morning. In fact, I was certain she would opt to drive to VetMed in lieu of riding her bike just to avoid me.

"Everything all right?" asked Nate.

"Fine," I said.

His brows shot up. "Yeah, sounds it."

"I need to go somewhere tomorrow morning," I said. "How about if you check on the grades, and I'll meet you back here?"

He took a long draw from his beer. "Yeah, okay."

Chapter 19

-Rae-

BENNET HAD ARRIVED. Through my bedroom door, I could hear his and Father's voice as they greeted one another with trivial comments—none of which were truly meant, I was sure.

I sat on the bed wearing the pale blue gown Father had set aside for me. The one, he claimed, set my eyes afire and my skin aglow. He also instructed me to wear my hair down and loose about my face. It had a natural wave that framed my features well.

Amy, his personal attendant, was ordered to come and help me get ready. He did not trust the servants to assure my readiness. They had bent to my will too often in the past.

Amy had spent nearly an hour grooming me and prepping my clothes as if I were a fancy poodle about to strut my goods before the judge. She had left only moments ago to fetch a bottle of perfume. Apparently, the one my mother had used wasn't good enough.

She knocked quietly before entering the room. She

was a tall woman with hard features. Given her abrasive manner and strict attention to discipline, she would have made an excellent schoolmarm at Auchinleck House finishing school.

The bottle hissed as she squeezed the gold-threaded bulb. The scent that emanated was akin to star jasmine in full bloom—pleasant, but far too strong for my taste.

She stood back, looking at me with self-pride. "There, now you are fit to meet your mate."

He's not my mate, I thought. He's merely a man posing to be one. In reality, he was nothing more than a collector of females looking to build his harem.

When she lifted my hands, she shook her head at my stubby fingernails. "Tsk, tsk, tsk," she said. "These are beyond repair for now. If I had more time, we could fashion acrylics over this disgrace."

"I cannot work in acrylics," I said.

"Darling," she chimed in a polished London accent, "you will be united soon to a very powerful man. I doubt he will want you to work, let alone get your hands dirty with those filthy horses."

My stomach roiled at the thought of being denied my passion. I closed my eyes and took a few breaths. Seth's handsome face came to mind, and for a moment, I seriously considered leaving with him tomorrow. The hell that would surely follow, however, derailed that idea.

"Come," said Amy, holding out her delicate bony hand. "It's time to meet your mate."

Her death grip on my hand assured me that I was to follow her whether or not I wanted to. She had her orders and would follow them to the letter.

The men were waiting at the bottom of the stairs. When Bennet's eyes locked onto me, they glowed like new brick reflecting the sun. He was still very handsome, in a GQ sort of way—clean shaven, square jawline, dark eyes, and immaculately trimmed black hair that looked too perfect to be real. He reminded me of Richard Gere in Pretty Woman—tired, sad, and filled with a self-loathing that rested deep within the hardened walls of his soul. I felt the hum of his energy as he scanned me from head to toe. Given the intensity of his look, he was extremely gifted and had honed his skills over many years.

"Lovely," he sighed. "Those eyes are like silver sapphires, and that hair. It flows like chestnut silk."

My father gave Amy an approving nod. Her chin rose a notch as her pride swelled to nearly palpable levels.

I continued down the stairs, feeling like a horse at an auction.

Bennet reached for my hand. "Raeiza, my lovely, you are a sight to behold."

"I'm glad you approve," I said, not really keeping my tone in check.

Father immediately reprimanded me with a sharp jolt that made my knees waver.

Bennet kept me from falling. "New shoes?" he laughed.

"Come," said Father. "We have hors d'oeuvres and white wine waiting for us in the den." He led the way.

Bennet's tight grip on my arm matched his possessive nature. Jenico followed us, brushing his hand over my shoulder for reassurance.

Bennet chose the Victorian loveseat, pulling me tight against his side. The fire crackled in the background, warming the space with orange light.

Father handed him a plate of stuffed mushrooms, cheese bites, and thinly sliced meats along with a glass of Sauvignon Blanc.

I, of course, was to wait for Bennet to serve me whatever portion he chose. As his mate, or future mate, he determined what I could and could not have.

He handed me his glass of wine, clearly intending us to drink from the same glass and eat from the same plate. After I took a sip of the clean, tart wine, he picked up a fancy toothpick loaded with a nibble of aged Gouda and a thin slice of prosciutto, and hovered it before my mouth.

The look he offered was more of a warning to part my lips so he could feed me, thus establishing his position as my mate.

Reluctantly, I did as he asked.

"Good girl," he chimed close to my ear.

"Excuse me," I said, starting to stand. Before he could stop me, I rushed out of the room and toward the nearest privy. Without ceremony, I spat the mouthful into the loo. The reflection staring back at me was shocking. Pale face, dull eyes, and a disgust that could only be spawned within the soul. What had I become?

My mother would never submit to a male who insisted on feeding her. She would have politely refused anything offered, which explained my father's constant frustration with her.

A knock sounded upon the door. "Rae, are you all right?" my brother asked from the other side.

"Fine," I choked. "I'll be out in a moment."

I heard him sigh before walking away. Muted male voices echoed from the den, followed by laughter and pinging glasses. Apparently, they had found something to celebrate.

After a few more dry heaves and a quick wash with cold water, I was ready to face the remainder of the evening—or so I thought.

I walked into the den to find my brother frowning, and the other two men grinning like cats who had just cornered a rabbit.

"Fabulous news," my father boasted. "Bennet wants to move your union date up to next month."

Again, my stomach roiled. It took everything I had just to remain standing. I must have wavered a bit because Jenico was at my side in a blink.

"Easy, Rae," he cooed. "Come, now. Let's sit down." He guided me toward the winged-back chair by the window.

Bennet walked over and took my hand. "I'll collect you next month on my way back from China."

My throat was so dry it was difficult to make any sound at all. After clearing it a few times, I finally cracked out, "I was hoping to finish med school before leaving."

"Nonsense," he laughed. "There is no need for such a trivial thing. You have no need to work, my dear."

"I want to work," I said.

His dark eyes grew cold. "Your job is to bear me many gifted children."

I started to open my mouth, but the energy radiating from my father coaxed it to close and remain silent.

"I believe dinner is ready," he said. "Shall we adjourn to the dining room?"

In silence, we meandered into the large dining hall where the long oakwood table lay stretched out under white linen, gilded bone china, silverware and elegant wine goblets that looked so fine that I worried they would shatter in my hand.

Bennet unwrapped his arm from mine to slide my chair out. Just as I was taught in finishing school, I smoothed my skirts and timed placing my full weight onto the chair until it had been slid all the way in—not an easy feat when not practiced regularly, I assure you.

Bennet's eyes crinkled with approval as he took the seat beside me.

Banal chatter filled the room as the first course of julienne beets and tender red potatoes were served. Next came a cup of spicy leek soup with cucumber curls and a smidgen of sherry.

Bennet leaned over to whisper in my ear. "Eat, my dear. I like a bit more meat on my females."

That comment alone was enough to kill my appetite for the rest of the year. I laid my spoon along the side of my cup and dabbed the corners of my mouth with the napkin.

The thin line of his lips indicated my response was not missed.

"Perhaps you would like me to feed you?" he said.

I immediately picked up my spoon, ignoring the smug look of satisfaction on his perfectly groomed face.

"Your spirit pleases me very much," he said, almost as a growl.

I took a deep breath, desperately trying to keep my stomach from lurching.

"What gifts does she possess?" Bennet asked my father. Of course, it would be below him to ask that same question of me.

Father spewed the list of common gifts that most Spirian females demonstrated: intuition, telepathy, shielding, blah, blah, blah. Although, he used dressed up words to make them sound far more spectacular than they really were.

Bennet was not a fool, however, and saw past the verbal fluff. "Any specialized gifts?" he asked, interrupting my father.

Father cleared his throat, chasing it down with an improper swig of wine. "She is hardly mature enough to have developed any. Spirifaes are slow to blossom. Her mother didn't show any signs of gifts until we had been mated for at least three years." He continued justifying my lack of gifts like a young child who didn't know how to stop talking.

I could feel Bennet penetrate my shield, trying to extract whatever he could. Jenico quickly responded, placing an invisible shield between Bennet and me. When Bennet sensed nothing, he pulled out.

Sitting back against his chair, he proposed, "Perhaps we should renegotiate our price?"

Father's eyes narrowed. "The price has been set."

"She is giftless."

"Fae females have never birthed ungifted children. For this reason, they are worth investing in."

"Apparently, there is a chink in this bloodline," said Bennet. He lifted my chin with his hand. "Still, this one is very beautiful and will be delightfully challenging to tame." His eyes met my father's. "I'll give you 500,000 for her."

Father tossed down his napkin. "That's half the agreed upon price."

"It is my offer," said Bennet.

Father growled. "I want 500,000 now," he said, "and another 500,000 when her offspring shows their worth."

Bennet laughed, obviously enjoying the debate. "Fair enough."

Father cast me a warning glance. I could feel the sting of his energy making my heart pound with fettered effort.

I endured the rest of the meal in silence. Bennet's hands roamed freely over my arms, shoulders, and lower back. Each touch made my skin crawl with disgust. How will I ever survive our union? I thought.

At the end of the evening, after we had retired to the den to sip a snifter of brandy, I was emotionally spent and ready to take a long hot shower.

Bennet had said his goodbyes with a promise to return at the end of June—only a short month away. He sealed his farewell with a deep, lingering kiss, one which I didn't return.

Father said nothing to me as he turned toward his master suite to retire. Jenico and I were left standing in the corridor.

I collapsed against his broad chest in a gut-wrenching sob. He simply held me close and allowed me to cry.

After a few moments, he stepped back to look at me. "Go with Seth in the morning," he said.

I shook my head. "No, Nico; I can't. It would place him and his clan in danger. You know that."

"He is stronger than you think, Rae. Please, I'm begging you to think of yourself for once. Mother would want that—I want that."

Another wave of sobs racked my body. Nico walked me up the stairs and helped me back to my room, my quiet sanctuary where things appeared to be at peace.

"I love you, Rae," he quietly said. "Please make the right choice."

He touched my cheek, then retreated from the room, closing the door behind him.

Chapter 20

~ R a e ~

THE SUN WAS JUST BEGINNING to rise over the hills as I pulled into Seth's parking lot. I needed to ride my bike this morning. The crisp morning air and physical exertion were just what I needed to clear my mind.

Leaving with Seth this morning was a tempting persuasion. The wrath that would ensue, however, was a stronger deterrent.

The lights in Seth's flat were still off, indicating he had not yet awakened. The sun hovered below the horizon but would be brightening the sky soon enough. I wanted to be long gone before then. Seth had mentioned leaving first thing this morning. I did not want to be around to face him.

My heart sank at the thought of Seth being gone for three months. I would be mated by then, and probably bound for the Americas before he returned. Perhaps it was better this way, I thought, riding past his door and through the slowly widening gates.

The air was chilling as I made my way down the quiet

streets. The soft rhythmic sound of my wheels rolling over the worn cobbled streets lulled my thoughts and eased my apprehension of the days to come.

I waved as I passed the groundskeeper at VetMed, rolling my bike up to the barn where my supplies were kept. I really didn't have much to attend to today. Many of my previous patients had been picked up by their owners. I had only one gelding in my care and he would be going home tomorrow. I just needed to be near the horses and the smell of a familiar barn.

Later, I had planned to join my brother at Musselburgh to watch him work. He was a master at bringing out the best in horses. His human clients would never understand how he connected to the magnificent animals under his care, but I did. I called it a gift. Nico called it intuition. Either way, his interaction with the horses was akin to watching a powerful ballet with inspiring orchestrations of strength, speed, and grace. It was the perfect distraction—one I desperately needed.

I entered the gelding's stall and lowered my bucket of brushes to the ground. The gelding stood calmly as I picked up a curry brush and began slow circular strokes over his bronze coat. I started at the top of his neck and worked my way to his strong hindquarters.

After giving him a thorough brushing, I checked his injured leg, and then gave him a quick healing to ensure his complete recovery.

Days ago, healing the foal of his eye condition had left me with much to explain—my claims sounding irrational as the vet inquired about my treatments. The healing was too quick and miraculous to be real. I had to be more careful to ensure a much slower healing from now on, I noted.

Cleaning up, I heard a noise at the end of the barn. Leaning over the stall door, I saw Seth pick my bike up and load it into his still running Range Rover.

Had he changed his mind about me having it? No, that didn't sound right. Seth was many things, but being a reclaimer of gifts was not one of them.

I gathered my things and left the gelding to finish his breakfast. When I reached my storage area, Seth took the things out of my hands and placed them into the bins.

"I need you to come with me," he said, as if there were no room for argument.

"I can't."

"Yes, so you've told me."

I locked up my storage area up and began shedding my coveralls.

For a long, silent moment, he just stood there, looking at me.

"Have you decided to take the bike back?"

His eyes narrowed. "Don't be ridiculous."

"Then, would you mind removing it from your truck so I can be on my way?"

The tension he emitted was palpable. His mind and body were obviously battling between wanting to pick me up and carry me off and trying to talk some sense into me. I prayed his mind would have a stronger influence on that decision.

His jaw rippled with frustration. "Can we talk?" His words sounded strained.

"About?"

With a thought, he killed the Rover's engine. "We both know that after I leave, you will be mated to a man you really don't want. We also know we will probably never see each other again. I don't know how you feel, but I can tell you that I'm not willing to let that happen."

I sighed and leaned against the cool stone wall. "And how, pray tell, will you stop the inevitable?"

"If you come with me, it will buy us some time."

"And then what?" I asked, arms folded under my chest.

"We take things as they come."

"Yeah, well I'm not willing to do that."

"Can you honestly bear the thought of never seeing me again?" His words were choked and spoken with pain.

I turned away from his piercing gaze. "I would like to remain friends," I quietly said.

"Friends?"

I nodded.

"I have enough friends," he spat.

Without warning, he closed the distance and pressed his lips against mine, his strong, shaking arms, pulling me tight against him as the intimacy deepened.

My mind screamed for me to end the kiss, but my body ignored the request, needing and wanting the affection to continue and never stop. I had wanted this for so long, but now that it was happening, I fought the urge to enjoy it—ironic.

Seth pulled back, his golden eyes boring deep into mine as if touching my soul. "I want you, Raeiza Tomei, and I am willing to do whatever it takes to have you. Even dying is better than letting you fall as another man's claim."

"Don't say that," I rasped, my breath feeling the strain of yearning.

"If you choose this man over what I can offer, I won't force you to come with me. But, if you are choosing to stay here only because you fear I may die defending you, know this: in losing you, I am already dead."

Silence lingered between us like dense lead.

"Please," he added. "Give me something to live for."

"God," I sighed with resignation, "how did it come to this?" I paced back and forth, fighting the urge to lash out. I was angry, frustrated, scared, and tired of all this drama.

I turned to face him. "Seth, you have managed to live without me for many years. You are not dead; nor will you be dying to save the likes of me. You will find a woman who suits you, have many children, and will eventually forget I ever existed. End of story."

Poor choice of words. His expression gave way to determination that would not be swayed.

He cleared the distance between us, picked me up over his shoulder, and carried me to the Rover.

Despite my screaming and slapping against his hard flesh, he willed the door open, placed me inside, and buckled me in.

All my efforts to release the belt and open the door were futile. He had bound them, a gift with which he was very efficient—to the point of being frustrating.

"Seth, please. This is a bad idea—a very bad idea."

"I've made my choice, Rae."

"And what of my choice?"

He looked over at me, his golden eyes glowing like the setting sun. "I don't agree with it."

I sat back in a huff. "I won't go with you," I said.

He didn't respond.

The remainder of the short ride was silent and filled with tension. His anger was riled, but so was mine. Was he crazy? Had he even thought this through? My mind reeled with possible scenarios: my father tracking me down—which he surely would; Bennet challenging Seth with fatal accuracy; my punishment for encouraging Seth. My face paled.

Seth reached over and took my hand as if sensing my fear. Somehow, his gentle squeeze calmed me. I felt oddly safe with this man—I always had.

Nate was waiting for us outside the gates. Seth pulled past him and pushed a button to open the back door. Nate tossed a few bags in before sliding onto the backseat.

"Things went smoothly, I see," he mocked.

One look from Seth encouraged the cheeky Kiwi to keep his mouth shut.

I looked back at Nate with a pleading expression. "Perhaps you can talk some sense into your friend?"

Nate smiled. "I believe the appropriate Yank saying is, if it ain't broke, don't fix it."

I groaned. "Do you not see the insanity of this?"

He shook his head and then shrugged with resignation. "The man knows what he wants."

I slammed back against my seat, closing my eyes and forcing my lungs to expand with air that seemed too heavy to be much good.

When Nate started singing, Seth reached over and turned on the radio.

By the time we reached the long stretch of M90, my nerves were frazzled. Seth continued to hold my hand.

I looked over at him, wondering what he was thinking that made his features look so serious.

"Do your uncles know I'm coming?" I asked.

"Yes, they both know."

"And they're okay with two Shadows entering their territory?"

He glanced over at me. "Once they get to know you, they will be happy to have you there."

"Know me?"

"My uncle Khalen reads intention, and my aunt Lenore senses your thoughts and feelings as if they were her own."

"Nice gifts," said Nate.

"I told them about you. They are...eager to meet you."

Nate chortled, "Well, that doesn't sound good."

I stared out the window at the passing trees and rolling hills. It was hard not to feel like a rabbit destined for a den of wolves.

"What if they don't like us?" I said, my voice barely audible above the chiming voices of U2.

Seth lowered the volume. "If they believe you are dangerous, my uncle Khalen will bind you to the camp."

We turned onto A9 in Perth, passing the small town that looked as if it belonged to a century gone past. I half-expected to find horse-drawn buckboards lined up at the local hardware store instead of pickup trucks.

"What's that look for?" asked Seth.

I shrugged. "Do these people know that it's the twenty-first century?"

He chuckled, shaking his head. "When I was younger, there were times I doubted it. Now, I understand their passion for the simpler ways of life."

I raised a brow, looking at the small town with simple buildings sporting aged wood siding and stone accents.

"First time to the Isle of Skye?" he asked.

Both Nate and I scoffed.

"This is not exactly Shadow territory," I explained, as if it needed to be.

Seth smiled. "For a moment, I had forgotten you two were from different clans."

"I'm beginning to wish we weren't," said Nate, staring

out at the green landscape and rugged hills. "New Zealand is beautiful, but I've never seen anything like this."

We continued to drive over winding roads, through thick forests, and past majestic meadows. This island seemed to offer a bit of everything. The beauty of it all, however, did little to easy my nerves. Entering an enemy clan was not exactly my life ambition. If I managed to survive this experience by some miracle, my father would, no doubt, pick up where this clan left off. Either way, I was doomed.

"Our clan is different," said Seth, reading my thoughts.

I nibbled the tips of my fingers. He reached over and pulled them from my trembling mouth.

"They won't hurt either of you."

Chapter 21

~Seth~

THE TENSION IN THE AIR as we drove up the long winding path leading to Shanuk's castle was palpable. Rae and Nate were leery—and for good reason. Entering an enemy clan was not something that even the most powerful leaders would attempt without serious motivation.

We passed the many small homes, barns, and pastures that bordered the massive garden areas. Just as it was back at home, this camp was self-sustaining with everyone contributing his or her own unique skills to the everyday chores that helped the clan survive.

Children playing a game in the fields came to a halt as their eyes followed the path of our car. Adults stopped what they were doing as we passed, all curious about the newcomers.

I pulled the Rover around to the back of the large castle that dominated the grounds with its massive stone structure and towering height. It looked like something that should be on a postcard instead of in the center of community of modern souls.

Rae's eyes were big as saucers as she took in the glorious site. "I've heard about Shanuk's castle, but I never thought it really existed."

Nate, too, looked to be in awe. "It's much larger than I thought."

"Wait until you see the inside," I said, putting the car in park and setting the brake.

I exited the car, noticing that Rae and Nate had not opened their doors. I leaned in through the open window. "Are you coming?"

Just then, I saw Darius and Khalen coming around the corner to greet us. Their energy radiated. I hugged them both, relishing in the comfort of familiar arms and strength.

"Welcome home," said Khalen.

"Damn, boy," Darius chimed, standing back to get a better look at me. "Ye look fine, lad."

I walked around the car and opened Rae's door. "Come on," I encouraged, offering her a hand.

With hesitance, she stepped from the car, keeping her eyes trained on the ground.

"This is not a Shadow camp," I whispered to her. "Women are viewed as equals here. Meet their eyes and be confident with who you are."

She looked up at Khalen first, obviously sensing the leader of the clan. "I'm Rae," she said. Her shift in stance and sudden stiffness indicated her shock over Khalen's resemblance to me.

Khalen maintained his intimidating look. His actions could be just as deadly as he appeared. He took her hand in his and looked directly into her eyes. "Rae," he repeated. "I'm Khalen, leader of the Gradhun clan."

Rae met his eyes, obviously mesmerized by his charming looks and British accent with a Scottish flair. Khalen often had this effect on females. That he was mated didn't seem to be an issue or a deterrent.

Darius took her hand next. "I'm Darius, keeper of these glorious grounds." He had not changed much over the years. He was still a stout Highlander with dark red hair and pale green eyes.

"Nice to meet you," she said, bowing her head slightly. Her eyes returned to Khalen.

He shifted his attention to Nate, who had silently exited the car while Rae made her introduction.

Nate confidently stuck out his hand. "Nathaniel Dronel," he announced formally.

Khalen studied the man, saying nothing. "And what is your birth name?" he asked, surprising both me and Rae.

Nate's face paled a few shades as he swallowed hard.

"Your secrets are safe here," Khalen added.

Nate looked over at me. I nodded, validating Khalen's statement.

Nate squared his shoulders and met Khalen's eyes, taking a long breath before speaking. "I am Taholin Daboi, son of Huli."

Khalen nodded, a slight smile softening his lips. "I know Huli. He is a good man."

Nate's eyes widened.

Khalen laughed. "Do not worry, young Nate. Your claiming father, Danube, is no friend of mine. He will not hear of your existence from me or anyone in this clan."

Nate's shoulders relaxed.

Aunt Skye came around the corner, her dog, Maiyun, right beside her. She wrapped her arms around me and held me tight. "Seth, it is so good to see you. Evening fires are not the same without your stories. The children miss you so much."

"Are they here?"

She nodded, glancing over her shoulder toward a group of young ones playing in the field. Skye was a simple woman, but her beauty shown from deep within. Her long blonde hair hung loose, falling to the back of her thighs. Though she was blind, her gray-blue eyes sparkled with life giving no indication of her impairment.

"I will tell them a story tonight," I assured her.

She smiled, warming the area like a summer breeze.

"Aunt Skye, I want you to meet Rae and Nate, my friends from Edinburgh."

I helped Skye find Rae's outstretched hand.

"Skye is blind," I explained. "This is her guide dog, Maiyun."

Maiyun, having heard her name, started wagging her tail. I leaned over to scratch her ear.

"I'm Rae."

Nate took Skye's other hand and placed his left one on top of it. The intimate act drew a growl from Khalen.

"Delighted to meet you," Nate said, stemming his typical penchant to kiss the back of her hand. One look from Khalen convinced him to release his grip and step back instead.

Khalen moved beside his mate and drew her close against him, making it very clear that she belonged with him.

Skye rolled her eyes. "Forgive my mate," she said.

A squeal of delight drew our attention to a pack of children running toward us. My mother, Sunjia, and her mate, Aidan, followed behind.

I was bombarded with arms and bouncing heads,

nearly knocking me off balance.

Rae smiled, obviously enjoying my plight of greeting the group while struggling to stay on my feet.

"Seth, are you going to tell us a story tonight?" young Kaili asked. She must have grown a good three inches since I saw her last. Being seventeen years old now, she stood nearly as tall as her mother. Fine, blonde curls danced about my arms as I held her. Green eyes sparkled up at me.

Her identical twin, Shaiya squeezed me tight, adding a very convincing plea of, "Pleeeease." She was the bolder of the two and often the one to get into trouble.

"Yes, yes, of course," I answered.

The group squealed with excitement, then ran off just as fast as they had come.

My mother laughed and held her arms open to me. "My turn?"

I pulled her into a tight embrace. I had missed her earthly scent of birch and bergamot flowers. She looked much older than when I had seen her last, as if life had suddenly caught up to her.

"How have you been, Mother?" I whispered in her ear.

She smiled, but it never reached her eyes. "Well," she replied. The tone of her voice was not very convincing. The events that had led to Tria's death several years ago had taken their toll on her. Based on the dullness of her eyes, I assumed that she and Aidan were still struggling to rekindle their relationship with one another.

I looked over at Aidan. He, too, looked far older than his age as far as Spirians were concerned. His cocky charm was gone. He had lost his faith in my mother when she held vital information from him and our leader. Though she did it to save my sister, the crime was not something easily forgiven. Aidan had every right to end her life that day, when Tria's true intentions were learned, but he chose to let Mother live. Looking at them both now, I wondered whether either of them would find the love they had once known.

Aidan reached over and pulled me into a bone-crushing hug. "Damn good t'see ye, lad." He slapped the back of my shoulder.

"It's good to be home," I said.

After introducing my friends, I looked around for Gabrihen and Zhentu.

Skye must have noticed. "They'll be joining us later this week," she said.

I nodded, trying to hide my disappointment.

"Come," she said, holding her hand out to me. "You must be hungry."

I glanced back at Rae and Nate. "I think we all are."

Nate nodded enthusiastically.

I held my hand out to Rae, but she fell in beside Nate, keeping a leery eye on Khalen as we made our way to the large fire burning in the main courtyard. An entire pig was roasting over a bed of coals not far away. Aunt Lenore, was busy orchestrating dinner preparations as we entered the yard. When she saw us standing there, her eyes grew bright with excitement.

She came running, her large frame gliding effortlessly over two stout legs. For a large woman, she moved like a dancer. Having seen her fight, I knew she was not a woman to be reckoned with; the people around her knew it also. Auburn hair, held back in a tie, swayed to and fro as she continued her way toward me.

The air purged from my lungs as she swept me off my feet and swirled me around like a child no bigger than a toddler. "Seth, ye handsome lad, so good t'see ye."

Struggling to breathe, I slowly pulled away and introduced my friends. She met them with the same scrutiny the others had shown, but she was pleasantly polite.

"C'n I get ye somethin' t'eat?"

I nodded.

"Please," said Nate.

She looked him up and down with a tsk of her tongue. "By the scant looks of ye, I'd say you're in need of a good meal."

"You too," she added, giving Rae the once over.

"How 'bout somethin' t'drink?" asked Darius.

"I fancy a beer," said Nate.

"Water, please," Rae said sweetly. She was like a new person out here among my clan—not quite docile, but not her usual sassy self either.

"Do you have some of your lemon tea brewed?" I asked.

A smile brightened her face to near glowing. "A fresh pitcher of it in the cooler." She nodded to a young woman to fetch the drinks.

Khalen and Darius moved some logs around to form a circle where they could all sit.

Skye studied Rae with curiosity before stating, "I would like to show Rae and Nate to their rooms."

Khalen stiffened, clearly not comfortable with the idea. After a few silent words with his mate, he conceded with a curt nod.

Rae followed Skye and Nate into the house, looking back over her shoulder. Maiyun stayed close to her mistress.

"They are good people," I said, looking at Khalen.

"Like you and me, they were simply born unto the wrong side, but their hearts are good and their intentions are pure."

"He is a listener," said Khalen. "And she is protected by an outside source."

I nodded. "Her brother. He suggested I bring her here."

The look on his face told me that I better know what I had done.

"Would you like us to leave?" I asked.

His eyes grew cold. "You know better than to ask that of me."

I did, but said nothing.

Skye came back alone, her expression revealing nothing. She sat beside her mate.

"Interesting pair," she reported. "They have decided to settle in a bit before joining us for lunch."

Khalen growled deep in his throat, clearly uncomfortable with them being unsupervised.

I stood. "I think I'll bring in our things and settle in myself."

I didn't care for the tension I was feeling; nor did I care for the mistrust of my leader. He had always trusted me before.

I grabbed the bags from the back of the car and hauled them over my shoulders. I had an idea of where my friends would be staying so I headed in that direction.

Knowing Skye, she would want them to have a comfortable stay so she would avoid showing them the lower rooms where it was always cold and dark. No, she would want them to stay on the second floor, the same as her and Khalen.

I walked up the stairs and turned left. Passing Skye

and Khalen's room, I continued down the long corridor until I heard voices.

"I shouldn't be here," said Rae.

"Neither of us should be," Nate agreed. "But yet, here we are."

"Khalen scares me."

He scoffed. "Yeah. He's a leader, and from what I hear, a very powerful one."

I stepped into the room. "I brought your bags."

Both of them looked up at me as if they had taken my last dollar and were caught discussing how to spend it.

"You have nothing to worry about," I lied, knowing full well how quickly things could turn ugly.

"I think we should go," said Rae. "We clearly don't belong here."

I sighed, lowering the bags to the floor. "Why don't we discuss it over lunch?"

"I'm not hungry," she exclaimed.

"Have you eaten anything today?" I asked.

She shook her head.

"Please," I said, holding my hand out to her. "Come with me."

With hesitance, she offered her hand. I could feel it tremble in mine as I led her out of the room.

Nate willingly followed, never one to pass on a meal, be it within enemy territories or not.

By the time we had returned to the circle near the fire, plates filled with sandwiches, fruit, and cucumbers awaited us, sitting next to our cold drinks.

Nate eagerly took his seat and dug in. I sat beside Rae, handing her a plate. Taking her hands in mine, I said a quick prayer in Gaelic.

Nate stopped chewing, lowered his plate, and said his

own quick prayer, adding a hasty thanks to the one who had prepared such a meal.

Rae kept an eye on Khalen as she nibbled at the sandwich and fruit on her plate.

Skye, noticing her discomfort, nudged her mate, probably asking him to look more friendly. It had little effect.

I could feel him reaching out to Rae with his energy and I didn't like it. My own protective shield slowly wrapped around her like a thick blanket. The gesture did not escape Khalen's notice.

A slight sting traced through my body, letting me know he didn't appreciate my actions.

Finding it hard to eat, I lowered my plate and met Khalen's eyes.

What are you doing, Seth? he asked me in thought.

I care for her, I responded.

Too much by the feel of it.

I stood, urging him to follow me away from the circle. He did.

When we were out of earshot from the others, I turned to face him. "Khalen, I need you to trust me on this."

"You have bonded with a Shadow female."

My jaw tensed. "Yes, so I've been told."

"What do you know about her?"

I looked away from him. "Enough."

The sting of his energy pierced my body. "Do not toy with me, Seth. You have placed our clan at great risk. I deserve to know why."

I met his eyes, glowing with the intensity of the sun. "Like you and me, Rae and Nate were born unto the wrong clan. They are Shadows by blood, but then so are you and

I. Their intentions are pure and they need our help."

He glanced toward Nate. "Your friend is listening to us now."

"He feels threatened. What do you expect?" My tone was a bit more harsh than I had intended, and Khalen's sharp reprimand was felt with a vengeance. I stifled a groan and fought to keep my legs from crumbling.

"I have no choice but to bind them both to this camp."

Knowing what that meant, I closed my eyes and raised my face to the warming sun. Khalen's reasons could not be challenged, but the thought of my friends being stripped of their gifts and bound to the camp made me feel like a traitor of sorts. "For how long?"

"Until I find out what the hell is going on," he growled.

Not waiting for my reply, he turned and headed back to the group. I followed, gritting my teeth and holding back my own emotions. Pitting myself against Khalen was not conducive to earning his trust—and that is exactly what I had to do.

By the time I had returned to my seat, the energy had shifted. Rae and Nate looked as if they had been betrayed. Neither of them met my gaze.

"Rae and Nate, I have bound you to this camp until I can better assess this situation. Seth tells me that you need our assistance. Until I know exactly what that entails, I must provide adequate protection to my clan. I'm sure you understand."

Rae lowered her unfinished meal. Nate continued to eat as if this situation were expected. Given his gifts, he probably knew what would go down long before I did. When he laid a comforting hand on Rae's arm, I growled.

All eyes trained on me.

Khalen cleared his throat, offering me a warning

glance before shifting his attention to Nate. "After lunch, I want to examine your condition. Your color is not right."

"I'm feeling much better, just a bit congested is all."

"I'll be the judge of that."

Chapter 22

~ Rae ~

SLEEPING SO CLOSE TO THAT horrid leader made it difficult to get any real rest. I had seen powerful leaders before and had felt their wrath, but nothing compared to the intensity of this man called Khalen. His mate, Skye, seemed completely opposite to him. She was gentle, trusting and calm.

Nate didn't act too alarmed, even when our gifts had been stripped. That part didn't bother me much, but being bound to this camp did for some reason. I should be grateful, I thought. So long as I was bound, my father would not be able to track me.

I wished Seth would come talk to me, but he seemed so distant all of a sudden, as if Khalen's binding of us affected him as well. Did he feel responsible?

I stood and started to pace the sizable room. It was elegantly decorated with rustic woods, a simple four-poster bed, a rosewood trunk at the foot of the bed, oak floors, and an elegant armoire that matched the trunk. In the corner was a valet where clean towels had been draped. Early morning light filtered in through the large window, its sheer drapes fluttering in the soft breeze flowing through the screen. The old castle had been modernized, I was sure. Somehow, though, it hadn't lost its charm.

The bathroom was down the hall. Gathering a thick towel and a clean set of clothes, I padded my way down the stone corridor toward a large partitioned room that Skye had shown us yesterday.

Pictures on the walls depicted generations of people. One in particular drew my attention. It was a portrait of a man with amazing blue eyes. His silver hair looked stunning and framed a powerful face. Below was a brass caption, "Shanuk."

I ran my fingers over the glass-covered portrait, disbelieving that I was actually standing in the hall of this great man's castle. I had heard stories about him—none of them seemed to be true. However, after looking at his face, I could believe most of them now. If Khalen's power was intense, I could only imagine what Shanuk could do.

Continuing down the hall, I passed Seth's closed door, hesitating there for just a moment. It was too early to disturb him so I walked on.

The shared washroom was much larger than anything I had seen. The privy was in its own section with a privacy door. Two large sinks took up the adjoining section with plenty of storage for supplies and fresh towels. The bathroom was in yet another section.

The large oval tub, nearly four feet deep and three feet wide, was constructed of a material that felt and looked like white marble. Along the far wall were five showerheads. I had never seen such a shower with no enclosure. The water flowed into a hidden drain cleverly disguised within the heated stone floor.

The inviting scent of lilac candles filled my nose. It was lovely. I lit the candles with a lighter Skye had placed on a hook near the door. They gave the room a warm glow. I then draped my towel over the warming rack and placed my clean clothes on the bench beside it.

The large faucet on the tub resembled an old-fashioned well-water tap. Adjusting the temperature, I filled the tub with steaming water, adding a small amount of flora-scented bath salts from an oak barrel that rested near the towel warmer.

As the tub filled, I removed my nightgown and folded it on the bench. I could get used to this, I thought, sinking down into the hot fragrant water.

When the water flowed up to my neck, I turned the faucet off and laid back, eyes closed, and ears tuned to the lulling sound of water, flickering candles, and blissful silence.

My thoughts drifted into a world that only lived in my mind. Seth and I were walking along the water's edge, holding hands and talking about our future. We were not bound by our heritage or anything else. We were free. Visions of my mother smiled upon me, warming my heart with a familiar love I had long forgotten.

A sharp bang jolted me back to reality. My eyes flew open as I abruptly sat up, sloshing water over the tub's sides. Someone was using the privy. The water felt cool against my skin, making me wonder how long I had been in here.

Pulling the plug, I climbed out of the tub, dried quickly, and then struggled into my clothes, now damp from the heavy steam. When I opened the door, Seth was just leaving the privy.

"Morning," he said.

God, he looked great with his mussed hair and his golden eyes still glossy from sleep. His bare chest and baggy pants only added to the charm. I looked away, feeling the heat rise to my face. "Morning."

I caught a glimpse of his smile as I buried my head in the towel to dry my hair.

He peered into the bathroom, waving away the fog of steam. "Is there any hot water left?" He turned on the fan to lift the condensation from the room.

"Um, I'm not sure."

When I removed the towel from my head, I saw him standing there with my nightgown draped over his arm. "It's a bit damp."

"Yeah," I chuckled. "I didn't really plan things out well." I pulled the damp shirt away from my body.

"Better put some dry clothes on before you catch a cold."

"Yes, good idea." Not meeting his gaze, I pulled my gown from his arm and hurried out of the room. I felt his eyes on me as I left. I could just imagine him laughing at my stupidity. Why hadn't I turned the fan on? The walls had been dripping with moisture when I left.

Returning to my room, I closed the door, grateful that no one else had seen my pathetic condition. Lord, my shirt clung to my bare chest, leaving little to the imagination. No wonder Seth was smiling.

I peeled my clothes off. Shivering from the cold, I donned a pair of jeans and a pink sweater, grateful for the dry warmth they provided. I hung my damp clothes over the valet to dry in the sun spilling in through the windows. I slipped on a pair of socks and my comfortable Bailey Button boots.

My brother, I had learned, had packed a few things for me and had delivered them to Seth for our journey. At first, I was angry. Now, I was grateful he had chosen practical clothes that offered comfort.

I had just picked up my brush to tackle my hair when a knock sounded on my door.

"Rae, you up?"

I opened the door to find Nate standing there fully dressed, twigs and branches clinging to his damp flannel shirt and mussed hair.

I looked him up and down. "Are you all right?"

"I'm beaut, yeah. Darius took me huntin' with him this mornin'. We caught a few rabbits for dinner."

The aroma coming from his clothes assaulted my senses. I pinched my nose. "I'd welcome you in, but you're a bit ripe, yes?"

"Sorry," he said, stepping back a bit. "I'm gonna get cleaned up. Lenore just wanted me to tell you that breakfast is up in an hour."

"Thank you."

He nodded and shuffled his feet a bit. "Uh, you look nice." Not waiting for a reply, he sauntered toward his room. Odd display of shyness from him, I thought, closing my door.

After brushing my damp hair and taming it with a thick braid down my back, I made my way toward the kitchen.

Lenore was orchestrating a group of young men and women as they prepared and cooked the morning meal. Skye sat at the table dicing onions. I scooted in beside her.

"Need some help?"

Lenore plopped down a cutting board before me, and

then topped it with a colorful array of peppers. "Ye c'n chop these up, love."

Skye smiled and handed me a butcher knife. "Did you sleep well?"

"Yes," I said. "That bed is extraordinary."

Her smiled deepened. "Lenore has the mattresses stuffed with fresh goose down each year."

"She's a busy woman."

Skye huffed. "She's amazing. I can't imagine a better person governing my grandfather's castle."

I thought about the portrait of the man I had studied earlier on my way to the bathroom. "Shanuk?"

Skye's face brightened. "Yes."

I nodded. "I saw his portrait in the hall this morning."

"He was a very powerful Spirian leader," she explained, expertly cutting an onion without even looking.

I chopped the stem off a bright red pepper and began dicing the top. "His legend is very familiar."

After dicing the red pepper, I moved on to the yellow and orange varieties, marveling at their brilliant colors. "I've never seen peppers as beautiful as these."

"Lenore keeps a fabulous garden. I can show you after breakfast if you'd like."

I smiled. "I'd like that."

This woman seemed so opposite to her mate. She was inviting, warm, kind, and easy to talk to. Khalen, on the other hand, was like dancing around a pot of bubbling grease, threatening to explode on you at any moment.

When Skye chuckled, I knew she had been reading my thoughts. I offered another image of a minefield under a bank of heavy fog.

"He's not that bad," she sighed.

I looked at her with a raised brow. Just then, the hairs

on my neck stood out like porcupine quills. Khalen had entered the room. Everyone else felt his presence as well. The hum was evident.

"Speak of the Angel," Skye muttered, "and he appears."

He leaned over and gave her a gentle kiss on the side of her neck. "Hey, beautiful," he whispered.

Then, his luminous eyes focused in on me. My body felt suddenly chilled.

"Morning," he chimed.

"Morning." My response was clipped and came out more like a choke.

Lenore handed him four platters of meat. "Make y'rself useful and carry these out to the dinin' room."

"Is there any coffee?" he asked, stacking the platters on his arms as if he had done it a thousand times.

"On the table," said Lenore, ushering him out of the room.

"Honestly," she added after he left. "That man c'n stop the momentum of the finest tuned machine with his presence." She clapped her hands. "Come now; back t'work."

Skye laughed, shaking her head.

"Is he always that...commanding?"

"Always," she said. "We can't even go to a restaurant without having the wait staff fall all over him."

"That must be frustrating."

"For him, yes. For me, it's quite entertaining."

I thought of Seth and the way he effortlessly drew the attention of every female in the pub, especially when he danced. He, too, was commanding.

The rest of the meal was colorfully displayed on platters that we carried into the adjoining room. The table was massive as it curled into the shape of a giant horseshoe, which enabled everyone to eat and talk with one another.

Seth stood with Khalen and Darius, drinking coffee and talking. His eyes locked onto me as I lowered a platter of hot cakes and a bowl of fresh blueberries onto the table. When Nate came around to my left to slide a chair out for me, Seth's back stiffened.

I smiled back at Nate. "Thank you."

Nate took the seat beside me.

"You smell better," I replied, trying to break the uncomfortable silence between us.

From the corner of my eye, I saw Khalen hold Seth back as he tried to advance toward us. Seth had never allowed anyone to stop him before so it was odd to see it happen now. Then again, Khalen was his leader.

Everyone took a seat, with Seth sitting across from me at the table's opposite end. When it came time to pray to the Father, he stood and walked around to my back, placing his hands on my shoulders. At the end, he gave me a gentle squeeze as if reaffirming his claim. Since our clan rarely, if ever prayed, the entire ritual felt odd, but strangely comforting. My father claimed that the great Spirit knew about our gratitude and there was no need to voice it. This clan, however, thought differently. It was delightful to hear what everyone was grateful for, including the young, who gleefully thanked the Spirit for desert and a later bedtime. The laughing that followed warmed my heart.

At the end, Nate cleared his throat, avoiding Seth's warning glare.

What was going on between them? I wondered. Nate had never shown genuine interest in me, and Seth was acting like a possessive mate.

"Did you sleep well?" Nate whispered, pulling me out of my reverie.

I shook my head. "Not really."

"Y'feel a bit like a rabbit in a snake den, yeah?"

"Very much so."

"No worries, Rae. Seth won't let anything happen to us."

I glanced over at Khalen. "Are you sure about that?"

Chapter 23

-Rae-

AFTER BREAKFAST, NATE AND SETH joined a few other men in the pasture where they were planning to remove a diseased tree. Nate's color had greatly improved. He attributed it to Khalen's administrations and Skye's healing touch. This clan life suited him well, and he seemed to blend in far easier than I did.

I followed Skye and her dog around the massive gardens. Crops were planted in sections for each season. Potatoes grew in large sacks that were already bulging at the sides.

She led me into an area that resembled a large rugby field encased in insulated plastic. Fans had been secured on each side of the enclosure for air circulation. The place smelled like crushed basil and rich earth.

"Here is where we grow our tomatoes, peppers, and other sensitive vegetables that require a particular environment."

"This is incredible," I said, looking around at the numerous tables supporting an endless spectrum of colorful foods. Misters hovered above, doling out sprits of moisture at programmed intervals.

"Do all your clans live this way?" I asked.

"Yes," she replied. "We own quite a bit of land and prefer to be self-sustaining."

"Our clans own businesses and factories. We purchase everything we need." I ran my hand over the velvety leaves of Italian parsley and dill.

"Do you like it?"

I looked at her questioningly. "Like what?"

"Your clan life?"

I followed her outside as we walked toward the pastures. "I really had nothing to compare it to until I came here."

"What's it like to be a Sh—. To live in your clan?"

I chortled. "To be a Shadow, you mean?"

"I'm sorry," she said, placing her hand on my shoulder. "I didn't mean to sound—"

"Don't worry. I'm fully aware of the differences between our clans."

We walked in silence, Maiyun prancing by Skye's side.

"It's not like this," I finally explained. "Our clans are private and often stick to their immediate families. Here, I feel as if you are all one big family, even the servants."

Skye chuckled. "We have no servants. Everyone contributes to the work that needs to be done."

"Even you and Khalen?"

"Yes, even us."

I shook my head, smiling at the image of my father doing menial tasks. He'd had a hard enough time allowing me to work at the pub. "In our clans, we have servants. My father would have had kittens if he had seen me chop food in the kitchen this morning."

"Really?"

"Yes. I would be feeling the sting of his reprimand for days following, I assure you."

"He sounds strict."

"You have no idea."

A series of shouts pierced the air, followed by a sharp crack and a thunderous roar as a large tree fell to the ground.

"Seth!" someone yelled.

"Uh, oh," said Skye, hurrying toward the commotion.

I kept pace, my heart pounding against my chest as my mind conjured the worst.

We approached to find five men pulling Seth out from under a heavy branch. His left leg twisted at an odd angle. His femur was broken; I was sure of it.

"How bad is it?" asked Skye, hovering beside her mate as he examined Seth's body. He was conscious, but his eyes were glossy and unfocused.

I remembered Seth telling me that Khalen was a skilled surgeon at one time. My hands shook, itching to heal the injury, but my gifts had been stripped by Khalen's bond.

"His femur is broken here and here. His tibia is cracked here, and his hip is injured here."

My eyes widened. Khalen was looking at Seth as if he were studying an x-ray. It was a rare gift for sure, but nothing could prepare me for what I saw next. Skye placed her hands on Seth. His bones melded as Khalen held them in position. I looked around at the crowd. None of them seemed surprised or concerned. Skye was healing Seth without fear of judgment against her.

My knees wavered as I sank to the ground next to Seth.

"Tell her," he said, peering at me through slitted eyes. His hand reached for mine. "Tell her now."

"I can help," I blurted.

Skye and Khalen glanced up at me.

"I'm a healer. I can help."

Khalen reached over and touched me. I felt a shock of power flow through me as if I had been struck by lightning. My gifts were back.

With shaky hands, I began working on Seth's hip. Together, Skye and I had him back together and completely out of pain in less than five minutes.

"Take him to the castle," Khalen ordered two young men. Then, his golden eyes settled on me. "You, come with me."

I glanced over at Skye. Her brow was furrowed with concern. I silently begged her to follow. Khalen didn't seem to object.

When we reached an area sheltered by a thick canopy of trees, Khalen gestured for me to sit on a stump across from him.

"Who shields you?" he asked.

"My brother, Nic—Jenico."

"Why?"

I twisted my hands together.

Skye came over and offered some comfort. "Don't be afraid," she said.

Khalen must have issued a warning because she glared up at him and stepped away. I could feel the energy building between them.

"There is no need to frighten her," Skye whispered.

He took in a deep breath and closed his eyes for a moment. "Why does your brother shield you?" he asked again in a softer voice.

His reaction surprised me. If Skye had said that to a male of our clan, she would be writhing in pain by now. Khalen clearly had more control than I thought.

My confidence rose a notch. "To protect me from our father."

"Who is?"

"Drake Tomei."

Khalen's face grew pale. "Son of Zorid?"

I nodded slowly.

"Christ," he seethed. "What was Seth thinking, bringing you here?"

"I asked him not to."

"Why does your brother need to protect you from your father?" asked Skye.

"He is not a kind man. My mother warned me never to reveal my gifts to him. I don't have the gift to hide it, so Jenico shields me from anyone who can sense such things." My voice started to quaver, knowing I was revealing myself far beyond my comfort level.

"Your mother is a smart woman," Khalen muttered.

"Yes," I said, raising my chin a notch, "she was."

He looked surprised. "Was?"

I bit my lip, wondering how much I should share with them.

"Everything," Khalen warned. "You will share everything with us or you will leave this moment without a trace of memory for Seth or this clan."

A shiver rose up my spine. How was he able to read my thoughts when he hadn't been able to before? I had no doubt this man would fulfill that threat to the letter if pushed to do so. I could handle being banned from this place, but losing all memory of Seth. That thought alone filled me with dread.

"My mother was banned after coming between my father and me during one of his punishments. We were told she died shortly after."

"You are not full-blooded Spirian," Khalen said.

"I am a Spirifae."

"Spirifae?" asked Skye.

"Half-Spirian, half-Fae," Khalen explained. "Very gifted."

I shrugged.

"Have you any other gifts?" he asked.

I shook my head. "My mother kept me very subdued, especially when she learned I could heal. I was afraid to explore other talents."

"Your brother's shield is very strong—impressively so."

I said nothing, not really having anything to compare Nico's gift to. Then again, he was the son of a leader.

"He's not your full brother," Khalen stated.

He clearly knew everything about me now, perhaps due to the binding? I determined it was best to be honest and not try to hide a thing. "No, he's not. My mother had only one child. Jenico's mother still lives and is our father's primary mate."

Khalen started to pace, rubbing his chin as he thought things through.

"Seth said you were in trouble and needed some help. What kind of trouble are you in?"

There it was—the loaded question. Taking a deep breath, I decided to spill the entire horror of this situation. "I am betrothed to a man who wants to join with me by the end of this month or sooner. He paid my father a half-million dollars for my safe delivery. I don't want to unite with him and Seth knew it. He thought it would be best to bring me here until a better plan could be devised."

"A better plan?" Khalen's voice was stressed. I could feel his anger peak and it frightened me.

"I should leave," I said, starting to stand.

"No," said Skye, "you can't."

"I won't tell anyone about this place or about your clan, I promise."

Khalen continued to pace, saying nothing. In a flash, I felt my gifts fade and the constant hum of his cursed bond. Once again, I was a prisoner.

"My father will find me," I said, more as a warning than a threat.

"Not through my bond," Khalen growled.

"He's a binder," I explained. "He will find me."

Khalen growled, his intensity reverberating through my bones. "Seth," he muttered. "What have you done?"

Chapter 24

~ R a e ~

THE NEXT FEW DAYS HAD been tense. I had not seen Seth, nor Khalen for that matter. Skye claimed they were around but offered no other information. Earlier this morning, I had gone to knock on Seth's door, but there was no answer. When I questioned Nate, he simply shrugged.

As the ladies and I sat in the sun, the men played a modified game of rugby on the lawn. Men and young children ran from one end to the other, shouting and laughing while a leather ball was passed from one person to another.

Nate was good with the children. It was clear he gave them every possible advantage without making it too obvious. Their delight in escaping his tackle was evident as their laughter reverberated off the trees. The children in our clan rarely laughed this freely.

Skye sidled up next to me. "Do the people of your clan play such games?" She was weaving something out of silky rope.

I shook my head. "No. Children of our clan are pressed to study and learn the strategic and manipulating skills of good business." The venom in my voice surprised even me.

"You sound like you disapprove."

"I never quite fit into my clan. My only joy was riding my bike to the neighborhood farm and mingling with the animals."

"Seth tells me you are studying to be a vet?"

My eyes searched the grounds for him, desperate to catch a glimpse. "I am, though I doubt I'll be able to finish."

"Why's that?" she asked, tying another knot in the piece without even looking at her work. I had to remind myself that she was blind and had no reason to look.

"Because my intended mate does not wish me to do so."

Her soft hand enveloped mine. "Can I ask you something?"

I met her silver eyes, amazed at how well she could look at me when she could not see. "Yes, of course."

"Do you love Seth?"

My throat constricted. There was no use in lying to this woman. Seth had told me she read intentions. Gathering my emotions and feelings for Seth, I tried to herd them into words that would somehow make sense. Organizing cockroaches would have been simpler.

"I am attracted to him, yes." The words sounded empty and contrite compared to how I really felt.

Skye laughed. "Attracted to him." She laughed again.

"I amuse you?"

Her laugh deepened. If I had not been so curious, I might have been offended.

Maiyun trotted over to investigate her mistress' outburst. Satisfied that she was all right, she laid down beside her, vying for attention with a wave of her paw.

Skye reached over to rub her belly. "You love that man so deep, you cannot find words to describe it. And because you fear your love is not reciprocated, you add a layer of safety by claiming that you are merely attracted to him."

The woman was far too perceptive. "Seeing I cannot be with him, the point is moot, is it not?"

Her expression turned serious. "Seth has bonded with you. He will not allow another man to claim you."

Now it was my turn to laugh. "I once thought he had, but now I'm not so sure," I tried to assure her. "I have seen him night after night in the pub where I work, with one female after another. He does not lack for their company."

"But he wants you."

I gestured around the area. "I have not seen him in days. That hardly seems like the action of a man who is bonded. Besides, he is no match for my father, let alone the man who has purchased me."

"Are you sure about that?"

I lifted the bundle of rope she wove together. "What is this?"

"It's a feed net for the goats, and don't change the subject."

I shifted my tingling legs beneath me and tried to find comfort on the warm lawn. My eyes drifted to the group of men and children playing in the field. I would miss this clan and the happiness it radiated.

"The truth of it is, I don't want him hurt because of me. My mother tried to protect me once and look where it got her. She's dead because of it."

Skye stood. "Come; let's hang this net for the goats." She reached for my hand and pulled me to a stand.

"Don't worry for Seth," she said. "He is with Khalen."

The thought of Seth with that man disturbed me, especially given the anger he had shown during my last interrogation.

Skye led the way toward the pastures. "What Seth has done is very dangerous for you and this clan. Khalen must fully understand the situation."

"Is Seth in trouble?"

"Khalen is not happy with him."

I stopped and gripped her arm. "I don't want him hurt."

"Seth made his choice, Rae. He knew the consequences."

My knees shifted beneath me and I fell to the soft ground. My stomach lurched, threatening to purge my meager lunch. "I need to know he's all right."

Her brow compressed with concern. "Khalen will not harm him."

THAT NIGHT, WE GATHERED AROUND a large fire to enjoy supper. Still, there was no sign of Seth.

"Eat," said Nate, pressing a full plate of food before me. "You look like you're ready to shatter."

He and I had been spending time with one another. At times, he acted as though our friendship had escalated to a whole new level. Knowing he would never trump Seth for my affections, I dismissed the idea that Nate was feeling anything serious for me.

"Have you seen Seth?"

"Earlier today, yeah."

I glanced up to find two weary men walking toward the castle. I stood and moved toward them. When Seth turned toward me, I stopped, stunned at the bruised and battered face staring back at me.

"You bastard!" I roared at Khalen, launching myself toward him. Without much thought, I began pounding his rock-hard chest.

Seth pulled me back. "Rae, stop."

My hands shook as they reached up to touch his swollen face. "My God. What has he done?"

Skye and the other clan members came running toward us.

"What have you done?" I asked Khalen. "You had no right."

Before I could land another blow to the arrogant leader's chest, Seth grabbed my arm. "Stop!"

My hands shook, my knees felt weak, yet still, my drive to hurt Khalen fueled a strength in me that would surely get me killed.

"You are no better than your Shadow rivals," I seethed at Khalen.

The blow of his energy sent me to the ground with such force that the air escaped my lungs.

"Khalen, please," Skye pleaded.

Darius ushered the clan back and instructed them to return to the fire. "Go on, now. Leave 'em be."

Tears stung my eyes as I endured the sting throughout my body. Khalen's eyes glowed like the sun. Through the din, I heard Skye and Seth plead with the leader.

My energy drained now, I collapsed in a heap, drawing in what air I could through my lungs. The sting resigned as the hum faded.

Seth pulled me into his arms and carried me back to

my room.

"Are you mad?" he asked, laying me down on the bed.

"He hurt you," I mumbled.

"Yes, to prepare me."

My eyes blinked back the tears blurring my vision. He wiped them with his warm, strong hands, making me want to press my face against them, craving the comfort they offered.

"He has been training me, Rae, not punishing me. I grow stronger because of him."

"He hurt you."

"No, he didn't. He's helping me."

I brushed my thumb over his swollen mouth. "I'm sorry."

"Don't be. For the first time in my life, my uncle sees me as a man. Because of you."

"Does it hurt much?"

"No. Skye removed most of the pain. I didn't want her to heal me."

"Why?"

"I need this, Rae. I want this. I want to learn what it's like to be strong."

"You already are strong."

"Not enough to keep you safe—to make you mine."

I buried my face against his chest, breathing in the raw scent of him. For years I had dreamed of belonging to this man. Now, the reality of it terrified me.

How many people must suffer to keep me safe? The numbers were too great already. My mother had sacrificed her life for mine, and Jenico was taking considerable risks by keeping me shielded. I couldn't stand placing another at risk, especially Seth.

"I don't care much for your thoughts," he said,

frowning. "Come, you need to apologize to Khalen before the clan."

I nodded, knowing he was right. If Seth were truly bonded with me, which I still had a hard time believing, nothing I could do would stop him from confronting my father. I had to have faith and concentrate on the desired outcome. This fear-based thinking wouldn't do anyone any good.

With Seth's help and support, I managed to urge my legs beneath me and support my weight. "He packs a good blow," I said, my voice cracking a bit.

"You're lucky you're able to stand at all. You must never challenge him like that. And under no circumstances at all, should you ever compare him to a Shadow. It's a bit of a sore spot for him."

"Apparently."

As he led me back to the fire, his hand held mine firmly in his grip. It was a possessive hold and one that provided great comfort.

I stopped before reaching the circle's perimeter and looked into Seth's golden eyes. "You respect him?"

"More than you know," he said, his words thick with sincerity.

I nodded, allowing him to guide me into what felt like a den of hungry wolves. The conversations came to a fading halt as I stood now before the formidable leader.

"I owe you an apology," I stammered, disgusted with the fear lacing my tone.

The man said nothing, his eyes glowing like the flames warming my back.

Swallowing hard, I continued. "I should not have compared you to the Shadows; nor should I have accused you of hurting Seth. Please forgive me." I offered a slight bow of my head.

"You understand that what I do is for Seth's own good?" he calmly asked.

"I do, and I'm grateful to you."

Khalen stood, his six-foot-plus frame towering above me. I felt his strong hands upon my shoulders and shuddered at the immense power he bestowed. "Your situation has placed our clan at great risk. Seth believes you are worth that risk."

He paused. "So do I."

I looked up, straining my neck to do so. "Thank you," I choked out.

He nodded, and then sat back down.

Skye gave me a beaming smile.

Seth urged me to sit, handing me a glass of red wine. "See, he's not that bad."

My hand shook as I took a healthy sip of the tart velvety drink.

Nate seemed to be blending in well with the other men, laughing, telling jokes, and sitting with a young child on his lap. He looked at peace here, healthy and vibrant.

"Ye played well t'day, lad," said Darius, slapping him hard on the back. "I half-expected ye t'toss the lot of us away to make your goal."

"The thought crossed my mind a few times."

Khalen came over and whisked the young child up from Nate's lap, swinging the boy around and making him giggle. "Time for bed, Zhentu."

"Can Nate tuck me in, Father?"

Khalen glanced over at Nate who winked back with hopeful eyes. He did not fear this leader as I did. No, there was respect in his eyes, and something else beyond my understanding.

"I'd be honored," he said, standing and offering a gallant bow, making the boy laugh.

Khalen handed him Zhentu after giving the lad a kiss on his cheek. "He can tell you one story, and then lights out."

"Yes, Father."

"Best make it a long one, yeah?" muttered Nate as he carried the boy back to the castle.

"He's a good man," said Darius, "and a fine hunter. Good instincts, that one. We're goin' out again tomorrow. I urge you t'join us."

Khalen glanced over at Seth. "We could do with a bit of a break in training. What do you say, Seth? Are you up for it?"

Seth smiled. "Sounds perfect."

Skye came over with Lenore and Sunjia in tow. Lenore carried a bottle with four cordial glasses.

"You look like you could use some company," said Skye, sitting beside me.

Lenore began doling out the glasses, and then proceeded to fill them with a thick amber drink. "Liquid gold," she said, giving me a wink.

We all clinked our glasses together.

"T'fine wine, good friends, and handsome men," Lenore announced.

"Here, here," the women chimed before downing the sweet spicy drink.

Chocolate with a strong bite of clove and cinnamon in a base of Brandy. I nearly choked as it burned down my throat like molten lava.

"M'own concoction," said Lenore, eagerly pouring me another ration. "D'ye like it?"

I nodded. "It's quite...strong."

"It'll burn the cobwebs from y'r mind, that's f'r sure."

The distant hum of conversation filled the space as I stared into the flames dancing around a twisted root.

"You seem deep in thought," Skye said, placing her hand on my back.

I smiled and sipped at the drink in my hand. "Just wondering how much time I have before hell breaks loose."

"We're no strangers to it, lass," said Lenore. "We've a strong clan 'ere, no worries for that."

I smiled. She was such a strong woman and one who seemed to thrive on challenge, even when it meant certain destruction.

"I hear a man paid a half-million dollars for you," said Sunjia, a quiet woman who was introduced as Seth's mother. Her exotic looks did not resemble her son one bit. I assumed he must have taken after his father.

"Yes," I confirmed. "Though I doubt he'll think I'm worth it."

Lenore brushed the tops of her fingernails against her smock. "Men rarely know our true worth."

Sunjia leaned forward. "He must be very powerful to afford such a dowry."

"He is," I admitted. "His name is Bennet Graves."

The women gasped as if recognizing his name.

"The, Bennet Graves? Leader of the East Coast clans?" asked Skye.

"Yes," I sighed.

"That man is gorgeous," said Sunjia. "What's not to like about him?"

"Everything," I said. "The only reason he wants me is to strengthen his lineage. He believes, like most males, that my children will be gifted with Spirifae blood."

"I've heard of Spirifaes," said Sunjia, "but I never knew they actually existed."

Lenore refilled everyone's glasses. "I hear the original females were protected by a fealty that would curse any man who lay harm to them."

I sighed. "If only that were true."

Chapter 25

~ R a e ~

THE MEN LEFT EARLY THIS morning. I helped prepare breakfast and clean up after the meal before setting off with Skye to feed the animals. She told me about her horse back home, and about the ranch she used to work at with her father. For the first forty-five years of her life, she had believed she was human. That fascinated me.

"Were you born blind?" I asked, pouring a bucket of grain into a feed trough.

She shook her head. "No, I was diagnosed with a rare form of Retinitis Pigmentosa, but my grandfather, Shanuk didn't agree with the doctors."

"Why's that?"

She stacked the empty buckets and we carried them back to the barn, our breath leaving white trails in the cold morning air.

"He believes it was all part of the prophecy."

"Would you like me to try and heal them?"

She smiled. "I wouldn't object." She was silent for a moment. "I tried healing them myself." Again, she looked distracted. "We need to return to the castle, now."

"Why? Is something wrong?"

I started to stack the buckets against the wall.

"Leave them." She took my hand and we hurried back to the castle.

Needing to take my mind off the worry, I started to talk. "Seth mentioned that you removed his pain."

She turned her head toward me. "It's part of the healing, I suppose."

"I cannot remove pain." I frowned. "At least, not that I know of. It certainly would have been useful during Father's punishments."

She chuckled. "Unfortunately, it doesn't work against that."

"Leaders have all the advantages, yes?"

She smiled. "They wouldn't be leaders if they didn't."

"True," I said, glancing down at her bare feet. "Do you ever wear shoes?"

"Only when we leave camp or when Khalen asks me to."

"Yeah," I chortled, "he's kind of hard to say no to."

She nodded. "Sometimes," she agreed. "Believe it or not, he can be reasoned with."

When we returned to the castle, it seemed eerily quiet. I removed my soaking wet shoes in the mud room while Skye dried hers with a towel.

"Where is everyone?" I asked.

"The children are probably studying and the others are off doing chores, I imagine."

"I don't remember it ever being this quiet here."

Lenore peeked around the corner, locking the door to the mud room.

"Lenore?" Skye asked. "Is everything all right?"

"Come inside," she said, gesturing us to follow her. She poured us both a cup of steaming hot coffee. "Somethin's amiss. I c'n feel it."

"Feel what?" I asked.

"There's a Shadow about."

Skye laughed. "Only one?"

"Aye, only one."

My back stiffened. "Oh God, he's found me."

"Your father?" asked Skye.

I nodded. My hands shook as I tried to sip my coffee. She laid her hand on my arm. "Surely he won't try to take you by himself?"

"He's a binder, Skye. He can strip you of your gifts and leave you helpless for hours at a time. I've seen him do it."

Her color paled a bit. "Khalen told me to come back. He knows."

"Yes," Lenore confirmed. "I contacted Darius the moment I felt the threat. He instructed me to get everyone inside. The men are on their way back now."

"I dunno' like this one," she added, looking around at the walls. "He's...different from the others."

"He's strong," I said, "but indirectly so. He can turn your own gifts against you if he chooses."

Lenore's face looked blank as if all her senses had been stripped. "He's gone. Just like that?"

"He's not gone," I warned. "He's here."

An airy explosion erupted around me as Khalen's binding was destroyed. Skye and Lenore flew back from their seats, landing hard against the stone wall. Blood trickled from Skye's head. Knowing I only had seconds before my father entered the room, I offered a quick healing to stem the blood flow.

With that blast, he would have destroyed Jenico's

shield as well, so risking my father's witness to my healing was not much of a deterrent.

The blood stopped flowing from Skye's head. Before I could search for other injuries, my father's strong hand reached down and lifted me clear off the ground by my collar, the sharp seam digging into my throat.

It didn't take long for me to pass out from lack of air—something he was counting on, I was sure.

~ S e t h ~

K HALEN SLAMMED BACK AGAINST A TREE. He was unconscious.

"Good God," said Darius. "What t'hell was that?"

"Rae," I whispered, taking off through the forest, my mind and body fueled by adrenaline and fear.

Nate followed close on my heels.

We entered the camp to find it empty but unharmed. I ran toward the castle. The door to the mud room was torn off its hinges. My heart slammed against my chest. Each breath was an effort.

"Rae!" I called. "Skye, Lenore!" I ran through the halls like a madman, calling their names. There was no reply.

"Seth," Nate called from the kitchen.

I ran toward him, then stopped as I saw Skye lying in a shallow pool of blood. Lenore was not moving either.

"Good God, what happened?" I muttered.

I tried contacting Khalen telepathically to tell him that Skye was injured. There was still no response.

Lenore started to come around. I knelt beside her, supporting her head. "It's all right, Lenore; we're here."

When she tried to move, her eyes dilated and she

screamed in pain. "Argh, m'arm is broke."

Maiyun came running in, panting and looking concerned. She had stayed with Khalen after the blast. The dog sniffed Skye and began licking the sticky blood from her head.

Darius stumbled in carrying a very limp Khalen over his shoulder. "The bloke weighs a ton," he said, lowering Khalen's body onto a chair. He slumped against the table.

Darius moved over his mate, tenderly brushing aside the hair that covered her face. "It's all right, love. I'm 'ere now."

He lifted her onto a chair.

"Gather everyone in the castle," I said. "One of them may have seen something."

Lenore coughed. A spittle of blood spoiled her blouse. "He took Rae," she struggled to say.

"Easy, love," Darius cooed. "We'll get 'er back."

He stood and left to find the others as I had suggested.

I examined Skye but found no source for the blood. Maiyun continued to lick a spot on her head. It felt soft to my touch.

"Nate, see if you can wake up Khalen. I need his help."

Nate walked over to the sink and filled a pan full of cold water. He then tossed it onto Khalen.

What happened next was too fast to recall. One moment Nate was standing beside our unconscious leader; the next, he was slammed against the counter, rubbing his head.

"Easy, Khalen," I said, holding up my hand.

When his eyes fixed on Skye, he rushed over to her side. "What happened?" he asked me.

"My guess is that your bond was destroyed and Skye and Lenore were too close to the blast."

Fealty

After careful examination of Skye's head, he concluded, "Someone tried to heal her but didn't have time to finish."

"Rae, no doubt," I said. "Her father has come for her."

Khalen lifted Skye into his arms. "Follow me to the surgery. I need to release the pressure in her head."

Nate helped Lenore, who was bent on helping, even though she looked as if she needed surgery herself. We followed Khalen to the lower levels of the castle. Telepathically, I told Darius where to find us.

"Fetch my bag," Khalen ordered, pointing to the large black case on the counter.

From it, he retrieved a sharp scalpel.

Lenore sidled up to him, holding a package of bandages, sponges, and a few instruments.

I watched in amazement as he expertly opened Skye's head and drained the fluid.

"You've done this before," I exclaimed.

He dabbed the sweat from his brow. "A few times."

I offered to tend the wound for him, but being the over-protective mate that he was, he wanted to do it himself.

I busied myself with taking care of Lenore. Her arm had been broken in two places from what I could feel. She would need to be tended to if it were going to heal properly. I secured her arm in an air cast and sling until Skye was able to heal her properly.

Darius showed up a few moments later. "No one saw anything," he reported.

"Skye," Khalen said, rubbing his mate's bloodied hair. "Come on, love. Wake up now."

Twenty minutes later, she finally came around, disoriented and in pain. "My head," she groaned.

"You're injured," Khalen explained.

Blue mist rose from her hands as she placed them upon her head. In seconds, her wound closed and the discoloration around her forehead paled.

Khalen helped her sit. "How are you feeling?"

"Better," she sighed. When she glanced over at Lenore, she tried to stand.

"Wait a moment," Khalen said. "Give yourself time to recover."

"I'm fine," she argued, struggling to gather her feet beneath her. "Help me up."

Khalen pulled her to her feet as if she weighed no more than a child. In moments, Lenore's arm was healed.

"What do you remember?" I asked them.

Skye sat beside her mate, burying her head in her hands. "We were sitting with Rae at the table, drinking coffee. Next thing I knew, I was out cold."

"I felt the Shadow clear as day," said Lenore. "Then, he just disappeared. I felt nothin'." Her brows pulled together. "I remember Rae saying something like, 'He's here,' and then, wham, m'mind went blank."

Nate must have left during all the commotion because he returned with Gabrihen. "The lad can help."

Khalen looked to me. "Seth, can you sense her?"

I closed my eyes and thought of Rae. Her presence touched me like a faded light. "They're heading for Portree."

Khalen gripped his son's shoulders. Gabrihen was only twelve years old, but his body was already starting to fill out. "Gabrihen, can you stall them?"

He nodded his head and beamed a smile. "I can disable their car."

"Perfect," I said.

"Do it quickly," said Khalen, "but do not get in their

way, understand? Report back to me when you are done."

"Yes, sir."

I sent the boy an image of where Rae was and the Mercedes her father was driving.

In a blink, he was gone. Apparently, his training with old wizzard Tetris was paying off.

~ R a e ~

THE HUM IN THE CAR was deafening. I had never seen my father so intense. His bone-piercing energy kept me still in my seat, the pain of it radiating throughout my body. I was used to this pain he so often inflicted, but it still made my stomach queasy.

"How have you kept your gift hidden from me?" he asked.

"I recently discovered it," I lied. The pain increased, making me double over.

The car sputtered and lost power. My father pulled over to the side of the road, swearing under his breath.

"What's this bloody about, now?"

"Father, please," I groaned.

He ignored my plea as he exited the car and raised the bonnet for a look.

His harsh punishment continued as he pulled out his phone and called for roadside assistance.

"Father!" I cried.

The pain subsided. He sat back down in the driver's seat and pocketed his phone.

"I don't like being lied to, Raeiza. Now, answer my question."

I said nothing, though it wouldn't take long for him

to comb my thoughts; and that alone frightened me more than any punishment he might choose to dole out.

"Jenico," he growled.

"No!" I cried. "It wasn't him. I—" I collapsed as another wave of pain racked my body. Tears streamed down my face, my throat too tight to make any sound.

"I warned you once, Raeiza. Do not lie to me again."

My eyes lost focus as my mind drew close to fading with blissful darkness. He wouldn't allow that, though. The reprieve would be far too merciful for him. The pain subsided just enough to keep me conscious.

"If I had known about your gift of healing, I could have asked for ten times what Bennet is willing to pay for you now."

He grabbed my left wrist and turned it over. "Thank God that whelp didn't claim you," he seethed. Tapping his fingers against the steering wheel, he pursed his lips. "What to do with Jenico now for shielding you from me for God knows how long."

Nothing I could say would sway him from hurting my brother. Even if I claimed it was my choosing, Nico would be punished for not coming to our father about it.

"Enough!" Father roared, ceasing his punishment. I took a deep breath, trying to calm my rattled thoughts and battered body. I felt as if I had been tossed from a truck and dragged for several miles. Every muscle ached, every joint felt pinched.

A tow truck pulled around us and started to back up. I stayed in the car as Father left to talk to the driver.

In twenty minutes, we rolled into Portree. Our car was unloaded in front of a small repair shop. My father lifted me from the cab since I was still too weak and sore to move.

"Stay here," he instructed, leaving me propped against a stone wall.

I watched as he disappeared into the shop to talk with a man behind the counter.

"Are ye all right, miss?" the tow truck driver inquired.

"Yes," I stammered. "I'm fine, thank you."

"Ye look a bit sore."

"Too long in the car, I'm afraid."

"Aye. Me mum has the same problem." He eyed me from head to toe. "Yer a bit young for that, though."

"Can I help you, sir?" boomed my father's deep voice.

The tow truck driver visibly paled. "N' n' no sir. Just havin' a bit o'conversation with your daughter 'ere."

My father gripped my hand and nearly dragged me toward a tea shop across the street. "Damn small towns. It'll take at least an hour before they can even look at our car."

I was surprised he hadn't offered to purchase another car.

"I offered to purchase the owner's car, but the bloody bloke refused my offer. I offered well over the value of the thing, I assure you."

I bit back my laugh, not really looking forward to another bout of pain. When I glanced out the window, I saw young Gabrihen run out of the repair shop. In another instant, he was gone.

Chapter 26

-Seth-

KHALEN, **DARIUS**, **GABRIHEN**, **AIDAN**, **NATE**, and I took the Land Rover, while the other men in the clan followed in their own vehicles. Khalen wanted to make sure we showed numbers when confronting Drake.

"What's the plan?" I asked.

"To get your female without losing our heads."

Gabrihen popped into the cab, making me jump back. "They're in Ned's Tea Shop," he said. "I spoke with everyone in town. They promised to do their best to delay them."

"Good job, son," said Khalen.

Gabrihen beamed a smile, obviously pleased to have been asked to come along. The other boys his age were ordered to stay behind.

Nate offered the boy a high five. The two of them had gotten close during the past few days. The children seem to take to the Kiwi quite well. I wondered whether it was enough to persuade him to join our clan.

Many of the folks in this town were our clansmen.

Gaining their cooperation was easy. Getting Drake to back down would be something entirely different. It was careless of him to venture into our territory, especially alone. He was not a man to take such chances, angry or not.

"Do you sense he has company?" asked Khalen.

I shook my head. "It just doesn't make sense for him to come here alone."

"Perhaps he thought he would have enough time to leave before we discovered what happened?"

I shrugged. "Perhaps."

Khalen pulled into a dirt parking lot. "Keep your head about you, Seth." He silently told the others to stay back.

I nodded and followed him out of the car.

Nate cocked his head left and then right, cracking his neck. "I sure hope this turns into a brawl."

Khalen cast him a hard look. "No brawling," he warned.

Nate frowned. "He's a bit of a damper, yeah?"

"Stay here," Khalen told him.

We walked across the street toward the shop. It didn't take long for Drake to sense our presence. He stood, dabbed his mouth with a napkin, and then headed out of the shop to meet us.

Drake's eyes settled on me. I felt the hum of his energy and immediately shielded myself against it the way Khalen had taught me.

"You dare take my daughter without my consent," Drake seethed.

"I did."

"What is this?" he asked, looking between me and Khalen.

Rae walked out of the shop, looking as if she had

suffered a beating. A low growl rumbled deep in my chest.

Stay calm, Khalen silently warned me.

"Father, please. Leave Seth be and I will return with you willingly."

He turned sharply to address her. "You will return, willingly or not. I told you to stay inside."

I started to move between them. Khalen held me back.

"Get inside," he told her.

She winced as if he had backed that command up with a reprimand. Still, she did not move.

"Raeiza!" he yelled.

"Enough," said Khalen, dispersing Drake's energy. "The female has suffered enough."

Drake's face turned red. His chest expanded as he drew in a deep breath. He was not a man used to being disobeyed or challenged. "Khalen Dunning, young leader of the Gradhun clan," he drawled.

"Drake Tomei, son of Zorid."

"You're a bit out of your territory, are you not?"

"This is my father's region."

Drake's eyes narrowed. "I was told your father was dead along with your twin brother."

Khalen smiled. "Hardly. My father is alive and well, I assure you."

"And you believe you can stand me down?"

"I believe I can make you see the wisdom of doing so, yes."

Drake drew in another deep breath. He didn't seem the least bit alarmed, and that worried me.

"I could have destroyed your little castle, young Khalen, and everyone inside with a wave of my hand. Out of respect, I left them whole, with the exception of those two females." He waved his hand as if dismissing the incident as a mere inconvenience.

Khalen stiffened. The energy between the two men increased, causing my insides to rumble.

"You are stronger than you look," said Drake. Then, his dark eyes shifted to me. "However, this little qualm is between young Seth and I."

"The female is under my protection," said Khalen.

Drake's eyes grew darker. "She is not your concern."

"You're right," I said. "She's mine."

Drake laughed. "You're an ant crossing the path of a lion. Be careful, young Seth, lest I crush you under my stride."

"Your self-imposed importance is no—" A jolt of pain ripped through me.

Khalen dispersed the energy, no doubt taking the brunt of it.

Do not challenge him here, he silently warned me.

"This is not the place for this," he reminded Drake.

Drake looked over at the repair shop, observing that his car was still unattended.

There are others, Nate warned me in thought. Khalen must have heard him too because he became suddenly alert.

"Do you really want a battle here, in front of all these humans?" asked Khalen.

Drake knew the consequences of such an act. If humans were exposed to the high vibration of a Spirian battle, it would cause irreversible damage. The High Council would become involved and the Spirians responsible for such a horror would be destroyed—immediately. His energy calmed a bit.

A car pulled over to the side of the road, followed by

five others. Twelve huge men stepped out of the vehicles, all Shadows.

Our clan instinctively gathered across the street. Onlookers slowed in their paths, others filed out of the stores to observe the commotion. Already, we were drawing far too much attention to ourselves.

"Raeiza, get in the car," Drake ordered.

She looked between me and her father. Slowly, she made her way toward a blue Mercedes.

Telekinetically, I picked the car up and tossed it across the adjoining field. I then pulled Rae against me. "She's coming with me," I growled.

Drake's men started to advance. He stilled them with a raised hand, looking around at the stunned faces of the onlookers and the ready stance of our clansmen. It was clear that he and his men were outnumbered. The attention we called was unwanted.

"This is not over," he said calmly. Gathering his men, they piled into the remaining cars and drove out of town.

Rae collapsed against me, shaking. "Seth. What have you done?"

Khalen tossed me the keys. "Take her back. Aidan and I will stay to clean things up."

"How will you get back?"

He smiled, then gestured toward Drake's car. "I have a feeling he won't be back for it."

Rae and I piled into the Rover along with the others who had come with us. I turned the key and followed the other cars back to the castle.

"Quite an impressive display of power back there, Seth," said Darius. "You're fortunate Khalen is able t'repair the wake of your damage."

He was right, of course. If my outburst of energy wasn't

so focused, it could have been my undoing. The Spirian
law was clear and completely nonnegotiable. No human
could be harmed by any Spirian without consequence of
death. My hands trembled against the steering wheel.

"Scary," added Nate.

Rae simply looked out the window, lost in thought. I
reached over to hold her hand. It was cold and shaking.

"Hey, you okay?"

She nodded, but continued to stare out the window.

"Looks like we've got a bit of a skirmish comin', eh?"
said Darius.

Nate pressed his hands together and rubbed them
with anticipation. "I'm lookin' forward to it."

Gabrihen turned to stare out the back window. I knew
that he would rather be with his father right now.

"You did well today, Gabrihen," I said.

He turned back around in his seat, his dark brows knit
with concern. "What did Father mean when he said he
and Uncle Aidan were going to stay and clean things up?"

Darius patted his hand. "It means their goin' t'right
the damage, lad, and clear the observers memories of it."

"How?"

Darius laughed. "It is a gift that only a few of us
possess, lad. Perhaps when you're old enough, yer da will
pass it on to ye."

A slight smile brightened the boy's face. He reminded
me of myself at his age. I had tried so hard to please my
father and gain his good graces. It was a feeble dream, for
nothing impressed my father, and he didn't have room for
grace of any kind.

At times, I thought there was hope for him. When he
returned from his training with Case, Khalen's adoptive
father, something had changed in him. He even smiled

with genuine joy. The Shadow clan changed that, however, and quenched that light like an unwanted ember in a pit of stone.

Khalen was his twin, yet he was the opposite of Traeger. I had never shed a tear when Khalen killed him. Part of me was relieved. I was destined to take over my father's clan, but I wanted nothing to do with it—nothing to do with the Shadows who squelched his light.

I glanced over at Rae, wondering whether she would think differently of me if she knew I was born to be a Shadow leader—the very thing she learned to despise.

The reflection in the window glistened with the tears streaming down her face. I squeezed her hand, limp and cold in mine.

"I need to warn my brother," she said.

I handed her my phone.

She dialed the number with shaky fingers, closing her eyes as the phone started ringing.

"Nico," she said. "Are you all right?"

"I'm fine, Rae," I heard him say.

"He knows, Nico. About your shielding."

"Yeah, I felt it burst. Don't worry, Rae; I'm safe. He won't find me."

"Please don't confront him, Nico."

"Are you all right?"

She sniffed. "Yeah."

"Is Seth with you?"

She glanced over at me. "He is."

"Good. Stay with him. He'll keep you safe."

"Nico—"

"Don't say it, Rae. I'm going to be fine. Trust me on this, yes?"

"Yes."

"I love you. Stay with Seth. I'll see you soon."

More tears fell as the call disconnected.

"This is not your fault," I assured her.

She pulled her hand away. "It's all my fault, Seth. I never should have come with you. I should have just—"

I jammed on the brakes and pulled the car over. "Look at me, Rae."

When she refused, I opened my car door and reached for her hand. Again, she pulled it away. In my current state, it took nothing for me to lift her out of the car.

"Let me go, Seth." The venom in her tone stung, but I didn't care.

I set her down but didn't relinquish my hold. I forced her to look at me. "This is your father's doing, not yours. Do you hear me?"

"He will destroy you, Seth, and your entire clan will suffer his wrath."

"Have you so little faith in our abilities?"

Her jaw tightened. "My father does not fight unless he knows he can win. He will bring forces you cannot possibly imagine in your worst nightmare, Seth. He won't stop until he brings you down."

"You speak from fear."

"Yeah," she countered. "I have felt his anger, his need for justice."

"I speak from faith, not fear, when I say we will win this war and you will be my mate."

I pulled her in against me, ignoring her fight to break free. She pounded my back with her tight fists as trembling sobs shook her body against mine.

"Damn you for doing this, Seth. Damn you for making me love you and forcing me to bear your death."

I said nothing, continuing to hold her until the hitting

and sobbing subsided.

"I love you, Raeiza Tomei, and you will be my mate."

Another fist slammed against my back.

I guided her back into the car and then continued our journey.

She'll come around, mate, Nate said in silence.

I didn't respond.

When we arrived home, we were greeted by the clan. Skye was completely recovered now, as was Lenore.

"I hear you had quite an adventure," said Skye. When she saw Rae, her smile faded to concern. "Rae, come with me." She helped Rae out of the car.

Lenore placed her hand on my arm. "She's in a bit of a state, eh?"

I shook my head and ran my fingers through my hair. "She believes this is all her fault and is convinced that her father will destroy us all."

"Darius has alerted Case and Arcadie. When the Shadows do attack, we'll be ready."

Chapter 27

-Rae-

SKYE SAT ME DOWN ON a log overlooking a pond. Then, we just sat there. She said nothing. I took advantage of the silence and wallowed in my thoughts. What was I going to do now? My father would retaliate and this clan would suffer the consequences of my disobedience. I had caused enough people enough harm. What would happen to Nico?

I leaned forward and pressed my face between my hands, as if trying to will the horrid thoughts from my mind. I felt as if I were trapped in a cage while the people I loved were being mangled and tortured right in front of me.

"When you are finished tearing yourself apart, talk to me."

I looked over at the gentle woman sitting beside me. "I have much to berate myself about, Skye."

"And your self-lashing is doing your loved ones good?"

"Right now, I'm doing more harm than good."

Skye reached down and scratched Maiyun behind her

soft ears. "Instead of focusing on what you have lost and what you cannot do, try thinking about solutions and what you can do."

"My hands are tied. If I leave, Seth will find me. If I stay, my father will kill everyone I love."

"Leaving is not the answer. So again, why are you looking at all the problems and not seeing what is right in front of you?"

I sighed, finding this discussion frustrating and unhelpful. "Tell me, then. What are my options?"

"You have a man who loves you, a man you have wanted for many years. Now that you have him, you hold him at a distance because you feel you don't deserve him. You have a clan willing to die for you, yet all you want to do is leave them. Your brother risked his life to save you from a fate you are too willing to accept." She huffed. "Honestly, Rae, you're like a captured rabbit, staring at an open door but too afraid to walk toward freedom."

I laugh at the absurdity of her accusations. "Freedom? Having freedom means nothing to me if everyone dies because of it."

She shook her head. "You are so certain that we will lose in this game."

"I know my father and the company he keeps."

Her brow raised. "Apparently you haven't considered the company we keep. We are not new to Spirian wars, Rae. Shanuk's clan has survived far longer than most and for good reason. Have faith in us, and in Seth."

"My father is a leader as is Bennet Graves. What chance does Seth stand against them?"

"Seth is the son of a leader, Rae. He has strength he hasn't even tapped yet. When push comes to shove, I believe he will discover just how powerful he can be."

When her hand closed over mine, I felt a surge of warmth and strength that could only come from the Holy Father. I squeezed her hand. "Thank you."

"You're welcome. Now, should we return and see how we can help to prepare for this adventure?"

"Adventure?"

"Believe it or not, this clan loves a good battle, like wolves before a hunt."

We stood and headed back to the castle. "Funny, I always thought the Protected ones reveled in peace, love, and unity."

She smiled. "Chardonnays are lovely in the summer, but on a cold winter night, I want something with attitude, like a spicy Zinfandel or a bold Barolo. Occasionally I want brandy or a zesty spiced rum."

I held up my hand, "Okay, I get it. A little spice in life adds dimension and interest."

"Partly," she said, "but these challenges in life enable us to grow stronger and wiser. Our clan doesn't turn away from such challenges. Instead, they face them with vigor and faith that victory brings about positive change and fortitude."

"People die in battles, Skye."

"Death comes to all of us. To die fighting for something you believe in is a death of honor."

"You sound like a warrior."

She smiled. "Leaders and their mates are the most powerful warriors of all."

We crossed the courtyard and entered the castle where the door had been blown from its hinges.

"Do you ever fear for Khalen's life?" I asked.

"No," she said bluntly. "I pray for his survival."

There was a low hum of conversation coming from

inside the castle. Skye led me to a room filled with pool tables, a full-size bar, dartboards, and plenty of comfy sofas and chairs. The conversations grew silent as we walked in.

I felt the weight of several eyes as Seth stood to greet me.

"Can I get you something to drink?" he asked. His thumbs rubbed the backs of my hands. The simply gesture felt comforting and oddly reassuring. Somewhere in the back of my mind, I expected him to be angry with me.

"Yes, a glass of red wine sounds perfect." I glanced over at Skye. "Preferably one with a bit of attitude."

She smiled.

Seth handed me my glass and sat beside me in the group's midst.

"Case and Arcadie will be 'ere tomorrow," said Aidan. His pleasant Irish accent flowed like silk on a gentle breeze. "Ian and Drew will join the skirmish, along with Tetris and his lot."

Gabrihen scooted in closer to his father. "I can help."

"Me too," said his younger brother Zhentu.

Skye's eyes widened. "Absolutely not!"

The boys looked as dejected as two pups in a lonely den.

Khalen reached over and pulled the boys close. "There might be something you can do."

That earned him a warning look from Skye. "Khalen, I don't—"

He raised his hand. "Easy, my love. They will not be in danger." He looked down at his two boys. "But, they can be of some help. Gabrihen's skills at manifesting are strong and controlled. Zhentu's ability to shift into a wolf can be a distraction. Maiyun will watch out for him."

Maiyun's ears pricked up at the sound of her name. I had seen her and Zhentu run in the fields and surrounding woods like litter mates who longed to be together.

"It's too dangerous," Skye countered.

"Mom, we want to help," said Gabrihen. Though only twelve years of age, he acted far more mature.

She sighed, knowing she had lost this battle. "Very well, but you will listen to your father and do what he says."

The joy that shone on both of their young faces could light up the darkest room. Skye had been right. This clan relished a good battle. I prayed none of them would die.

Khalen stood and started to pace—something I noticed he did when thinking something through. "Lenore, you're in charge of the women. Keep me informed of the Shadows' intentions. Skye, you're in charge of the children. Make sure they know what to do and when to do it. Skye and Rae, I need you to be on alert should any of us need healing." His eyes rested on Nate. "You're a listener. I need you to relay the Shadows' thoughts."

"You will have to open your minds to me," he said.

Khalen hesitated, but then nodded. "I'll take care of that. We'll discuss further plans when the rest of the clan arrives."

Darius rubbed his palms together. "And I thought this would be an uneventful summer."

Khalen looked at Seth and me. "You two, come with me."

I set my glass down before following him and Seth to a small room littered with shelves upon shelves of books. The room was warm and soft with dark wood furniture, old tapestries, soft rugs, and plush seats. Khalen sat in a high-backed chair while Seth and I sat on the sofa.

Khalen willed the door shut. "I believe you two would make a solid union."

Seth squeezed my hand as if confirming that thought.

"I have spoken with Darius and he has agreed that you, Seth, would be a strong leader for this clan."

I felt him stiffen against me. "I am no leader, Khalen."

Khalen smiled. "We both know that isn't true, Seth. You were destined to lead your father's clan. You chose to step down from that position. I'm asking you to step up again and lead this clan."

"Darius has done a fine job so far," Seth retorted.

"He is not a leader; nor does he desire to be one."

Seth's grip tightened in mine. "I am too young to lead a clan."

Khalen's eyes glowed. "Are you questioning my judgment?"

"No sir," Seth quickly responded.

"Are you denying my request, then?"

Silence.

"Seth?" Khalen prodded.

"No sir."

Now Khalen's golden stare focused on me. I felt chills run through my veins. "Do you accept Seth as your mate?"

My throat closed. "Um, I...I don't know."

More silence. The weight of their stares felt like a lead shield shrouding my body. "I can't answer that now," I finally said.

"Because?" Khalen asked.

Seth was smiling now, obviously enjoying my dilemma. "Do you want him? Love him?"

I stood and started to pace. Skye's words echoed in my mind. I finally had the man of my dreams right before me, asking me to be his mate, and I pushed him away.

Everything I ever wanted had been pried from my grasp so many times that I accepted it as the norm.

"Is there someone else you would consider?" asked Seth, a hint of sadness in his tone.

I shook my head. "No. I've always wanted you, Seth; you know that. It's just that—"

Seth stood and pulled me into his strong arms. "Be mine, Rae. Please."

God, how could I say no to this and live the rest of my life knowing I had given up the one thing that would make me happy? "Yes," I said, the words flowing from my mouth on their own volition. "I will be your mate."

Khalen smiled. For the first time since I had known him, he genuinely smiled. He was quite handsome when he did so. Seth pulled me closer, burying his face in my hair.

"Thank you," he whispered.

"Arrangements will be made, then," said Khalen. "Tomorrow, you will join."

My stomach sank. "Tomorrow?"

"Yes," he confirmed. "By joining with Seth, you will be connected with the clan. We will hear your thoughts more clearly and can communicate to you as well. This will become important during the battle."

"What if I'm captured?" I asked.

"As my mate," said Seth, "I will be able to find you, even if they move you out of our territory."

"And," Khalen added, "once you are mated, Seth will have leadership status. His powers will increase tenfold—something your father will not have anticipated."

"But, I'm a Shadow. They can reclaim me and put your clan in danger."

"Not anymore," Seth growled, gripping my hand

tighter.

Khalen's expression changed to something that resembled a child recalling a painful memory. "I made the mistake of waiting too long to take my mate for almost the same reasons. I almost lost her because of it." His golden eyes rested on Seth. "I don't want you to make the same mistake."

"Tomorrow is fine," I blurted.

Seth's lips grew firm. "Are you sure?"

I studied his eyes, nearly as golden as his uncle's, but filled with a depth that had no end. "I've never been more sure of anything," I chuckled. "For the first time in my life, I know what I want."

"Do you have your promise pendant?" Khalen asked him.

Seth nodded. "In my bag."

"Get it. I'll announce your decision tonight."

With that, Khalen turned to leave. I hadn't realized I had been holding my breath until my lungs ached for air.

"Are you ready for this?" Seth asked.

I laughed. "I should be asking you the same question. Wow, mate, leader. That's a huge leap for one so young."

He flinched with that. "I am young, Rae, but I will take care of you."

"I know you will."

"Come," he said, offering his hand. "We should probably join the others."

Chapter 28

~ S e t h ~

AN HOUR LATER, I HANDED Khalen my pendant. Rae was sitting in the corner of the room, chatting with Skye and Lenore. She looked happy and her sea-green eyes held a sparkle I hadn't seen before. Soon, Khalen would announce our proclamation to join; something that was done prior to setting the ceremony date.

This would all be new to Rae. The Shadows rarely did anything with ceremony. A male would simply unite with a female and the deed was done—no proclamation, no ceremony, no pendant. All the female was left with was the mark of her male on underside of her left wrist.

Khalen stood and demanded the clan's attention. "I have an announcement to make."

The room faded to a low hum and then silence before Khalen spoke again. He held up the pendant Aidan had given me before I left for Edinburgh. The crystal was a sister to the one he had given my mother. It shone with a pale yellow hue that displayed tiny rainbows when the sun hit it just right. Every male, who came of age, received one from their father. The crystals were akin to an engagement ring used by the humans.

Aidan's status by birth was relatively low. Khalen had granted him high status when Aidan became Skye's templar. Along with that came the crystal pendants that reflected high status. The pendant from my birth clan was higher yet, but I wanted nothing to do with that clan—ever again. My mark on Rae's arm would show my lineage. In time, Khalen would grant me a better pendant for Rae.

"Seth, Rae, come up here please."

I waited as she stood and walked toward me. I reached for her hand. Her smile was brilliant, but there was trepidation behind her eyes.

"Last chance," I whispered.

"I'm not letting you go that easily," she said.

I smiled as we moved to stand before Khalen.

Khalen studied us both for a moment. "Seth, you have bonded with this female and have asked her to be your mate."

"I have."

Now, he looked at Rae. I felt her tremble beneath our leader's piercing eyes and squeezed her hand for reassurance.

"Raeiza Tomei, daughter of Drake and Jenna, do you accept this man as your mate?"

"I do." Her voice rang clear and true as if her heart held no doubt that this was what she wanted.

Khalen handed me my pendant. "Offer your pendant to this female to pledge your claim."

I slipped the pendant over her head and rested it just above her heart. The crystal seemed to glow.

"The ceremony will be tomorrow," Khalen announced.

The crowd cheered and drinks were poured all around.

Nate was the first to approach us. "This is sudden." His voice had an edge to it.

I saw Rae struggle to swallow. Nate noticed it as well. "You sound disapproving," I said.

"It just seems rather sudden; that's all."

"Nate," Rae said, hesitating to touch him.

Nate's eyes narrowed. "I guess status holds merit for you after all."

"That has nothing to do with this, Nate."

I knew that Nate had feelings for Rae, but I never would have guessed they ran deeper than a possible one-night stand. "What's this about, Nate?"

His eyes rested on the pendant at Rae's chest. "Nothin'. It doesn't matter." He pushed through between us and stormed out of the room.

"Go after him," said Rae. "He needs you now."

"I think he'd rather have you," I said, following after him regardless.

I pushed through the onslaught of congratulations and made my way out to the courtyard. Using my senses, I detected Nate in the woods near the pond. When he heard me approach, he stiffened and then continued tossing rocks into the pond.

"Did you have designs on her?" I asked.

"Of course not, ye dolt. I knew you had bonded with her." He tossed another stone, avoiding my eyes.

Something about his words didn't ring true. "Aren't you the one who swore you would never settle on one female?"

"And you the same," he countered.

"She's different."

"Yeah, she is." Another stone bounced off the water and landed on the other side with a rattling clunk.

"I want you to be her templar."

He stopped as if frozen. "A Shadow," he laughed. "Seriously, mate, do ya think that's a good idea?"

"To me, you are a good friend, not a Shadow. I trust you, my clan trusts you, and Rae trusts you. I know if anything happens to me, you will take good care of her."

"I would," he agreed, tossing another stone.

"So you accept?"

He finally stopped to face me. "I accept."

"Are we still friends?"

He laughed. "Bugger all, yeah, we're friends. I have every thought of challenging you for her, though."

"I pray you don't, my friend. I'm not sure I could best you."

Again he laughed. "I've seen you fight. I know you could best me, which keeps me from openin' m'big mouth and sayin' somethin' I'd surely regret."

"Come back with me then. We'll tell Rae together."

~ R a e ~

TWO GLASSES OF WINE LATER, Seth and Nate returned. My nerves were shot as the women drilled me on the details of the upcoming ceremony. I didn't have much to offer seeing I hadn't ever attended or even witnessed a mating ceremony. Our clan didn't do such things.

Somehow, my life had been set to supernatural speed and my mind was having a hard time keeping up. The look on the men's faces enticed me to run for my room and lock the door. I simply couldn't handle anything more this evening. I swallowed the last of my wine and started to stand.

"Rae," Seth called out. For a brief moment, I considered continuing along as if I hadn't heard him. Knowing Seth, he would follow me. It was best to get this over with. With a heavy sigh, I turned to face them. "Did you have a good talk?"

Seth frowned. "What's wrong?"

"Just tired; that's all."

His eyes studied mine for a silent moment before he spoke. "I have asked Nate to be your templar."

When I looked at Nate, he smiled like a cat who had just made a morsel out of the family bird.

"Well, he looks happy about it," I said, forcing a smile. Having Nate as my templar was like inviting your rival into the house and not expecting him to kill you. It's not that I didn't trust Nate, but he was a Shadow through and through and Shadows had a reputation for getting what they want, moral standards aside.

"Whatever you're thinking, my sweet," said Nate, "get it out of your head. I am a Shadow, yes, but Seth is like a brother to me, and if I'm to have his mate, it will have to wait until he finds his demise—the natural way."

"Define natural," I said.

Nate raised his hands and clapped them loudly. "May I have all of your attention, please."

When the room grew silent, Nate dropped to his knees. "Before you and this clan, I pledge my fealty to assure the safety of Seth and all in his charge." His eyes softened. "Including his mate."

Khalen pushed through. "Are you willing to spill your blood for it?"

Nate pulled out his pocketknife and with little thought, sliced his hand. He then handed the knife to Seth, who followed suit and drew his own blood.

Fealty

Khalen pressed the two hands together. "I verify this fealty and seal it with my approval."

"You know what this means, don't you?" Seth asked his friend.

Nate nodded. "I am now governed under the rules of the Protected—no longer a Shadow."

Tears glistened in Seth's golden eyes. "And you do this for me?"

Nate looked between Seth and me. "I do it for both of you." His eyes scanned the crowd. "And my family."

"We welcome you, Taholin Daboi."

Nate struggled to swallow, his eyes glistening at the sound of his birth name.

Now that was worth staying around for. As soon as Seth pulled him up from the ground, I wrapped my arms around the stout Kiwi and gave him a hug.

"Thank you," I whispered in his ear.

He gently pushed me away from him so he could look in my eyes. "I will take care of you both. You know that."

I nodded. "I do."

His smile was genuine.

Khalen slapped his shoulder. "Now we can see about expanding those gifts of yours."

"I'd like that."

Darius banged something metal against his glass. "We have much t'celebrate this eve: a strong union, a new clan member and skilled huntin' partner, and Seth, our new leader."

The clan members roared with approval, tapping their glasses with anything that made noise.

Seth smiled down at Nate and me. "Welcome to the family."

Two hours later, we all disbanded and retired to

our chambers. Nate said a sleepy good night before disappearing down the hall. Seth stopped in front of my door.

"Stay with me," I said.

"That is a tempting invite, my love, but a dangerous one. If I stay, I will have a hard time keeping my distance from you."

"I don't want you to keep your distance, mate of mine." He kissed my hands and then my lips. The power in that kiss caused my knees to weaken. If he hadn't had a good hold on me, I was certain to fall.

"Tomorrow," he said, his voice husky with need, "I make you mine."

The coldness that lingered when he left had me shivering. It would be a long night, I was certain.

I AWOKE WITH A START, sweat dripping down my forehead, my nightshirt drenched. A soft knock sounded against my door.

"Rae," Seth called.

"Come in."

He opened the door and hurried to my side. "God, Rae, you're drenched."

He opened my armoire and pulled out a dry sweatshirt. Without thought, he pulled my damp nightshirt over my head and quickly replaced it with the sweatshirt. He then sat beside me, pulled me into his arms and briskly rubbed my back until my shivering ceased.

"Your bed is soaked." He wrapped me in the blanket and lifted me into his arms. "You're staying with me tonight."

I didn't argue as he carried me to his room.

"How did you know to come?" I asked sleepily against

his shoulder.

"I felt your fear," he said, lowering me onto his bed.

"Is that a normal gift for you?"

He nodded and smiled. "Among others."

I giggled. "I'm sure."

He tucked me in before stoking the fire and building it up to a heated blaze. "Get some sleep."

I watched as he sat in a chair and stared into the flames.

"Seth."

"Hmm."

"Come lay beside me—please."

He looked at me for a moment as if weighing his choices. Like a true gentleman, he kept his bed clothes on as he slid beneath the covers beside me.

He groaned as I moved to find comfort close against him.

"Christ, woman, settle down," he growled.

"I need to feel you hold me."

His warm strong arms wrapped around me, his breath feathering across my head. "If you keep wiggling like that, you're going to get more than you bargained for."

I pressed my face against his chest. "Is that such a bad thing?"

"I will not join with you without ceremony, Rae."

I raised my head to look at him, trying to ease the pain from showing in my eyes. "Yet you have taken many women to your bed in the past."

"They were not you," he growled, his voice deep and strained.

"Why am I any different?"

His arms pulled me close as he pressed my head against his chest. "I didn't want them as I do you, Rae. If

I love you tonight, I will not be able to stop myself from claiming you forever."

Smiling now, I allowed the steady rhythm of his heart to lull me into a deep, much needed sleep.

Chapter 29

-Jenico-

IT TOOK ME LONGER THAN expected to find Jenna. Though she was not my biological mother, she was the one I always looked up to. Unlike my mother, Jenna was strong and incredibly intelligent. Her defiance often got the best of Father and typically ended badly for her.

When we were told of her death, I knew something was wrong. No body had been found that I knew of and Father kept the cause of her death a mystery. A few months later, I felt her presence and a shielding force that she had helped me develop. Though she couldn't shield herself, she knew about the gift and how to make it stronger. I reasoned another member of our clan must be protecting her.

I felt her again from time to time throughout the years, but I had never laid eyes on her until today. My God, she looked the spitting image of Rae, only a few years older. She sat with a stout, redheaded female at a London cafe sipping tea, no doubt.

Careful not to alarm her, I approached with my shield

up until I sat across from her. She stiffened a bit, her eyes alert. I waited for some recognition.

"Clara, wouldn't it be lovely to have one of those pasties from Tomas' market?"

"Oh yes, that would be lovely. Would you like me to get us one?"

"Do you mind?"

Clara stood with greater grace than most women her size. She was more round than tall, and she had a full head of hair that made her look top heavy.

After Clara was out of earshot, Jenna looked me right in the eye. "Unshield yourself, my son."

Her endearing term for me was not lost. I was not her son, but she always treated me as such. I did as she asked.

Her smile was warm and genuine. "How did you find me?"

"I felt your energy at each of my tournaments and figured I could follow your path one day. Unfortunately, that proved more difficult than expected."

She laughed. "Berkai told me he felt your presence."

"Your protector?"

She nodded. "It's very dangerous for you to be here, Nico. If your father finds—"

"He won't," I said. "He cannot see past my shield and cannot destroy it unless he knows where it is."

Her eyes searched mine. "How's Rae?"

My mouth tightened. "In trouble."

She sighed. "Oh, dear. What has she done?"

I filled her in with thoughts to save time. At the end, she sat back and pondered the situation.

"Does she love this...Seth?"

I nodded. "She has for many years. I asked him to take her away, and now his clan is in Father's radar."

"Yes, I'm certain. Drake never did like losing control, especially over a female in his charge."

I hesitated to ask my next question—afraid to hear the answer. "Is the clan still in my favor?"

Her brow arched. "Of course. But they are not stupid, Nico. They will not act on a half-baked plan."

I cringed at that one, remembering my first attempt to overpower my father. We had lost over a dozen lives that day—loyal followers who trusted me. Father had retaliated, putting me back in my place like a young wolf foolishly vying for a choice piece of meat. Oddly, Father said he was proud of me for trying to assert my dominance. He had claimed I would make a fine leader someday. Having just been beaten down, I seriously doubted it.

Her hand rested over mine. "Nico, to overthrow your father, you must outwit him. It is the only way."

"He will be gathering the men soon."

She nodded. "Sazar is loyal to him, as are a few of the others. To plan something, you must go through Sazar's son."

"Tomar? I asked, thinking about Sazar's eldest boy."

She shook her head. "No, you want to talk to his youngest, Kenik. He is a strong elementist and is disgusted with his father's heavy-handed treatments of the others. He will be your strongest ally in this endeavor."

"Can you arrange a meeting?"

She nodded. "Tomorrow at noon, meet us at Trafalgar Square by the statue.

"Who's this?" Clair asked. She laid two bags on the table before taking her seat.

"Clair, this is my son, Jenico."

The woman's eyes widened. I sensed her fear.

"It's all right," Jenna assured her. "He has protected

me against Drake."

Clair placed her hand over her heaving chest. "Oh, thank God. For a moment there, I thought I would have to leave these fine pasties uneaten."

I stood. "I'll leave you to them, then."

"No point in leaving on my account," Clair chimed. "There is plenty for all of us to share."

"Where will you be staying?" Jenna asked me.

"At a hotel."

"Certainly not one of your father's?"

My father owned nearly half the hotels in London and a dozen more in the outlying areas surrounding the city. I laughed. "No, not one of his."

"What about Bennet?"

I frowned. "He's another problem. No doubt Father has told him about Rae's gift of healing. Bennet will not relinquish his claim. His clan will band with Father's."

Jenna sat back, her eyes distant in thought. "You must take me to see Rae."

"Enter their clan, unannounced? When they are expecting a Shadow war?"

"Get word to her so they know to expect us."

"Expect us, yes? Trust us? Never."

"Try, Nico. Please."

T HAT NIGHT I CHECKED INTO the Thames Inn, a quaint little place on the river's bank. It was managed by an elderly couple who insisted I take at least two fresh-baked cookies back to my room.

I checked in under the name, Lucas Byrd. The identity papers were easy to obtain. My father kept company with many shady characters who often needed new identities. Mac was a talented forger who always kept a few passports ready to distribute. Having worked with him on many occasions, I had learned the trade and could easily add my photo to the passport. I then assigned the new papers to a man who worked for my father now and then, but not enough to make an impression.

I knew Father's business intimately. He had been grooming me to take his place. It must have been quite a shock to learn I had betrayed him. It was not something he would ever forget. My life had come to a crossroad. The direction I took would determine my fate.

After getting settled into my room, I sat on the bed and stared at my mobile phone, wondering how this conversation with Rae would go. She would either hate me for keeping my mother's presence hidden, or she would be thrilled.

I poured myself a glass of Bushmill's Black Bush and picked up the phone. Slowly, I dialed Rae's number. She picked up on the third ring.

"Nico?"

"Rae."

Silence.

"Are you all right?" she asked.

"Is this a good time to talk?"

More silence.

"Just a minute, yeah?"

"Yeah," I answered.

I heard some muffled conversation and then steps as if she were walking to another location.

"Okay," she finally said. "Talk."

There was no skirting around this issue so I decided just to blurt it out. "I found your mother."

I heard a muffled gasp.

"Rae, she wants to see you."

Silence, and then a loud bang, as if she had dropped the phone.

"Who is this?" said a man's voice.

"Seth?"

"Yes, who is this?"

"Jenico. Is Rae all right?"

"She's fine. What did you tell her?"

"I told her I found her mother and that she wants to come see her."

"You told her like that?"

"Um, yeah. I—"

"Hang on."

I heard conversation but couldn't make out the words.

"Nico," said Rae. "Does Father know?"

"No, she's safe, Rae."

"How long have you known?"

"A long time, Rae. I told you I didn't think she was dead."

"Yes, I remember."

"Can we come see you?"

More muted conversation.

"Seth wants to know when."

"Two days, perhaps?"

"Just you and mum?"

"Yes."

"You know Father's on the hunt?"

"Yes, I know," I said. "May we come?"

"Yes, of course."

"We'll be arriving under a shield. You might want to alert your leader."

"I'll let him know."

"See you soon, Rae."

"Take care, Nico. I love you."

"I love you too."

I hung up and took a long sip of my drink, praying Rae would forgive me for keeping this from her. She was not the type who reacted quickly. She stewed on things until the pressure became too intense to hold back. Then, she lashed out without restraint. I took another sip before settling in for the night. It was bound to be a long one.

T HE NEXT MORNING, I MADE my way toward Trafalgar Square to meet the young man I hadn't seen for nearly thirty years. I arrived an hour early and decided to have a cup of tea and a scone.

Dixie's was open. Using my shield so I wouldn't be recognized, I entered the cozy tea house. The place was packed with Shadows, each of them sensing my shield but not understanding its purpose.

A tiny young thing pranced over to my table, her dark ringlet pigtails bouncing like loose springs against the sides of her head. "What c'n I fetch'a?"

"Earl Gray and a black current scone, please."

She beamed me a smile that would have most young men craving for more. I preferred my females to be more mature.

She returned with my order. "Anythin' else, love?"

"No, thank you."

She pranced away, swinging her backside like a banner. The effect caught the attention of half the men in the room. My attention was outside on Nelson's Column, the statue at the center of the square.

A half-hour later, a shimmy in the air caught my attention. I sensed Jenna's presence as she reached out to me.

I'm here, I told her in thought. Placing my money on

the table, I stood to leave.

Kenik had grown into a large man with a solid frame, rivaling many of my former opponents in the ring. His black hair and deep blue eyes provided a stunning combination that I was sure attracted many females.

"Nico," Jenna said. "You remember Kenik, yes?"

"Yes, of course," I claimed. "You've grown into an impressive male, my friend."

Kenik offered his hand in greeting. "Jenico. I have never stopped following your competitions." His voice was deep and confident like a leader's.

"Not too disappointed, I hope?"

He offered a slight bow. "You are my idol."

I chuckled. "You must have missed my last fight."

"You were...distracted," he said, looking at my mother.

"Has she filled you in on the details?"

He nodded. "She has. What you propose is dangerous. Only a few of us will stand against your father. Many more are anxious for you to take the lead; however, they are not willing to help you take it under treason."

"My goal is to save my sister and the clan who has taken her in."

"A Protected clan?" he asked.

"Yes. Is that a problem?"

He stepped back and thought for a moment. "Why did you send her there?"

"She loved one of their kind."

His hand rested against his chin. "Interesting."

"I don't see it as a problem."

"Don't you, now? When you place a dragon in a den of wolves and expect them to love her as one of their own, you're a fool."

"I know this man. He will take care of her."

"The Protected ones killed our elders, or have you forgotten?"

"That was many years ago, and we were the ones who started the war, not them."

"They cannot be trusted."

"Funny, they think the same about us."

"Stubborn males," Jenna chided. "An alliance between the Shadows and the Protected has never been formed, but that doesn't mean one never will. You are all Spirians, are you not?"

"We are," I said.

Kenik nodded.

Jenna stepped between us. "This segregation of truths must be mended. This mending starts with two clans, theirs and ours."

Silence followed.

"Kenik, I need your help," I said.

More silence.

"I'll do what I can."

"Thank you."

Jenna touched my arm. "Have you spoken with Rae?"

"Yes. Can you meet me here tomorrow?"

"Not here," she said. "Where are you staying?"

"The Thames Inn."

"I'll meet you there at ten, yes?"

"Yes, very good."

I watched them leave and felt the hum of too many Shadow eyes upon me. No wonder Jenna wanted to meet somewhere different.

Chapter 30

-Rae-

SETH HAD REQUESTED THAT THE ceremony be performed this morning, giving the clan time to plan for the upcoming battle. He had talked to Khalen about the arrival of my brother and mum. The leader was not pleased and the tension in the clan was high.

Skye seemed preoccupied while working with my hair. The other females chatted wildly while my dress was fitted and the adornments prepared. It would be a simple ceremony at Seth's request. I was definitely fine with that. Personally, I wanted a short private ceremony, but that was not an option.

By eleven o'clock, we were ready. Skye escorted me to where Seth stood waiting. He looked amazing in his dark suit and royal blue cummerbund. His golden eyes sparkled as I moved to his side. He took my hand and held it firmly as if I would disappear from his sight should he relinquish his hold.

Khalen was dressed in a white ceremonial robe gilded in gold. He looked stunning. An acoustic guitar played in the background. The din of the crowd grew silent.

Khalen started the ceremony with a prayer spoken in Gaelic. After that, he pressed his hand against Seth's.

"Seth Dunning, son of Aidan and Sunjia, do you agree to take this female, Raeiza Tomei, daughter of Drake and Jenna, as your lifetime mate?"

"I do," he said with confidence, a slight smile curling the edge of his lips.

Never in all my years had I imagined him saying these vows, let alone saying them to me. My heart felt full and shone with hope I had never before experienced. I prayed I would never awaken from this dream—ever.

"Repeat after me," said Khalen. "I, Seth, promise to love and protect Rae for the remainder of my life."

Seth repeated the words with the vigor of a true leader.

"As a result of this union, I swear to lead this division of the Gradhun clan, under our regional leader, Khalen, our national leader, Case, and our elder leader, Arcadie."

Seth raised his chin a notch and repeated the vow loud and clear, indicating he fully understood the responsibilities of a leader and was ready to commit to the clan. Given his dominating nature and demanding demeanor, I guess I should have seen he had the blood of a leader in him. It was just masked beneath his humble attitude and quiet disposition.

As Khalen looked to me, I felt that familiar yet still disturbing vibration that always seemed to radiate from him when he offered his full attention. He pressed his hand against mine.

"Raeiza Tomei, do you accept this male, Seth Dunning, to be your lifetime mate?"

"I do," I said, my voice quivering. The obvious fluctuation caused him to smile. Seth squeezed my hand, offering comfort and strength.

"Repeat after me," Khalen instructed. "I, Rae, promise to love and respect Seth for the remainder of my life."

I repeated the words with more conviction in my tone this time, hopefully relating to Seth that I was committed to this union.

Khalen continued. "I vow to stand by his side as he leads this clan and to support his decisions. I accept the role as a leader's mate and commit to the wellbeing of this clan."

I repeated the words, fighting the swelling lump that quickly formed in my throat. I had absolutely no idea what I was promising or what that promise entailed.

He released my hand before prompting Seth to remove my pendant.

Seth and I presented our bare wrists to our leader. Using the edge of the crystal, he sliced a shallow cut over Seth's wrist. Then, it was my turn. The cut burned as the crystal drew a thin line of blood over my skin.

"With your blood, you commit to one another as mates, a union of two souls that can never be broken."

He pressed our wrists together and bound them with a red satin sash. Raising our bound hands, he announced our union to the clan. "I now present you with Seth and his mate, Rae."

Khalen handed Seth my pendant. Seth carefully lowered it over my head and positioned his crystal over my heart. "Forever mine," he whispered.

The clan members roared with approval, stomping their feet and clapping their hands. Seth leaned over and offered a kiss that had the power of removing the din around us. His lips, soft, warm, and commanding, claimed my spirit, heart, and soul. When it ended, I continued to feel the hum over my skin.

The crowd waited for the next moment when Seth chose an appropriate templar for me. When he walked toward Nate, the conversations amped up to an excited volume.

Seth kneeled before our mutual friend. "Taholin Daboi, do you accept the honor of being my mate's templar?"

Nate removed the red sash that bound our wrists with shaky fingers. Continuing to hold both our hands, he leaned down and pressed an endearing kiss to the back of my hand. "I am honored to accept this mantle."

Seth stood and then presented my hands to Nate.

The sting of our melding felt like a thousand bee stings before quickly fading. Nate and I were connected now with an unbreakable binding. He would be my protector, and my suitor should anything happen to Seth.

Again, the crowd roared.

Darius raised his hands. "Let the celebrations begin!"

Music played—a seductive tune that caused my belly to tighten with anticipation for the mating soon to follow. Seth, with eyes glowing and filled with desire, took my hand and led me to the area designated for dancing.

His intense stare held me entranced as he led me effortlessly over the soft grass. For years I had watched him lead one female after another through dances that I had only imagined sharing with him. This one dance trumped them all. Seth was mine now, and mine alone. Never again would I have to endure watching with painful envy as women swooned under his command only later to share his bed. Tonight, he would be my mate.

No one joined us. They were, no doubt, too entranced with Seth's ability to command a female through a dance with effortless elegance and strength. When the song ended, I was breathless, my mind in a zone that guaranteed this man anything he wanted.

He smiled. "Anything sounds good to me," he said in a husky voice.

Khalen wrapped his massive arms around us both. "You've never failed to impress anyone on the dance floor, Seth."

"You mean he's always had this gift?"

"Since he was a young teen," Khalen replied. "His ability to make a female swoon under his command is enough to keep my mate away from him."

Skye came up and gave her mate a hug. "You do a fair amount of commanding a female's swoon, yourself, my love."

"Really?" With that, he swept Skye up and carried her to the dance area.

Nate tapped Seth's shoulder and gestured to me. "Do you mind if I have a dance with her, mate?"

Seth looked over at me; then he hesitantly placed my hand in Nate's. "Make it a short one."

~ S e t h ~

I LOOKED OVER AT THE WOMAN I had once wanted more than anything else in this world. Elle was beautiful, elegant, and always just out of my reach. Now, I saw her as the infatuation Khalen had said she was. Though, at that time, I didn't believe him, and even harbored resentment toward him for stating such a thing. Tonight, I felt grateful for his wisdom.

Elle's eyes widened as I approached her with an

extended hand. Her mate smiled up at me as our eyes met. "May I?" I asked him.

Drew nodded. "Of course." He placed his mate's hand in mine.

Elle stood and allowed me to lead her to the dance floor, glancing back at her mate.

"I wanted to thank you," I said.

"For what?"

"For not taking me seriously when I tried to court you."

Her expression grew serious. "I did take you seriously, Seth. I just didn't feel the same toward you."

That hurt—a little. "I thought I loved you the way a man should love his mate." I looked over at Rae, dancing with my closest friend. "Now, I know that what I felt for you is nothing close to how I feel for Rae."

She smiled. "I understand that more than you know."

"I know you do. I just wanted you to know how I feel. You will always be special to me."

She quirked a smile. "I certainly hope so. After all, you are my templar."

When the song ended, I led her back to Drew. Bowing my head to him, I said, "Thank you."

Reading my expression and the thoughts behind those words. He smiled, his amethyst eyes glowing. "You are most welcome, Seth."

~ R a e ~

NATE LED ME ONTO THE floor and immediately swept me into his arms as we twirled into the center of dancing couples.

"You look radiant, Rae."

I nodded my head to him. "Why, thank you, kind sir."

"I still think I would have made a better man for you, though."

I laughed, knowing he was merely jesting. "Well, at least I can look into your eyes without straining my neck."

"Yes, being an overly short male has its advantages."

"You have other gifts as well, my templar."

A slight pinkish tone lit up his face.

"Nate, are you blushing?"

"Absolutely not." He twirled me around, lacking the fineness of my mate. I did my best to keep up with him.

"It's good to see you happy," he said.

"You will find a perfect mate, yourself, one day."

He rolled his eyes. "With my luck, she'll be six feet tall and double my weight."

"Careful what you put out there," I said, laughing at the visual image that his premonition conjured.

"This clan is much different from my own," he said.

"Yes, it's different from mine as well."

"In a good way, though, yeah?"

"Yeah, in a very good way."

"It'll take some time adjusting to it."

I laughed. "It seems you've adjusted quite well, judging by how the children love you and all."

"I miss all the females."

"No one said you can't enjoy females, Nate."

"Yes, but to mate only one?"

My laugh deepened. "Who knows, you might enjoy it."

Again, he spun me. "Never."

When the song ended, my mate came quickly to collect me.

"I'm done sharing you," he said, picking me up in his arms. "Now it's time to make you mine."

My stomach did a flutter. "I like it when your voice gets deep like that."

"Mmm," he growled, carrying me to the castle.

My heart skipped a few beats and I found it hard to swallow. I had never wanted a male as fiercely as I wanted Seth. My body craved his touch, starving for something only he could provide.

He carried me up the stairs and turned a different direction down the long corridor.

"Where are you going?" I asked, expecting him to take me to his room.

"To our chamber," he said. He stopped before a very ornate oak door with a carved bone handle. It looked like something out of medieval times. He opened the door to reveal a room that could only be real in dreams. A huge featherbed nestled in a cherry wood frame rested in the center along the far wall. It had two matching end tables with plenty of shelf space and reading lamps. An armoire took up most of the left wall, with two valets on each side. Along the right wall was the entrance to a private bathroom and a large see-through hearth. Seth set me down.

"Is this really ours?"

"Yes, my angel, it is really ours."

I walked toward the bathroom entrance. Two walk-in closets flanked both sides of the entrance. To the right were double vanities. A small privy occupied the left wall, adjacent to a spacious walk-in shower with a drop-down tub that could easily accommodate two people, all done up in white marble.

"This is amazing."

"This is Khalen," he said. "He has a flair for making the ordinary extraordinary."

"I wonder what his and Skye's room looks like, not to mention Lenore and Darius' chamber."

"They are similar to this one. There are a few more like it for when Case and Arcadie come to visit."

"Not even my father's room is this grand, and he considers himself rather spoiled." I giggled, unable to harness my happiness any longer.

I spun around, taking in the splendor of it all. "I cannot believe this is all happening to me."

He wrapped his arms around me. "I've never seen you this happy. Your eyes are sparkling like fine emeralds and you have dimples here," he placed a soft kiss against my cheek, "and here," another kiss on the opposite side.

My body felt the power of him and melted. With a laugh, he lifted me into his arms and carried me to our bed.

My heart raced like a jackhammer, pounding against my veins. He kissed me—gentle yet possessive, commanding. Taking his time, he slowly removed my gown, studying my naked body as a gemologist would a fine emerald.

"God, you're beautiful," he moaned.

With quick work, he dropped his clothes to the floor and hovered above me. I was breathless now, and apprehensive. Sex had never been pleasurable for me and I knew from listening to others how painful it could be when a male joined with a female. It was different than just making love. When a male and female united, their souls merged and the male possessed the ability to impregnate his female at the time of his choosing. I had heard from other females how good Seth was, but still, my body remembered the abuse it had endured time and again from other males.

"Rae," he laughed. "You look terrified."

I felt my face redden. "A bit, perhaps."

He smoothed the hair back from my face and smiled. "Do you trust me?"

"Yes, of course I do. It's just that...."

He rolled off of me, propping his head up with his arm. Slowly, his warm hand caressed my body, leaving a trail of bumps in its wake. My breath hitched as he continued his exploration with slow, methodical precision.

His eyes never left mine as he read my every reaction. I was in a spell under his command as he made my body yearn for more of what he offered. This was making love, I thought, not just sex. I never wanted the others like this. My belly ached, but in a good way.

"Please," I moaned.

He continued to kiss me, caress me, and to build that ache until tears trailed from my eyes. The power that hummed around him was soothing, commanding, and protective. I felt safe—very safe.

"Keep your eyes on mine," he said, his voice gravelly, yet smooth as silk. The moment his body met with mine, I felt my soul open to him. I was lost in a euphoria of desire and hunger. There was no pain, only pleasure.

Then, his eyes changed to a golden color that rivaled the intensity of the sun. It was almost painful to look at, yet I couldn't look away. The moment of our joining was close; I could feel the intensity build in the pit of my gut as his energy amped up.

His body arched. The surge of energy that followed could not be described by words. He took his time, seemingly relishing the pleasure as much as I did. The moment our spirits joined, the pain was sharp, but that pain was quickly overruled by the elation of our two souls becoming one. For several minutes, I couldn't breathe, couldn't move.

Still joined, he wiped his glistening forehead and grabbed my wrist, his need to mark me evident in his golden eyes. A sharp pain shot up through my arm as his hand squeezed me tighter. I stifled my cry.

"Shh," he cooed. "It'll be over soon, my angel."

When it was done, he rolled off me and pulled me close to his side. A wry smile curled at the corners of his mouth. "Now, you're my mate."

I brushed the hair from his eyes. "Mate," I sighed, loving the sound of it.

Chapter 31

~ Rae ~

WE REJOINED THE FAMILY THE following morning. There were a few new members to meet. The clan had nearly tripled in size overnight. I was a bit overwhelmed by the power emanating from the group. After numerous formal introductions, I was famished and ready for breakfast.

Seth and I sat on a warm log with our plates full of food. I sipped the hot coffee and nibbled on fried potatoes while Case, a powerful man, spoke of news from his home in Eastbourne.

Arcadie, his older brother, spoke of his plans for rebuilding the clan in Brazil. I had heard about this man from others, but sitting beside him was an experience beyond description. His mate, Kitta, was extraordinary. Dressed in blue jeans and a cashmere sweater, she acted more like one of the girls than a high-bred female mated to the most powerful Spirian since Shanuk. From what Seth had told me, Arcadie and Case were Shanuk's sons. That would explain their power.

Arcadie's blue eyes fixed on mine. "I understand your mother is Fae, yes?"

I nodded. Seth must have sensed my anxiety. He wrapped his fingers around mine and offered a comforting squeeze.

"She is," I wheezed out.

"You'll meet her soon," said Seth. "She and Rae's brother are due to arrive this afternoon."

The energy shifted as Khalen stood. Both Arcadie and Case followed him with their gaze.

"Forgive my son," said Case. "His history with Shadows has left many deep scars."

Again, I nodded. In my clan—my birth clan—it was inappropriate for a female of my stature to talk to a male of such power, let alone talk to an elder. I knew only a handful of elders, and they never spoke a word to me.

Case laughed. "You are welcome to talk to us any time, my dear. We are here to teach and protect, not to make you feel uncomfortable."

I nodded and continued to eat my food.

"Khalen tells me you're a healer," Arcadie said, his voice a deep baritone with a hint of an accent—Scottish, perhaps?

"I am," I acknowledged uncomfortably. For years, I had kept my gift hidden. It seemed odd and precarious even to talk about it.

Seth laughed and nudged me. "Relax, Rae. Case and Arcadie are so efficient at reading your thoughts that they probably know more about you than I do."

Arcadie chuckled. "I most certainly hope not, young Seth. After all, you are her mate."

I felt the blood rush to my face.

A kind woman came to my rescue. I believe she was

introduced as Case's mate, Eve. "Come, my dear," she said with an eloquent British accent. "I believe these men have interrogated you quite enough for one morning." She helped me stand, picked up my plate and coffee, and then led me to another area where the women were talking in a circle.

"She's had a tough life," I heard Seth explain. The rest of his words were muffled, but his mind was open to me and that made me smile. I glanced back at him and warmed in the light of his grin.

"I'm excited to meet your mum and brother," Skye said as I took a seat beside her.

I smiled. "I still can't believe she's alive."

Being connected to the clan now, everyone could tap my thoughts and I could tap theirs. It was odd, really. My birth clan's members always kept to themselves, never intruding unless it aided them to do so. The thoughts of this clan were lively, open, and hard to calm in my mind. The moment Seth and I had joined as mates, I had felt the severing of my birth clan, my brother and father. I wondered whether they had felt it too.

"Will this be the first time you've spoken to her?" asked Sunjia.

"Since her banishment, yes."

Skye looked lost in thought.

"I'd give anything to talk to my birth mum again," said Sunjia.

"Me too," Eve chimed in. With a chuckle, she shook her head and added, "She would never believe me if I told her that I had married a Spirian."

That caught my interest. "Why in heaven's kingdom not?"

"Because I was born human."

I looked down at her wrist. It clearly bore the mark of her mate. "That's impossible."

"It's true," claimed Skye. "She was human."

Eve's eyes sparkled like vibrant tourmaline. "Case was skilled enough to claim me, and I was strong enough to bear the change. It is rare, but now we know it is possible."

Skye turned my left arm over and examined my mark with her fingers. "You and I are sisters now."

She bared Khalen's mark to me. "See, we share the same family crest."

I frowned after looking at Khalen's bloodline. "This seems odd." It was a mixture of two bloodlines.

Eve laughed. "It's confusing, my dear, I know. Case and I adopted Khalen when he was nine. He is Seth's uncle by blood. Seth's father was Khalen's twin."

I remembered Seth saying something about him, but I couldn't recall the details.

"Khalen was forced to kill him when he tried to reclaim Sunjia and her children."

I shook my head, feeling more confused as the conversation lingered. I looked at the exotic woman sitting across from me. "I thought you were joined to Aidan."

"I ran from Traeger, Seth's father," said Sunjia. "He was a cruel man and I did what I had to for the sake of my children."

"Twins typically die together," I stated.

"If it weren't for Skye," said Eve, "Khalen would have died that day. It was her love and spirit that brought him back. We came close to losing them both because of it."

I sipped my coffee, pondering the information that challenged my sense of reality. Everything I was led to believe was impossible, this clan had proven otherwise.

Skye tapped my leg. "The girls and I were going to go for a soak. Would you like to join us?"

"A soak?"

Lenore gestured to a hill looming above the castle. "There's a hot spring on the other side o'that hill. The natural minerals make your skin feel like a baby's bum."

The other ladies laughed.

I glanced back at Seth.

Go with them, he said in thought.

Skye's eyes sparkled. "The men will be strategizing the war for some time."

"You don't seem the least bit concerned," I said.

Another laugh erupted from the group.

"Remember what I said," Skye chimed. "Focus on the desired outcome, not the possible disaster."

That gave me something to think about for quite some time.

I still had a few hours before my mum and brother were due to arrive, so I gathered a few things and followed the women up the hillside.

The swimming hole was large enough to fit at least twenty people comfortably and smelled slightly of sulfur. The soak was absolutely incredible. My muscles immediately loosened and my body released the stress of many years under my father's command.

It seemed almost too good to know that I was released from his charge forever. Now that I belonged to Seth, my father had no jurisdiction over me—unless he challenged my new mate and ended his life. Nate would no doubt step up in my defense, but he was no threat to my father.

"Change your thinking," said Skye.

"It's harder than you think."

"Perhaps. But if I keep harping on you about it, that

switch will eventually happen."

I smiled. "Keep harping, then."

"What do we do during the battle?" I asked.

Lenore smiled. "We distract the Shadow buggers."

My eyes widened. In my birth clan, women were always ushered into some dark cellar during a battle or a threat. "How?" I asked, feeling a tinge of excitement for being involved.

"Mostly by making ourselves seen," said Sunjia.

"How do you do that without getting killed or caught in their snares?"

"Ye work with the men," Lenore explained. "Stay open to them and they'll tell ye what t'do."

"Can you heal someone over a distance?" asked Skye.

"I don't know. I've never tried it."

Eve held up her hand. "I have a sore thumb. Give it a try."

I closed my eyes and imagined holding her thumb in my hands, offering healing energy. After a few moments, I peeked my eyes open. "Any better?"

Eve shook her head.

"You need to connect with her," said Skye. "Imagine her body as your own. Feel her pain. Connect with its source."

I tried again, but felt no such connection.

"Eve," Skye instructed. "Come sit here." She gestured to the spot beside me.

Skye placed my hand over Eve's. "Can you connect with her now?"

I nodded.

"Pull your hand away a few inches. Try to connect with her again."

I did as she suggested. Nothing. I released a sigh. "It's

not working. I must touch her to feel her."

Skye thought for a moment, pursing her lips and looking at nothing in particular as if searching her own internal database for a solution. "Lenore, do your have your knife with you?"

Lenore reached behind her and pulled out a rather large knife from her pocket.

My eyes grew wide as Skye dragged the blade over her palm, making a deep cut. "Now, heal me."

I connected immediately and closed the wound. "Did you do that or me?" I asked.

Skye smiled. "You did."

I frowned. "Then why can I not heal Eve?"

"Her injury is not serious. Your healing instincts are triggered by urgency."

I tried to imagine Eve's thumb bleeding and injured. Still, nothing happened. I shook my head.

Skye connected with Eve. "There is no injury there, just pain. There is nothing for you to heal."

"So I can heal but not remove pain like you?"

Skye shrugged. "It seems so."

"I couldn't heal your eyes, either," I said.

"Perhaps because it is due to an illness. I cannot heal illnesses, either."

I thought back to the colt with the eye condition. I had managed to heal him just fine and his condition was due to an illness.

Skye looked toward Aidan's exotic mate. "Sunjia, do you think you could tap into her gifts?" Skye looked back to me. "Sunjia is a seer," she explained. "If you have hidden gifts or ones you haven't developed, she can see them."

I nodded, not really sure I was comfortable with someone peering into my soul so intimately.

Sunjia moved closer to me and offered her hands with a gentle smile. "It will only take a few moments."

I glanced over at Skye for reassurance. Her eyes were soft and gentle.

With hesitance, I placed my hands in Sunjia's. The hum was immediate, tingly and warm.

Sunjia started to frown before pulling away.

A hollow feeling lingered in my gut as I started reading her thoughts. My gifts extended well beyond healing, but they were dormant.

"We must bring this to Khalen," she murmured. "Immediately."

Images of a young teen flooded my thoughts—Sunjia's daughter. Sunjia looked pale and frightened. She alerted Khalen. He and the men would be here soon.

The ladies and I climbed out of the pool, dried and donned our clothes.

Skye moved closer to me and offered a hand.

"I would never cause harm to anyone," I said.

Skye smiled. "All healers have the ability to cause harm and injury," she explained. "Sunjia is concerned because your Fae blood adds another variable into a dangerous, volatile gift. What she saw was the strength of your Shadow blood, your father's ability to bind and trap."

"And the young girl?"

"Tria, her daughter. Khalen was forced to take her life when she turned rogue and endangered the clan. Sunjia saw it coming, but she never alerted Khalen. I think it has made her overly cautious."

Khalen came over wearing a menacing frown. His eyes peered down at me. When he glanced at the other women, they quickly retreated back to the castle. "We need to talk. Sunjia, stay with us."

Skye stood with me as we waited for the other women to leave.

"She can learn to control it," Skye said to her mate. He did not respond.

Seth must have sensed my fear because he was not far behind Khalen and closing the distance fast. Nate followed on his heels.

When they caught up to us, Seth placed a hand on Khalen's arm. "What is this about, Khalen?"

"I'm not sure yet."

"Sunjia, you must share you vision with us and don't hold back anything. Understood?"

She nodded, holding one hand out to me. Khalen started to take my other one, but Seth respectfully brushed him aside, taking his place. Skye, Khalen, and Nate joined hands, completing the circle.

Khalen nodded to Sunjia. The familiar vibration ran up my arm, the one attached to the hand she was holding. I felt her presence in my soul: it sent shivers down my spine as if delicate feathers brushed against my skin.

Seth's grip tightened around me as we all shared in the image of my evil self, binding three men and causing them fatal injuries. As they crumbled in a screaming, bloody mass, I shuddered.

"No," I cried, sinking to the ground. I felt dirty and hollow.

Seth lifted me up and held me close to his side, kissing my head as if trying to remove the filth I felt.

"Something's wrong," said Skye. All eyes turned toward her. "Someone is interfering with Sunjia's vision."

"Yes," Khalen confirmed. "These images were tainted."

"Tainted?" I said, my voice shaky and trembling.

Sunjia dropped to her knees, grabbing her belly. A

sharp cry escaped her lips.

Khalen called to a man named Tetris, who manifested before us instantly. His gray eyes narrowed as they fell on Sunjia.

"Sunjia," Aidan called, crashing through the thickets toward us. He dropped down to cradle his mate in his arms. "What happened?" he growled.

"A binder has seized her spirit," said Tetris. "Aidan, put her into an illusion, now."

Aidan struggled but finally succeeded. Sunjia now sat calm and serene as if she were on a peaceful beach somewhere. Her eyes were soft and unfocused.

"Whoever this binder is," said Aidan, "he's strong."

Tetris nodded, and then looked at me. "He's trying to taint your mind, but someone protects you." He reached toward me as if I were in some sort of a bubble. "I've never seen such a shield." He looked toward Khalen.

Khalen looked at me and frowned. "Interesting."

"It's my father," I said. "He is a powerful binder."

"Yes," said Khalen, "but he is not the one who shields you."

"My brother, perhaps?"

Tetris' bushy white brows pressed together, forming a large crest above his eyes. "This is the work of multiple males, not just one."

Khalen's jaw tightened. "When your brother comes, we will get some answers." It was more of a command than a statement. Taking Skye's hand, he turned to leave. She looked over at me and offered a sweet smile. How did such a gentle female end up with that man? I wondered.

"They're good for one another," said Seth, obviously reading my mind. "Strong and gentle, fire and water, healer and warrior."

He lifted my chin, meeting my eyes with a warm golden glow that matched his uncle's. "Like you and I."

Aidan lifted his mate and carried her back to the camp.

Soon, we were the only ones who remained by the pool.

"I'm bringing nothing but trouble to this clan," I said.

His arms tightened around me. "Do not say that—ever."

I looked down at the empty steaming pool, remembering how happy I was just a few moments ago when the ladies and I were soaking and chatting. Now, the pool sat empty and hollow, like my belly.

"Come," he said, taking my hand. "Your family will be here soon. Let's get cleaned up and ready for them."

When we returned to the camp, everything seemed to be back to normal as if nothing weird had transpired. I half-expected to feel like Typhoid Mary, but no one tried to avoid me, nor did they avert their eyes. I received warm understanding smiles and felt love, not rejection.

"This clan is very special," I said.

He smiled and softly chuckled. "We try to support one another with compassion and understanding. None of us has lived a perfect life. Each of us has caused waves that have helped to carved the foundation of this clan. Without the fire to forge the steel, true strength cannot be achieved."

I chuckled. "You sound like an elder, my love."

He arched a brow with speculation. "Yet I'm far younger than you."

That earned him a slap. "Not that much younger."

He laughed, picked me up in his arms, and carried me to our chamber.

Chapter 32

-Rae-

SETH INSISTED ON MAKING LOVE to me after our long soak in the bath. I couldn't very well complain. When he turned on that charm of his and commanded my body with his magical touch, I melted like butter in a hot iron pan.

Dressed in blue jeans and a pink cashmere sweater, I was ready to face the clan once again, feeling completely loved and satisfied in all areas of my life.

I opened the door, but he closed it again. "Not yet," he whispered, closing the distance between us. My stomach fluttered at the sound of that sultry voice.

He closed his eyes and took in my scent. Slowly, he lowered his full lips to mine, gentle at first, then deeper, possessive. He tasted like cinnamon and mint.

Burying his face in my hair, he drew me in closer. "I love you, mate."

He squeezed me so tight that I couldn't have replied if I had to. Stepping back so he could meet my eyes, his expression grew serious. "Listen to me, Rae. You are worthy of this love, of me, and of this clan. I don't want to observe anymore thoughts to the contrary. Understood?"

I nodded. "I will try."

"No trying. Those thoughts end here, right now."

"Habits are hard to break, Seth."

"Then I will help you break them for good."

"And how, pray tell, do you intend to do that?"

He sent me images that made my face heat and blush. "You wouldn't dare."

The look in his eyes assured me he would—without hesitation.

"Shall we go?" he asked with a smile.

Hesitantly, I took his hand.

The courtyard was bustling with activity. Lenore supervised a group of young females as they learned to cook a side of venison over an open flame. Eve was laying out loaves of fresh bread on the table, while her children carried bowls of goat butter and honey.

Khalen, his mate, and several others gathered by the central fire, talking and sipping wine. I was introduced to Aidan's brother Ian, and his lovely mate Erika.

Over on the field, Nate was sparring with Drew. Elle, a charming lady I had met earlier, sidled up to me. "I think my mate has finally met his match." She was definitely American with a slight accent that could only be Washington.

I watched the two men wrestle each other to the ground, grunting and flailing like two fish out of water. Drew finally ended up on top, breathing like a billow and wiping sweat from his brow. He stood and offered Nate a hand up.

"I was told you were beautiful," said Elle, "but that's an understatement."

I blushed and shrank back into myself. Seth ripped me out with a firm smack to my backside. "Yes, she is very lovely, isn't she?" he said with a growl.

I looked back at him with a glare.

Elle pursed her lips, saying nothing—smart girl.

Drew and Nate ambled toward us, exhausted and soaked with perspiration.

Nate pointed a thumb at the large man beside him. "This bloke packs a good punch, yeah?"

Elle studied both their faces. "Well, judging by your battered looks, I'd say you both do."

Drew leaned down to give his mate a long, lingering kiss. I looked away, feeling the heat redden my flesh.

"Well," Nate said, pulling the clinging shirt from his belly. "I'd best get cleaned up before the feast, yeah?"

"Please," said Seth.

Nate smirked at him before passing his eyes over me. "You're looking great, Rae. This union suits ye."

My blush deepened. "Thank you."

Seth pulled me close to his side and whispered, "Good girl."

The surrounding energy shifted. All conversation stopped. My brother and mother had to be approaching. It was wise of Nico to announce their presence so clearly, I thought.

"Are you ready for this?" asked Seth.

I took in a deep breath. "Yes, I am."

Khalen summoned Seth in thought.

"I have to go," he said, leading me to the group of women gathered by the fire. "I want you to stay here."

I nodded, watching him run toward the other leaders.

Skye pressed up against me. "Seth will make a strong leader."

"Yes," I agreed. "I believe he will."

The tension increased as a car wound its way up the long drive. I expected to see my brother's shiny red SL convertible, but instead, he drove a dull blue Mini. How he ever fit in that tiny car was a mystery in itself.

My mother sat beside him, but through the window's glare, I couldn't see her clearly. My heart raced in my chest, echoing its powerful beat in my ears until it was nearly all I could hear.

As Nico stepped out of the car, Khalen ordered him to remove his shield. Nico did so, immediately. He met Khalen's eyes, and then offered a deep, respectful bow.

"Thank you for allowing us entry."

My mother remained in the car, no doubt under Nico's orders.

Khalen was the first to extend his hand. "Khalen Dunning, leader of the Gradhun clan."

After twenty minutes of formal introductions, my mother was asked to exit the car. When she did so, several audible gasps filled the silence. I, too, was stunned. My mother was my twin, only slightly older. When her eyes locked onto mine, I nearly fell to my knees. She, however, ran toward me, stopping short before we collided.

Her trembling hands rose to touch my face. "Rae," her quivering voice spoke. "My God, I never thought I would see you again."

"We were told you had died," I cried, no longer able to hold back the emotions that had welled in me for too many years.

"A part of me did, that day," she sadly admitted. "I have so much to tell you."

I introduced her to the women of the clan, all of whom greeted her like a member of their own clan. She was offered a glass of wine and a comfortable seat next to the fire. I sat across from her, still in awe of how much she resembled my own reflection.

Seth came over and rubbed my shoulders.

"Mim, I want you to meet my mate, Seth Dunning, leader of this camp."

My mum stood, looked my mate up and down. "Seth," she said with great hesitance and a disturbing bit of hostility.

Seth smiled. "Don't worry, Jenna. I will take care of your daughter."

That soft, sultry voice of his had the same effect on my mum as it did on most females. A smile curled her lips. "She is special, you know."

He pulled me close to his side. "More than she realizes herself."

I rolled my eyes and he pinched me. I winced.

"Do you love him?" she asked point blank. It was an odd question to be asked in the presence of a male. If this were a Shadow camp, she would be swiftly chastised for her insolence.

"Very much," I said with conviction. "He is good to me," my eyes narrowed at him, "most of the time."

My mother's eyes widened, probably expecting my mate to lash out for that last comment. When he smiled, she relaxed some.

"I'll let you ladies talk. I need to rejoin the leaders now." He bent down and kissed me sweetly on the mouth before taking his leave.

Elle started fanning herself. "That man has the charm to melt Alaskan snow in the dead of winter."

The other ladies laughed, all looking a bit flushed themselves. My mother's eyes sparkled.

Fealty

There was so much I wanted to know about her: where she lived, how she managed to escape Father's notice.

She patted the space beside her. "I'll tell you all that and more," she assured me, having read my thoughts.

"I thought my mind had been severed from you when I joined Seth."

"Yes, I felt the severing," she said.

"But you were able to read my thoughts?"

She nodded. "Only when we are close," she sadly admitted.

I reached over and took her hand before sipping my wine. It was a fine Pinot Noir, something light from Oregon. It was fabulous and perfect for chatting around a warm fire.

I felt Khalen's protective hum around the camp. He was still uneasy with my family's presence. Skye must have felt it as well. She seemed lost in thought, or perhaps she was monitoring her mate's thoughts as the men interrogated my poor brother.

Knowing Seth would fill me in later, I took advantage of the time I had with my mother. I wanted to give her my full attention. "So where have you been staying?"

She smiled sweetly at me, studying me with sea-green eyes that revealed many more years than her physical appearance. "You are so beautiful," she said, almost distantly as if speaking to a dream.

"I look like you."

She nodded. "Yes, you do. That must have really irritated your father, yes?"

I shook my head. "He was never happy with me. My life was miserable after you left."

Jenna's smile faded to a sadness I never wanted to see again. "I'm so sorry, Rae. I tried many times to release you from his bind."

"Don't be, Mim. He's a determined man."

"Nico told me how he treated you, the men he offered you to." She shuddered. "Curse his soul," she muttered.

"Don't," I said, squeezing her hand. "You're better than that. His fate will be his own doing. I'm happy now and with a man who loves and protects me."

"Does he know of your gifts?"

I nodded. "The entire clan knows."

She sighed a breath of relief. "You are safe here. I can feel it."

"Please," I said, bringing her back to my original question. "Where have you been staying?"

"Berkai's clan."

My brow rose. Berkai was Father's most trusted confidant. He was a powerful man in charge of three clans in my father's territory. "How?"

The other ladies in the circle, including Skye, leaned closer to hear her answer while Lenore refilled our glasses.

Jenna looked around at the crowd and smiled. "Berkai has been waiting for your brother to take over Drake's territories. Until then, Berkai has feigned his loyalty to Drake."

"Father would certainly sense the deception."

"I have gifted Berkai and Jenico with a shield that your father cannot detect or destroy."

"Is that what protects me now?"

She nodded. "Fae females have the ability to enhance a male's gifts and make them stronger. Five males protect you now. Drake and his army cannot touch you."

"Can you extend that protection to this clan?"

She shook her head. "Too risky. A shield that vast could backfire and destroy everyone it protects."

"That doesn't sound too comforting," I said, sitting back.

Jenna glanced over at Nico, talking with a serious expression on his face. "Nico is proposing that we join forces with you in the battle."

Lenore laughed. "Shadows and Protected fightin' in alliance?"

"Yes," Jenna said, eyes wide and promising. "Drake will never suspect it. Berkai will come with his clans, intent on backing Drake's forces, but things will take a turn and your father will be defeated."

"What about Bennet's clans?"

Jenna chortled. "Bennet. That buffoon is only a threat in the corporate arena. He and his clan know nothing about fighting a real war. Once he sees Drake has fallen, he'll turn tail and run."

"You sound so certain," I said.

"I am." She chuckled. "Rae, you've always been such a worrier. Always looking out for others before yourself."

I rubbed my hands together.

"That's exactly what I've been telling her," said Skye.

My mother placed her hands over mine, stopping my insistent rubbing. "When are you going to realize that you are loved and protected?"

"I don't want any more people getting hurt for the sake of my safety and happiness."

My mother's face grew serious. "If my Fae Master Tishar had known the fate of my slave sisters and me, I'm sure he would have given his life to save us."

"And you would have been all right with that?"

Her eyes studied mine with the intensity of stalking panther. "I would be honored and would repay that honor by living the best life I could."

I stood and started to pace around the soft crackling flames.

"Why does your mate believe you are dead?" asked Skye, always the inquisitive one.

"Berkai severed our bond."

Eve's eyes widened. "Is that possible?"

"It is," Jenna affirmed, "but there are consequences."

I returned to her side and sat. "What kind of consequences?"

"Neither of us can ever bond again with any mate."

I thought back on my father. He had not taken another mate since my mother was banished from the clan. I had thought he was merely too busy for one. He didn't even seem interested in Nico's mum, Terezza.

"That's terrible," said Eve.

"When our bond was severed, Drake assumed I had died."

"Are you lonely?" I asked.

She shook her head. "No, dear. I have many people who love and care for me. I'm not lonely."

Without a mate, she could never bear another child. The thought of that saddened me.

"Master Tishar envisioned a world where Faes and Spirians thrived together. Never did he imagine that his beloved females would be mistreated as we were. His fealty is the only thing that keeps me alive. When my slave sisters perished, the men who harmed them were bound by Master Tishar's fealty. They died shortly after. When Drake heard about the contract, he banished me, thinking he would be spared the curse."

"I remember the tale," said Lenore. "My grandfather recited it many times. His brother was awarded one of your sisters by Lord Tishar, himself."

Jenna brightened. "Which sister?"

Lenore shook her head. "I don't remember her name, but my granduncle was killed shortly after. Your sister was taken by the Shadows."

"We all were. After our worth was revealed, wars erupted and the evil began."

When Nate walked toward our circle, Jenna stiffened, obviously sensing he was a Shadow. Though he had joined this clan, his Shadow vibes would take some time to diminish. Even then, they would never dissipate completely.

"It's all right," I assured her. "He's my templar."

Jenna stood. "No." With purposeful strides, she walked toward Nate.

"Mim, stop, please."

My plea caught the attention of Seth and the others. Within minutes, everyone gathered at the spot between my mother and a very surprised Nate.

"He's a Shadow!"

"I'm a Spirian," he countered with equal fervor.

Soon, they were nose to nose.

"Stay away from my daughter."

"I'm not the one you need to be concerned with."

"Enough," Khalen roared.

Everyone grew silent.

"Damn, hotheaded Shadows," he grumbled.

"I am a Spirian!" Nate spat. "Not a Shadow or Protected." He started to walk away.

"Stay," Khalen ordered.

Nate ignored the request and quickly received a jolt that dropped him to his knees.

Khalen released his hold and helped the Kiwi up.

Nate brushed himself off, biting his lip.

"How could you allow this to happen?" Mother asked the leader.

Khalen held up his hand. "First, you need to calm yourself. Second, Nate was Seth's choice, not mine, and third, this man," he said, pointing in Nate's direction, "has never proven to be unworthy of the responsibility of being your daughter's templar. He is honest and has integrity that rivals any man here."

Nate stood a bit straighter, eying the leader with renewed respect.

"He is our friend," I explained. "He has protected me and has stood by Seth's side in battle."

"He is a Sh—"

"No," said Seth. "He is not. He is Spirian, the same as the rest of us."

Nico placed his hand on Jenna's shoulders. "Mother, I am born of Shadow blood. Do you find me so abhorrent?"

She stilled herself, quiet for words. "No," she said. "You are not like them, not like your father and his bloody henchmen."

"Shadows are not born," said Khalen. "They are merely those who have made a choice toward a particular lifestyle."

Jenna stared up at the man as if pondering his words. "Yes," she finally said, "of course."

Nate held out his hand to her. "Are we good?"

Hesitantly, she took his hand. "I'm sorry. It's just that—"

"I know," said Nate. "No worries, love. I understand."

Jenna looked into his eyes. "Thank you."

"Dinner's ready," Lenore called out.

"Crikey, I'm starved," said Nate. He fell in beside Khalen, nudging him as they walked. "Your energy binds are quite painful."

Khalen looked down at him. "They're meant to be."

"Right." Nate fell back, allowing the leader to walk with his mate.

Seth grabbed him by the nape of the neck. "Don't worry, my friend. Khalen does not hold grudges."

"He seems a bit miffed."

"He's just amped up from having so many new faces in camp. Also, when he issues an order, he fully expects it to be obeyed and not ignored."

Nate shuddered. "Yeah, he made that point quite clear." After a few more steps, he added, "I supposed that now you're a leader, you will have that same effect, yeah?"

"In time. I have always had certain gifts reserved for leaders because of my blood, but as time goes on, those gifts will increase in breadth and strength."

"Oh, goody," I said, under my breath, remembering how demanding he had already proven to be.

He squeezed me close to his body. "You, my angel, will always be treated with utmost respect."

"Except when I do something you disapprove of."

A slight smile curled his lips. "Well, you being the obedient mate that you are, that shouldn't pose a problem."

I laughed and so did Nate.

My mother walked in silence beside us. I nudged her. "Hey, are you all right?"

"I apologize for overreacting, my dear."

"It's fine, Mim."

"I have witnessed so much savagery from your father's clan. I didn't want you subjected to that ever again. What he did was inexcusable."

"This clan isn't like that, Mim. The females are treated

very well and with respect."

"My father was cruel as well," said Seth. "He was raised to be so. My mother had suffered by his hand too many times for my level of tolerance, so when I became an adult, I made the choice to join Khalen's clan."

"And you weren't hunted down for treason?" my mother asked.

"Yes, Seth said. We all were, my mother and sister. Khalen was forced to kill my father for the sake of us all."

"I'm sorry," replied my mother.

"Don't be. We are all better for it, including my father. Although he feigned otherwise, he was rarely happy."

"Shadows rarely are," I said.

Chapter 33

-Seth-

IT WAS INTERESTING OBSERVING THE conversations during dinner. Khalen once told me that good leaders listen more than they spoke. Tonight, I understood a bit of the truth behind his words.

Jenna talked about what it was to be a Fae female. Their primary purpose and devotion was to ensure that the males in their lives were as powerful as they could be. Women were their males' spines. They provided the structure, strength, and balance that enabled them to function to the best of their abilities.

I saw a bit of that in Rae. She was definitely my world now, my purpose for being the best that I could be. God, I would do anything to ensure her safety and happiness. It felt good. I felt complete and whole beyond what any words could possibly describe. Now, I understood my uncle Khalen's protectiveness toward his mate.

Being a leader offered a sense of power that was strangely foreign to me, yet familiar at the same time. Khalen said I was a natural during our training. At times,

I believed him. Other times, I doubted my abilities as he pushed me beyond limits I couldn't comprehend.

Tomorrow, we would begin our preparations for battle. My gut instinct warned me that those preparations would never be complete. Drake wouldn't fight fair, and he would attack even though Bennet's clan had not been assembled.

I offered that thought to Khalen and watched as he pondered the possibility.

Jenico and Drew discussed fighting strategies and even stood to put some of them into practice, each being an equal to the other. Watching them spar was like watching a dance of sorts, all liquid movements and anticipated maneuvers.

Nate jumped in, unable to stay out of a good match. They quickly shut him down, though, when his cockiness got the best of him.

Tetris worked with Gabrihen, teaching him the finer points of being a wizzard. Gabrihen was a natural and seemed to pick up on complex concepts quite easily, much to Tetris' delight.

Zhentu was adept at changing into his wolf form and blending into the landscape to be virtually undetectable.

I looked over at the ladies, all chatting and working with Rae to strengthen her healing skills. Having her mother so close seemed to help. Jenna knew quite a bit about healing. She had an apothecary shop in London, we later learned.

Khalen came over to sit beside me. "Fascinating, yes?" he said as we observed the activities around us. "In all my years, I never would have believed that Shadows and Protected could work together toward a common goal."

I nodded. "I believe Nate is correct in saying that we

are all Spirians. To define ourselves as one type or another is to deny ourselves the power of being one."

"Yet there are distinct differences, Seth."

I nodded. "As there are in all things."

"You've made some very powerful friends."

"It seems so, yet this battle is not yet won. Drake does not act in ignorance."

"You believe he knows about the mutiny?"

I nodded. "He must."

Khalen smiled. "You are a fine leader already."

"I have a good teacher and impressive antecedents to follow."

His gaze followed mine to where Case and Arcadie sat and sipped brandy in front of the fire. They were unoccupied by the upcoming battle.

"We need to have a plan if this war turns sour," I said.

Khalen huffed. "I've never had a plan that came to fruition. In war, anything can happen. The best you can do is keep your head, react quickly, and never expose your weaknesses." He glanced over at the women.

"Have you ever been able to keep Skye from a battle?"

He shook his head. "Can one keep the waves from brushing the shore?"

We sat in silence for a moment as I thought about Rae and the vengeance her father must be craving. How far would he go to satisfy it?

Khalen looked around at the stars. "The air is getting thick and cold. It won't be long before they attack."

"Tonight, perhaps?"

He nodded. "Perhaps."

A shiver ran down my spine. Was I ready for this? Could I keep Rae from harm as I had promised?

"Never doubt your strength, Seth. Doubt is the weak

link that will enable Drake to sever your bond to all that is right and just. Keep your head in the game and your emotions under control lest you fall under the illusion of his confidence."

He looked over at me, nudging me with his broad shoulders. "This is not your first battle, and it won't be your last. Nate and Jenico will watch your flanks as Ian and Aidan watch mine."

Arcadie and Case headed toward us. Arcadie's eyes glowed like neon orbs.

"Time to gather everyone inside," he said.

"Right," Khalen agreed.

With a thought, he alerted the clan, and within five minutes, everyone had filed inside. The children were tucked away in the basement with direct orders to leave through the tunnels should the castle be breached. Kaili and Shaiya, Khalen's twins were instructed to lead the young to safety.

Being the son of a leader, I knew what it was like to bear far more responsibilities than most children of the clan. The young women, however, looked ready for the task, taking charge already as they ushered the children to the lowest level of the castle.

The women had ensured the space had plenty of soft beds and enough wood for warmth. Eve, of course, made sure there were cookies and cocoa for all of them.

The rest of us gathered in the game room, the most central place in the castle and the only room with multiple exits. When Shanuk had built this place, he had made sure it was built to withstand battle and protect those within its walls. It had survived many skirmishes and would stand for many more, I was sure.

"Seth, extinguish the flames," Khalen ordered.

Using the gift he had taught me, I telekinetically removed the oxygen from around the pits. The fires dwindled before completely extinguishing to plumes of black smoke.

"Darius, we could use a heavy downpour."

Khalen had explained to me that Shadows did not perform well in a rainstorm for reasons not entirely clear. Darius was a skilled elementist who had a strong command over water and fire.

"Tetris, Gabrihen, add a mist that disorients intruders," Arcadie said.

As I watched my elder leaders give orders and directions, I registered their commands so I could lead this clan with similar efficiency during future battles. They knew everyone's strengths and used them with impressive precision.

"Zhentu," Khalen called. "You and Maiyun prowl the camp's perimeter. "Let us know what you find but do not get involved, understand?"

Zhentu nodded, changing form with grace and fluidity. In his place stood a large gray wolf with glowing silver eyes, just like his mother's. He and the Malamute headed outside, stalking the perimeter like two stealthy shadows in the night.

Case looked over at Lenore, who looked to be in a trance. "Talk to us, Lenore. What are they thinking?"

"Underground," she muttered. "Earth, elementist."

"Skye," Khalen growled. "Get the children, now!"

So much for plans, I thought, remembering what my uncle had said about wars.

"What is he thinking?" I asked Jenico.

"Father is a strategist," he said. "He will come at you from all angles, not just one."

"There are too many of them," said Lenore. "Too many."

"No," said Jenico. "That's an illusion."

Skye returned with the group of frightened and confused children, settling them down in the game room's center. "Keep them calm," she instructed Kaili and Shaiya.

"I don't sense the illusion," said Aidan.

"Father can shield it from you," Jenico explained.

"We need to split up," I said.

"They're coming," said Khalen. "Zhentu has reported at least twenty. Maiyun senses more, but she can't bloody count."

"They're planning to draw us out," said Lenore.

Khalen frowned, then looked at his old friend. "Darius, take Tetris with you down to the basement." His gaze shifted to Arcadie.

"Right," he said, "out back."

"I'll come with you," said Case.

Khalen's eyes settled on his oldest son and me. "Gabrihen, Seth, come with me. The rest of you surround this room. Don't let anyone through."

To Aidan and Ian, he added, "Keep them safe."

The brothers nodded.

I gathered Rae into my arms. "Stay with Skye and Lenore," I told her. "Stay safe."

She pulled me down for a kiss. "You too."

Khalen settled on Skye. "You know what to do."

She nodded. "Go; we'll be fine."

The hum that surrounded us was deafening, rattling my bones with vibration.

"Keep your head about you," Khalen said.

My heart pounded so loudly in my chest that soon

it was all I could hear. Khalen was leading us out to the courtyard, the first line of defense.

Khalen looked down at his eldest son. "If you get into a fix, dematerialize. Understand?"

"I won't leave you," said Gabrihen.

Khalen shook him. "You will do what I ask."

Gabrihen's eyes widened. "Yes, Father."

I squeezed the young man's shoulders, silently understanding how it felt to be subjected to that kind of power.

"Get ready," Khalen warned, positioning himself against my back. He positioned Gabrihen between us to form a triangle.

To my surprise, Gabrihen had an impressive command over projection which enabled him to attack from a distance.

Maintaining our triangle, we rotated, picking off Shadows three or more at a time as they approached and tested the castle walls.

As the numbers increased, we struggled trying to ward them off.

"Gabrihen!" Khalen shouted.

The young wizzard dematerialized. Now it was just Khalen and me. We fought until the motions made me numb.

Sensations flooded my senses like a vengeful horde of bees. I could feel my mate's fear, and the clan's screams, death, pain, and the will to forge on.

Khalen fought like a machine, killing one Shadow after another.

Rae called out to me and I froze. That's when a Shadow's blade sliced through my chest. The next blow was meant to sever my head. I blocked it and countered the attack with an energy blast that shattered the Shadow's bones.

Another cry pierced my heart. "I have to get to her," I yelled.

"Go," Khalen called out. "I'll hold them back."

"Not alone."

As if reading my thoughts, Nate and Jenico raced out the door.

"Go to her," Nate yelled. "Now!"

I ran back to the castle, slaying Shadows who stood in my way. When I reached the game room, it was empty. The women and children were gone.

I called out to Rae, but there was no answer. Panic washed over me.

Stay in your head, Khalen silently warned. *Keep your weakness at bay*.

More Shadows attacked. I fought them all, ignoring the wound in my chest. Looking down, I noticed that the bleeding had stopped. Skye must have healed me. That meant she had to be safe somewhere.

Rae still remained silent. I made my way back to the courtyard where the three men I had left stood fighting. Shadows came at us from all angles. The battle seemed endless, unbeatable.

I was tired, numb, confused.

Don't let them wear you down.

I looked over at Khalen, still fighting as if on auto-pilot.

Three Shadows ambushed Nate as he slayed his last opponent. He was now down on his knees as two of the Shadows pounded their fists against him.

I pulled them off and nailed them with enough energy to launch a jet. They flew back, pounded into the side of the castle, then slumped to the ground in boneless heaps.

Jenico killed the third, before fending off another. Nate remained unconscious. I gently kicked at him.

"Get up!"

Jenico, Khalen, and I formed a circle around him.

A fire erupted at the back of the castle. Another blaze blasted a wall of Shadows we hadn't even seen.

Gabrihen directed the fiery blasts from the canopy of a large elm.

A yelp echoed from the trees, followed by a whine and a chorus of howls. Rain continued to fall, drenching our skin and clothes. My energy felt drained as I continued to fight one Shadow after another.

Gabrihen manifested before us, grabbed Nate, then disappeared again with my friend.

The sounds of night amplified in my head as my eyes filled with colors that didn't make sense. If Spirians could get drunk, I imagined this is what it would be like— disorienting, surreal.

"Something is wrong," said Jenico. "Berkai is not here. His clan is missing from this horde."

Chapter 34

-Rae-

MOTHER AND I HAD NEVER been in the midst of a battle before. Females were never brought into the thick of things. Battles were always fought away from the clan—mostly because Shadow clans initiated the fight.

I watched in awe as Lenore and the others fought the Shadows off with efficient elegance and speed. Elle's hand-to-hand skills were impressive and caught many of the Shadows off-guard. Skye's ability to blast them with a shield offered the females time to finish the surprised and stunned Shadows before they could fully recover. The entire show reminded me of how wolves hunted in packs, each supporting one another during an attack.

The children had been sent away, but I didn't know where. The twins seemed comfortable with the idea and led the children down a hidden corridor.

Now that I was a member of the clan, I would have to learn my own skills so I could contribute. As it stood now, I was clueless.

I felt my father's presence long before he breached the

castle walls. Mother must have sensed him as well. She gripped my hand. He was not one for engaging in physical battle; that brutal practice was reserved for his minions and reckless teens. Father surrounded himself with elders who watched his back with impressive skill. As he drew closer to us, my belly quivered with fear. He was searching for me, but he was not entirely certain where to look.

As injuries occurred to the clan, I did my best to heal them with Skye's assistance. Things happened so quickly; everything was a blur. I kept my communications open to my mate, but when my fear and internal screams distracted him, I had to close him off. Healing his wound was easy for me due to the connection we had. Skye handled most of the other injuries.

I could hear Seth calling for me and wanted to assure him that I was all right, but not when my father was so close. Father wanted me. God only knew what he would do should Seth interfere with his plans.

Gabrihen contacted me, asking me to heal Nate. They were in the basement area. I offered a quick healing, but the energy attracted my father and drew him to me.

My mother shook me. "No, Rae."

Too late. My father was making a beeline toward the game room. I warned the others to leave.

"Not without you," said Skye. "Come with us, now."

Mother and I followed her and the others down a hidden corridor. Father's presence grew stronger. I knew if I continued to follow, my new family would be annihilated.

Shivering from the cold damp space, I glanced over my shoulder, half-expecting my father to be on my heels. I felt nothing, and that in itself seemed alarming.

"They can't sense us in here," Skye said over her

shoulder.

I wasn't sure why that was, but it offered a sense of relief just the same. Unfortunately, it also cut us off from the clan. The voices were silent in my head.

The corridor ended at a room surrounded by earth and rock. Skye worked at opening a door, but it wouldn't budge. Lenore and a few others offered assistance.

"It won't open," said Skye.

A sinking feeling anchored my gut. Here we were, deep in the earth, cut off from our clan, and trapped.

Father appeared at the room's entrance with three elders, all laughing. Due to the Earth's shielding effects, their powers were diffused and had little effect. That didn't seem to matter much to Father. He had us cornered.

Skye reached over and pulled me behind her. She placed a dagger in my hand. When my father spotted my mother, his expression cycled through snippets of shock, fear, and anger.

"What is this?" he roared, accentuating each word. He stepped toward her. Mother met him in the center of the room.

"Hello, Drake."

"Impossible," he said, reaching out to touch her.

"Improbable, but not impossible."

"Our union was severed. I felt the separation."

"That is correct," she explained. "We are no longer joined."

His eyes narrowed. "What sort of crafting is this?"

"Not crafting, old man. Our union was severed. Neither of us are able to bond with another mate ever again."

He went after her. My dagger flew with alarming accuracy, piercing the hand that reached for my mother.

Drake roared. His elders tried to cast an energetic blow, but all that resulted was a slight tingle, something I was well immune to.

Drake pushed my mother aside and gripped my hair, pulling me down before him. Telekinetically, he removed the blade and allowed it to fall to the ground with a dull thud.

"She will suffer," he promised her.

Grabbing my neck, he blasted through the door that had been stuck and dragged me through the dark tunnel leading outside. The elders ushered the other women behind us. As we approached the fresh air, I found it difficult to breathe. Once we were outside, my mother launched herself toward Drake. He dropped me to the ground and held me with a painful, nearly blinding bind. I wanted to scream out, but air would not escape my lungs.

Without the earth den's protection, the women and I were easy prey to his gifts and those of his elders. My mother went flying over the wake of Father's blast before crumpling to the ground.

"You are bound," she murmured.

Drake huffed.

Seth approached with Khalen, Jenico, Arcadie, Case, Aidan, and Ian. I saw Maiyun peer at us through the trees, but there was no sign of Zhentu, Gabrihen or Tetris. Nate, too, was missing, along with Darius.

Father looked around him, smiling. "Is this all that's left of your clan, young Khalen?" He gestured to the small band gathered around us.

Father clapped his hands and from the shadows, another legion of minions appeared.

"It looks as if you're outnumbered this time."

Seth eased his way toward me, his eyes bright as the

sun. He was amped up. I could feel the hum of his energy through the ground.

Breaking through my father's bind, a feat that few males could do, Seth reached down and lifted me to my feet. I knew it had to have been painful, but he never showed any hint of discomfort. His only concern was for me.

"Release her," my father roared, sending a blast of energy toward us. Seth redirected it toward the three Shadow elders. They deflected the blow but were not unaffected by the blast. Stumbling, they fell against the wall, stunned.

Case and Arcadie blocked the counterattack.

"Stay out of this," Arcadie growled.

The three elders held up their hands, capitulating under his power.

Father waved his minions forward, though none of them moved. "Come," he roared.

Looking over at Aidan and Ian, I knew they had placed the army under an illusion of sorts.

Father must have realized it as well. "Impossible," he grumbled. He looked around at his men, all of whom stood with catatonic expressions.

His eyes locked on to Jenico. "You treasonous ingrate. Did you really think that Berkai would help you?

Nico raised his chin a notch. "Your time of ruling has come to an end, Father."

Drake laughed. "Berkai will not come, son. You stand alone and weak with this lot. As soon as I confronted that old fool, he turned tail and ran, taking his sorry coterie with him. My men hunt him down as we speak." He shrugged. "He's probably dead already, spineless bugger."

My mother's expression remained collected. Limping,

she staggered toward him. "Are you so certain?"

He looked down at her but didn't give her an answer. Instead, he cast his eyes upon me. "You will go with Bennet now."

"No," said Seth, "she won't."

Bennet and his horde moved toward us, hands raised in surrender. "I'm merely here to collect what is mine. There is no need for bloodshed."

"She is my mate," Seth announced, "and you will not have her."

Father directed a blow toward Seth. He blocked it, sending it to the earth. Seth countered with a blow of his own, causing my father to stumble backward, eyes wide and mouth hung open. I had never seen this side of my father—shocked, concerned.

Drake grabbed my mother. She fell against him, wincing in pain.

"Remember the fealty," she gasped.

Drake laughed. "The fealty is dissolved. Your precious Tishar is dead."

The glow in mother's eyes dulled. "No," she whispered.

To prove his point, he twisted her arm, causing her to scream in pain as the bone splintered.

Arcadie and Case made a move to save her, but Khalen motioned them back, his eyes fixed on Seth.

Skye and I worked together. She removed my mother's pain while I repaired the arm.

Drake's huge hands squeezed around my mother's neck, cutting off her air. He could have killed her instantly, but he was making a point. Father always loved making a point.

"Please," I begged him. "Stop."

Seth positioned me between Khalen, Arcadie, and

Case before confronting Drake with ominous confidence. "Let her go," he said calmly. This battle is between you and me."

With a quick snap, Drake twisted my mother's neck. She fell limp at his feet.

"No!" I cried, trying to get at her. Case and Arcadie stopped me.

The hum between the two men increased to deafening proportions. I had never seen Seth so intense. He faced my father with absolutely no fear.

When Bennet and his men made a move toward me, Seth stopped them with a look. Bennet foolishly called him on the threat, inching his way closer. Seth waved his arm, sending Bennet and his men flying back. This seemed to surprise even my father.

Khalen smiled.

"It seems the gauntlet is thrown," said Drake. "But know this, young Seth. You are merely a whelp, I will crush you slowly and enjoy how you squirm."

Seth did not reply. He was far too amped up for rational discussions.

When Father aimed his deadly blast toward me, Case, Khalen, and Arcadie shielded it. Nico countered the blast with one of his own, but Father quickly dispersed it and sent him flying into the castle walls. He crumpled to the ground.

He was injured but not dead.

With Nico out of the way, Father was free to bind the camp. I felt it build, though I knew the clan was unaware of the snare building around them.

I sent an image to Seth and Khalen. When Khalen tried to counter the binding with one of his own, it felt as if hell had torn loose. Fire, wind, and an ear-piercing wail erupted around us.

"Get everyone out of here!" yelled Seth.

Khalen hesitated for a brief moment before ushering everyone into the castle.

"No, I won't leave him," I said.

"You cannot help him out here," Khalen argued.

Seth and Father were trapped in a whirlwind of fire and dust. I could no longer see them.

"Come on," Skye said, taking my arm. "We must hurry."

Unable to see anything, I allowed her to guide me back to the castle. "We need to bring Nico and Mother," I said.

"Case and Aidan have them."

Once inside the castle's belly, everything seemed calm, yet I could still feel the rumble of the turmoil in the courtyard. The heavy stone walls vibrated as if they were being pummeled. Lightning lit up the sky and trees cracked.

"C'n ye feel that?" asked Aidan.

"Aye," Arcadie replied. "Another moment and we'd all be dead."

Khalen sat in silence, obviously monitoring the fight in thought, the same as I.

Seth's mind was so focused it hardly seemed real. Through his thoughts, I saw my father, grinning, but there was a hint of fear behind his eyes.

I said a prayer to the Father, silently begging him to spare my mate.

"Rae, help me," Skye said, leaning over my brother's limp body.

I knew she could heal him without my help, but I was grateful for the distraction all the same. Together, we mended his wounds and healed his bones. The healing as well as the day's events drained me. I felt numb and nearly paralyzed with fear.

Send Seth your strength, I heard my mother say, though her body was still as night.

Do it now, her voice said again.

I had absolutely no clue how to send Seth my strength. Mother had never revealed that skill to me. All I could do was imagine my mate as strong. With every move, I was with him, adding my will to his own. I felt the connection to him. I writhed with his pain and stared into my father's eyes through Seth's.

"I will kill you," my father said. "Then I will make her suffer for the remainder of her days. I want you to know that. She will suffer."

A surge of energy pushed through me from the ground like a bolt of lightning. A bright light flooded my eyes before darkness consumed me. No more pain, no more— anything.

Chapter 35

~ Rae ~

PEACE, DARKNESS, AND UTTER BLISS surrounded me now. Memories of the battle, of my mate's pain and dwindling strength, lingered in my thoughts but didn't register as anything real.

A pale fog surrounded me. The scent of lilacs filled my nose. In the fog, a figure emerged.

"Mim?"

Her hazy figure drew closer. "Save him, Rae. Save your mate."

She looked away from me and to the left. I followed her gaze to where Seth lay, still and pale. I tried to run to him but had no legs to propel me forward.

"Seth!" I called. "God, please; Seth, answer me."

Nothing. He was too still, too pale. I floated toward him.

"You can save him," my mother said.

"How?"

She placed my hand over his heart. Through my ethereal touch, I felt his pulse grow stronger along with mine as two merged into one.

"Come with us," I told her.

She shook her head. "No, my dear. My time is done."

"Please, Mim; don't leave me; not again."

Her smile brightened. "I've never left you, Rae."

Her image faded as the fog grew thick and very cold.

~ S e t h ~

I AWOKE AS IF FROM A very bizarre dream. I was in my bed—alone. The room was quiet. I bolted up, eyes wide, heart pounding.

"Rae!" I called, also summoning her in thought. My senses told me she was close. I started to calm down.

The door to the room opened. Rae entered with a tray of food and steaming coffee.

"Hey, you're awake."

I ran my fingers through my thick sticky hair. It was disgusting. "How long have I been sleeping?" She set the tray down on my nightstand. "Five days. You stirred long enough for us to get some soup in you before drifting off again."

I racked my brain, trying to conjure some memory that made sense. "Was I sick?"

A knock sounded on the door. Nate and Nico stood on the other side.

"Hey," said Nate, "you're alive."

Rae arranged the pillows behind my back and helped me sit.

My eyes narrowed at the sight of Nico. Then, the memories came like a tidal wave.

Rae poured me a cup of joe before sitting beside me

on the bed. "How are you feeling?"

I huffed. "A bit like Alice in Wonderland after she took the pill that made her small." That first sip of coffee was like heaven, bold, rich, hot, and completely satisfying. "God, this tastes good."

Rae laughed. "You must be hungry?"

As if on cue, my stomach issued a mighty roar. More laughter. My eyes roamed over her, craving her more than food. "A bit, perhaps."

Nate cleared his throat. "Right, well, we'll let ye get settled, then, mate." He grabbed Nico's arm and backed out of the room, closing the door behind them.

Rae giggled, a sound that roused a deeper hunger. I wanted to pull her into my arms and love her into the day, but my body was weak and my fingers were numb.

"Ut, ut, uh," she said, holding up a finger. "I hear your thoughts, my love, but they will have to wait until you regain your strength."

She picked a strawberry from the plate and slid it into my mouth. The taste of it was fresh, sweet, and enticing. I wanted more.

My senses were hypersensitive. The light streaming into the room was nearly blinding. Sounds in the castle traveled as if the walls were made of paper, not stone. And food, good God, it tasted surreal with flavor. Even the texture was amplified.

Reading my thoughts, she brushed her hand over my cheek. "Khalen said you'd be hypersensitive for a few days."

She positioned the food on a tray over my lap. "I'll let you eat, love."

I reached for her hand. "Please stay."

"I'll come back. Eat now. Khalen wants to talk with

you." She left, closing the door behind her.

I made quick work of the meal and hungered for more of the same. On shaky legs, I staggered into the bathroom. A hot shower was what I needed, and clean clothes.

The simple act exhausted me. Clean, dressed, and groomed, all I could do was sit on the bed and stare out the window toward the courtyard. What I saw nearly floored me. The trees had been burnt to stubs. The grass was ash, and the once colorful grounds stood barren. Everything was gone. My heart sank.

A soft knock sounded on the door before it opened. Rae entered with Khalen and Skye.

"Welcome back," said the deep familiar voice of my uncle.

I tore my eyes away from the destruction. "What could have done that?"

Khalen laughed. "You did."

I closed my eyes, falling back onto the bed. "I thought it was only a nightmare."

"Only a nightmare?" Khalen mimicked. "Good God, man, you almost annihilated us all. If you hadn't sent me a visual on your intent, we wouldn't have retreated to safety in time."

"I don't remember anything except an immense surge of power and will coursing through my body."

Rae cleared her throat.

"We need to talk," said Khalen.

I sat back up and spun around to face them all. My lovely mate wore an expression of shame.

"What's wrong?" I asked her.

She came over and sat beside me on the bed. Khalen pulled two chairs over for him and Skye.

Rae closed her hand over mine. "My mother told me

to give you strength, so I did—all that I had to offer."

"Oh boy," I sighed.

"What we have," said Khalen, "is a highly volatile situation. You are a leader with substantial power of your own. Rae simply accelerated your development. Now we must couple it with control."

Skye leaned forward, offering comfort as only she could. "I have already begun asking other clans for anyone with Fae training."

"Arcadie has agreed to train you, Seth, and help you control that power." Khalen's eyes dropped to the ground, something he only did when he had something difficult to admit. "There's another thing."

"What?"

"You took Drakes life."

I huffed and gestured to our desecrated courtyard. "Yeah, I took more than that."

"No," said Khalen. "You separated his soul from his body."

That got my attention. "Are you saying I'm a reaper?" Khalen was the only one I had heard of who bore that gift. It was very rare among Spirians, and one that could easily get away from a man, as I had clearly demonstrated.

"I believe you are, yes, but Arcadie will help you control it, Seth. It doesn't have to be a bad thing."

Knowing my uncle and his impeccable control over the gift, I knew that to be true.

"Coupled with Rae's accelerated strength she has gifted you with, the power can be overwhelming but I have no doubt you will use that power wisely."

"Drake and his army?"

"Gone," said Khalen, "along with half of Berkai's troups who were fighting in our wings. Bennet's clan was waiting to ambush us when we thought the fight was over."

"Where's Bennet now?"

Khalen shook his head. "We don't know." A sadness touched his eyes.

I looked over at Skye, who was taking a deep breath and fighting back the swell of tears in her eyes.

"Where is Zhentu?"

"We don't know," said Khalen. "He's alive, but out of our reach."

"Out of our reach?"

"He's being shielded somehow," Skye replied. "We think he was captured and placed in an iron cage so he cannot communicate or change back into human form." Her voiced hitched.

I reached over and held her hand. "We will find him, Skye."

She nodded. "I know we will."

"Zhentu is a survivor," Khalen admitted. "He's smart and knows what to do. It won't be long before we find him." He sighed. "Right now, I'm more worried about Gabrihen."

"Gabrihen?"

"Aye. He feels responsible for his brother's disappearance. He took off shortly after the war. Tetris followed him, of course, but we haven't heard from either one of them."

"Surely Tetris would have kept you informed?"

Khalen shrugged. "They are wizzards. Their sense of time holds little bearing to what is real. A minute to them may be years to us."

I nodded sadly. "Any other casualties?" I asked.

He named at least fifty members of our clan who had

perished during the fight, and thirty more with extensive injuries. "If Rae hadn't been here to help with the healing, the death count would have been much higher."

I pulled her close to me and gave her a squeeze. "My head feels close to exploding."

"Yes," said Khalen. "It's the acceleration and the powers of leadership. You will be hypersensitive for a few days before you grow numb to the new sensations."

"Get some rest," said Skye. "We'll talk more, later." She and Khalen stood.

"You fought well," he said as he repositioned the chairs against the wall. The pride behind his eyes was genuine.

"I had a great teacher."

When Rae and I were finally alone, I lowered her onto the bed and buried my face against her warm, familiar neck.

"I'm sorry," she whispered.

"Don't be."

"So many lives were lost."

I held her tighter, not having any words to share that would make that fact less horrible. "Losing your clansmen is never easy, Rae, but know this: they died protecting those they love. It makes our lives all that more valuable. We honor them in turn by living the best life we can."

"Interesting," she said. "That's what my mother said."

Chapter 36

~ S e t h ~

THE NEXT FEW WEEKS WERE spent restoring the camp. With Eve's help, the vegetation grew at a rapid rate with more vibrant colors than anyone thought possible.

It was late now and everyone had retired for the evening, leaving my mate and I to relish the peace of night. The fire crackled and sputtered as I tossed in a few twigs. Sipping my wine, I thought back on the past days.

Arcadie had helped me harness the newfound power that bolstered my ego. The elder quickly reminded me that egos were the doorway to darkness. The lessons were painful but necessary. My gift was not one to reckon with, and if I couldn't control it, I would turn into the very thing I despised.

Case and Khalen came in on a few of the training sessions, giving me a run for my time that I would not soon forget. Their powers combined was enough to dwindle my ego to a mere speck. Together, they ensured that it would never raise its ornery head again.

Skye had no luck in finding a Fae to help my mate, so

she and the other women did their best to help her, but I knew Rae really wanted another one of her kind to talk to. Losing her mother had been a hardship. Jenna was the last of the original five Fae females gifted to the Spirians. Now, they were all dead. Finding the children of those females had proved to be challenging.

Nico had stuck around for a couple of weeks, but he had much to do to stitch his own clan back together and mend the damage his father had wrought. Then, there was the issue of dealing with other Shadow clans and their accusations of treason due to his sworn alliance with us. Nico was a strong leader, however, and would deal with the issue efficiently.

Delicate arms wrapped around my shoulders as dark silky hair draped all around me.

"You seem deep in thought, my love."

"There is much to think about."

She moved to sit beside me, taking the glass of wine I offered.

"Everyone has gone to bed," she said. "Are you not tired?"

I shook my head. "God knows I should be."

She ran her fingers over the bruises marring my face. "I don't like this."

I took her hand and kissed it. "The training is necessary."

"Does it have to be so harsh?"

"Together, those three men could shatter my bones with merely a thought. Believe me, they were not being harsh."

"Does it frighten you to know you have the power to do the same?"

"Not so much anymore. Shanuk was far more powerful

than I, and he had the gentlest soul of any man I know."

"But you are not of his blood."

"No, I am not, but neither is Khalen and he has grown into a fine leader."

"And you will too," she said, leaning her head on my shoulder.

The fire crackled against the lulling sounds of night. I added another log and sat back as it fed the flames with an orange glow. The scent of alder and oak added a sweetness to the air.

"Seth,"

"Hmm."

"School will be starting up soon."

I wrapped my arm around her and refilled our glasses. "Yes."

"Will you be returning with me?"

I squeezed her shoulders. "Of course, angel mine. I have one more year to attend."

"One quarter," she reminded me.

"One quarter," I laughed.

A moment of silence passed before she spoke again. "Will we be staying in the same flat?"

"No. I was planning on moving us into the Penthouse."

She moved away from me, eyes wide. "The Penthouse?"

"Yes, Khalen owns the entire top floor. It's a larger suite, and Nate can stay at the far end."

"Is there anything your uncle doesn't own?"

I pulled her close. "Yes, he doesn't own you."

She snuggled in close, warming her hands on my body. The chill surprised me, but I didn't move away.

"Do you want to work after you graduate?" I asked her.

She shrugged. "Yes, I do." Her voice was guarded,

almost as if she expected a battle or something.

"I could build you a facility here in Uig if you wish."

She relaxed and laughed. "I doubt there's much need for one here in Uig, my love."

"Where then?"

She shrugged. "I thought about working at the track with my brother."

I didn't like having her so far from here, but I fought the urge to rebuff her plan.

"How about you? Any plans to practice?"

I sipped my wine, weighing my reply carefully. "I am a leader now, Rae. That will require most of my time."

Her brows furrowed with confusion. "Then why complete your degree?"

I smiled. "I still want to be a doctor. Like my uncle, my skills will come in handy, even if I don't have a practice."

More silence followed, her thoughts whirling through what she wanted and what was possible.

"Will we be living here?"

I looked at her. "As a leader, I'm required to be here, yes. Do you prefer to live elsewhere?"

She sat quiet for a moment. "I want to be wherever you are."

"That is not what I asked you."

"I will miss the city."

My heart sank, feeling the weight of our differences. I had hoped she would find her place in Uig. "We have animals here that could use a vet."

She sighed. "We have a year to figure this out, yes?"

She was right. It was silly to worry about this now. Both of us needed to finish school. After I completed my quarter, I would be traveling back and forth between Uig and Edinburgh. Life would be hectic for a time.

She leaned her head on my shoulder. "Do you want children?"

Her question startled me. "Eventually, yes."

"When?"

"After you graduate, perhaps."

More silence. I enjoyed observing her thoughts and emotions as they played through her mind. She was like a child in a toy store without boundaries. So many possibilities but no direction toward any one choice.

"I'd like to be a mother."

I laughed. "A vet, a mother, a leader's mate. That is a rather ambitious number of goals, don't you think?"

"How do Skye and Khalen do it?"

"Their main focus is the clan and their children. Both of them had to give up their practice."

Another long sigh. I brushed the hair from her face and pulled her tightly against my chest.

"I love being your mate," she said, "and I know you'll make a great father."

"But?"

"This all happened so fast, Seth. I'm confused."

"We don't have to figure this all out now, Angel. Time will sort things out. For now, concentrate on earning your degree and license."

"But what good is it if I can never use it?"

"Achieving a goal is never a waste, and who said you won't ever use it?"

She moved away from me. "Well, if we live here, and you're the clan leader, there seems to be little chance for me to practice veterinary medicine. Add kids to the mix and—I don't know." She tossed her hands up in the air. "Not to mention, we have the issue of Zhentu missing."

We sat there, staring at each other as the fire crackled

in the background. "I'm sorry."

"For what?" she asked in frustration.

"For bringing you into all this," I huffed. "I guess I'm just used to this chaos. It seems our clan is good for about three years between crises."

She stood and started to pace in front of the fire, wrapping her arms around herself. "I'm not sorry, Seth. If given the chance to do it again, knowing what I know now, I would still choose to join with you. It's just—"

I stayed quiet, allowing her to process her thoughts. My instincts told me to take her into my arms and protect her, but I knew she had to do this on her own. Shadow females were very protected and shielded from clan obligations other than being available for their males. I was sure this was all overwhelming for her.

"Part of me wants to have my own practice while another part wants to be a mother. Still, another part wants to explore my new freedom, but my obligations to you and this new leadership seem like—"

I waited, sipping my wine and tossing twigs into the flames.

"Well," she continued, "they seem—constricting."

"It is a huge responsibility."

"Not huge, Seth, more like overwhelming."

"I will never make you do anything you don't want to do, Angel. If you want your freedom, you have it."

Her eyes widened. "You're letting me go?"

"Yes."

"Um, we're joined, remember?"

"And nothing will change that. You are, and always will be my mate, my love, and the most precious thing in my life."

"But you're letting me go?"

"I'm giving you the chance to explore this world of freedom, to do what you've never had the chance to do."

"I don't want to do them without you."

"I have obligations, Rae. I gave Khalen my word. This clan is mine to lead, but that doesn't mean I'm stuck here day in and day out. Darius and Lenore are more than capable of running things here; God knows they've done it for more years than I've been alive."

"So how will this work, then?"

I shrugged. "If you find something you want to do or an endeavor that you want to explore, we'll find a way to make it happen."

"You and I?"

"If that's what you want."

She paced some more, chewing on her lower lip. "That sounds like a good plan." Her face started to brighten. "I'm not used to having freedom."

I smiled. "You'll get used to it soon enough."

I tipped the empty bottle of wine with a frown. "Looks like we're empty."

"No," she said. "Far from it." Her delicate arms wrapped around me like a blanket.

I picked her up and carried her back to our room. "I think I'm going to make love to you into the morning."

She giggled, nestling her face into the crook of my neck. "Or at least until we both collapse with exhaustion."

"I'm feeling very energetic right now," I growled.

"Me too."

- The End -

A Note From the Author

I hope you have enjoyed reading *Fealty*. This story reflects two wonderful people in my life who offered each other encouragement when life was too heavy to bear.

Many of us have a story to tell but are afraid tell it for one reason or another. My goal is to encourage and inspire you all to tell your story, be it as a memoir or as a fictional tale such as this one.

About the Author

Rowena started writing at a young age, feeling an inherent need to tell stories that inspire and reflect aspects of life that are rarely considered.

Being a descendant of James Hudson Taylor, author and founder of the China Inland Mission, Rowena comes from a long line of story tellers, including her mother and father. The tradition of writing continues through her daughter, Erika.

Rowena's goal is to inspire others to tell their stories and share the wonderful gift and adventure of life. She often speaks before groups, sharing her experiences of writing and telling stories. It is a passion of hers that she shares with her mate, Gregg.

Together, they are writing a book entitled, *Finding Peace Among Chaos*, due to be released in Spring 2013.

Though she is over 75 percent blind, she doesn't allow that to derail her ambitions. Her husband is deaf, so they make the perfect pair. They live on the Olympic Peninsula in Washington with her guide dog Skye-Bear.

Other Books by Rowena

Protected
Union
Legend
Aeon Pneuma
Illusions

www.Rowena-Portch.com

Book a Speaking Engagement with Rowena and Gregg

Rowena and Gregg love to inspire people to tell their story and to follow their passion no matter how unobtainable it may seem.

Both of them have been on their own since age fourteen and have some incredible stories to share. Though both of them are disabled—she's blind and he's deaf—neither of them allow their impairments to deter them from their dreams.

If you want Rowena and Gregg to speak at your next event, please email them at:

RowenaPortch@gmail.com